THE DEAD THING

Coop and Jersey stood in the foyer, their backs against a wall, and pulled out their Uzis as they peered up the stairs.

"We better be careful, Coop. These men may not be terrorists after all," Jersey said, just as a man carrying a Kalashnikov machine gun over his shoulder walked by on the landing to the second floor. She jacked a shell into the firing chamber of her Uzi.

Coop put his finger to his lips and started up the stairs, keeping his back to the wall. At the top, he peeked around a corner, then jerked his head back. He laid his Uzi down on the floor and took his K-Bar assault knife from a scabbard under his coat.

As a small, thin, dark-skinned man with a rifle in his hands walked around the corner, Coop slipped his left arm around the man's neck and pulled his face tight against his chest as he slipped his knife up under the man's ribs and into his heart. The muffled groan was barely louder than a gasp. Coop lowered him to the floor and whispered down the stairway to Jersey, "Scramble. The party's heating up fast."

Less than a minute later, another youth leaned over the stairwell above them on the third floor, and said, "Amal?" His eyes widened when he saw them, and he began to shout as he reached for his shoulder holster.

Jersey leveled her Uzi at him and loosed a burst of five rounds, cutting him down. Coop bounded up the stairs, screaming for Jersey to cover her ears as he lobbed a stun grenade down the hallway, then followed with a tear-gas canister. He didn't wait for the explosion, but ran back down the stairs and took Jersey in his arms, covering her body with his.

As he laid her down, he was grabbed from behind, his arms pinned, and thrown up against the brick wall of the building. "Let's see some ID—fast!" said a man holding a pistol to Coop's head. He was dressed all in black, and Coop knew immediately that the man was with the FPPS.

He quickly scanned Coop's ID, then lowered his gun and released Coop's arms. "Want to tell me what the hell's going on here, and what a medical team's doing firing off automatic weapons and getting shot in my city?"

Just then, Harley and the rest of Coop's team walked out of the door of the building, Uzis slung over their shoulders.

The FPPS man shook his head. "Oh shit, not more of you?"

Harley walked up to the man, holding out his ID. "I'll explain it all to you later, sir, but for now could you call for some more men. The terrorists ran out of the back of the building."

"Terrorists?" the FPPS man asked.

"Yeah. They plan to kill the president," Harley said, causing the FPPS man's eyes to widen and his face to pale in the light from the flames consuming the building down the street.

BOOK YOUR PLACE ON OUR WEBSITE AND MAKE THE READING CONNECTION!

We've created a customized website just for our very special readers, where you can get the inside scoop on everything that's going on with Zebra, Pinnacle and Kensington books.

When you come online, you'll have the exciting opportunity to:

- View covers of upcoming books
- Read sample chapters
- Learn about our future publishing schedule (listed by publication month *and author*)
- Find out when your favorite authors will be visiting a city near you
- Search for and order backlist books from our online catalog
- Check out author bios and background information
- Send e-mail to your favorite authors
- Meet the Kensington staff online
- Join us in weekly chats with authors, readers and other guests
- Get writing guidelines
- AND MUCH MORE!

Visit our website at
http://www.pinnaclebooks.com

DESTINY IN THE ASHES

William W. Johnstone

PINNACLE BOOKS
Kensington Publishing Corp.

www.pinnaclebooks.com

Destiny

'Tis all a Chequer-board of Nights and Days
Where destiny with Men for Pieces plays:
Hither and thither moves, and mates, and slays,
And one by one back in the Closet lays.

—Edward FitzGerald
The Rubaiyat of Omar Khayyam

One

Ben Raines sat at his desk, drinking his third cup of coffee of the morning, as his team members filed into his office. He'd called a staff meeting to discuss the latest intel on recent happenings in the USA.

Mike Post, his XO and Chief of Intel, took his customary seat next to Ben's desk, while Buddy Raines, Ben's son and heir to his command, sat on his left.

Cooper, known as Coop, was the next to enter, followed closely by Jersey, Ben's bodyguard. Coop had his left arm in a sling, courtesy of the final shoot-out in Mexico City a few months before.

The rest of Ben's team filed in and took seats around the large office, sprawling in comfortable chairs and sofas in no particular order.

After they were seated, Ben glanced at Coop's arm, then at Dr. Larry Buck, who'd taken over the previous year for Dr. Lamar Chase.

"Buck," Ben said, a wry smile on his lips, "how's Coop's arm coming along?"

Buck looked over at Coop and shook his head. "I can't understand it, Ben. All of the tests show the arm to be completely healed, but Coop still complains of stiffness and pain."

"Coop?" Ben asked, his eyebrows raised.

Coop assumed a pained look on his face. "I don't know,

Ben," he said, moving the arm around in his sling. "It just doesn't feel right yet."

"Hah!" Jersey exclaimed, a look of derision on her face. "Coop's just playing it up to the hilt, Ben. He knows you've ordered us all to undergo extensive training exercises to keep in shape between hostilities, and he's using that old wound as an excuse not to run the obstacle course."

"I think a little refresher course in hand-to-hand combat might be just the thing to get the stiffness outta that arm," Harley Reno said, smiling at Coop.

"Aw, Ben," Coop complained, looking injured. "They're not being fair. I think it just needs a little more physical therapy and it'll be good as new."

Jersey's eyes narrowed. "Is that what you call it?" she asked. "Having that big, buxom Swedish nurse over at sick call rub around on you all day?"

"It *is* therapy," Coop said, glaring at Jersey. "Just ask Dr. Buck."

Buck shook his head, grinning. "I guess you could call it therapy, after a fashion," he said, "though Helga tells me the arm seems pretty strong to her, especially when she's trying to keep it away from various parts of her body."

"That settles it then," Ben said, laughing. "The sling comes off and Coop will take the physical training with the rest of the squad from now on."

Coop shook his head. "Traitors," he mumbled, removing the sling and stretching his arm, as if in pain.

"Now, Mike," Ben said to Mike Post. "Tell us about the latest intel from the USA."

Mike took his pipe from his mouth, tamped the tobacco a little with his index finger, then snapped a Zippo lighter and fired the pipe up.

As clouds of cherry-scented tobacco wafted upwards, he began to talk. "So far, President Claire Osterman has been too busy trying to rehabilitate her country to get into any more mischief. The plague organisms she unleashed in concert with Bottger and Perro Loco last year have caused quite a bit of illness in the states bordering the SUSA."

Ben glanced at the doctor. "Buck, have we sent her an ample supply of medicines and vaccines to help stamp out the epidemic?"

Buck nodded. "Yes, sir, as well as a couple of hundred corpsmen and medical team members to help with the treatment protocols."

"Anything else going on up there we ought to know about?" Ben asked Mike.

Mike shrugged. "Just the usual aftermath of another unsuccessful attempt to take us over," he answered. "Claire has made a major change in her command structure, getting rid of General Stevens and replacing him with a General Maxwell Goddard."

"What do we know about this Goddard?"

"Pretty reasonable sort of fellow from what my men on the inside tell me. Not at all the usual 'yes-ma'am' type Claire usually assigns."

"You don't mean to tell us he actually tells her the truth about her hare-brained schemes to take out Ben Raines?" Jersey asked, a look of incredulity on her face.

Mike laughed. "I wouldn't go that far, Jersey, but he seems to give her fairly good advice. At least he has so far."

"Is there any report of widespread unrest among the citizens?" Harley asked. "I would think after all Claire's failures and what it's cost the country, the common people would be standing in line to get rid of her."

Ben laughed out loud. "You underestimate the greed of what is laughingly called a citizen of the USA nowadays," he said. "As long as Claire keeps the welfare state pouring money out to the scum who never think they ought to have to work to earn it, the bums will keep her in office over the objections of the masses who pay taxes."

Mike nodded. "That's about the size of it, Harley. So far,

there've been some scattered pockets of rebellion, but nothing so big Claire's Army couldn't handle it."

"Damn shame," Harley said.

"Oh, I don't know," Anna, Ben's adopted daughter, chimed in, glancing at Harley, whom she adored, sitting next to her. "At least with Claire, we know what we have . . . an idiot who couldn't plan a major war if her life depended on it." She shrugged her shoulders. "Who knows? The person who replaced her might even give us more trouble than Claire has."

Ben smiled. "Anna's right. Claire's been a huge pain in the neck, but she's also been so incompetent that each time she's moved against us, we've come out on top."

"At the cost of thousands of lives," Dr. Buck said.

"Thankfully, more thousands of USA lives than SUSA lives," Hammer Hammerlick reminded the doctor.

"So, to sum up, nothing north of our borders to worry about?" Ben asked Mike.

"Not from the USA, but there are some happenings across the ocean I've been monitoring rather closely.

"What in particular?" Ben asked.

"The situation in Iraq is becoming increasingly unstable," Mike said, pulling a pouch of tobacco out of his pocket and adding a pinch of brown leaf to his pipe, again tamping it down with his finger. "A man over there is raising all kinds of hell."

"Who are we talking about?" Ben asked.

"Abdullah El Farrar," Mike said. "He's the son of one of the richest oil families over there . . . at least they were rich before the United Nations took over the oil fields in that part of the country after the big war."

"You've lost me," Harley Reno said.

Mike glanced at him. "After the big war, when the United Nations started to try and put the pieces of the old world economy back together, there was a shortage of oil—that is, gasoline, etc.—just about everywhere. With the agreements of most of the Middle Eastern countries, which were devastated by the destruction of the war, the United Nations took over all of the oil fields, refineries, and most of the shipping facilities so that oil and gasoline could be transported around the world to the Third World countries that needed it."

Ben interjected, "Of course, this ruined many of the ruling families in those areas who'd grown immensely rich on the backs of the common people of the region."

"Not to mention what it did to the governments of those countries involved, including Iraq, Syria, Egypt, Saudi Arabia, Iran, and Jordan," Mike added. "Most of them became little more than figureheads, with the real power in the countries being the United Nations."

"And that pissed this El Farrar off?" Harley asked, grinning.

"Yes," Mike said. "He was pulled from his expensive schools in Europe and sent home, just another poor rag-head who used to be rich and powerful."

Ben leaned back in his chair. "So, what is he up to now?"

"He's become almost a folk hero to his countrymen. He calls himself the Desert Fox now, and has gone up into the hills of Iraq and has been recruiting an army of fanatical followers dedicated to taking back what they consider was stolen from them."

"You mean he's trying to retake the oil fields?" Coop asked.

"Not only that, but he has declared himself the rightful heir to the throne of Iraq, as well as the other countries in the Middle East."

"Sounds like just another egomaniac on the loose," Ben said.

"Yes," Mike agreed, "but he seems to be very appealing to an entire continent of people who feel their heritage and lands have been stolen from them by white, non-Muslim interlopers. My intel says he's developed quite a following."

"You can't be too worried about a bunch of Arab types riding around in the desert on horseback, can you?" Jersey asked.

Mike shrugged. "We weren't, until we found out that El Farrar has acquired huge stores of weapons and war matériel that the previous leader, Saddam Hussein, had stockpiled. There's even some talk that he may have some nuclear missiles in his arsenal."

"How large is his army?" Ben asked, leaning forward and putting his elbows on his desk, interested now.

"Over a hundred thousand at last count," Mike said, "and still growing. Intel has information that his forces are spreading out across the entire area over there, absorbing more and more matériel as they overrun the United Nations forces and confiscate their weapons and ammunition."

"What does Jean-François Chapelle think of all this?" Ben asked, referring to the Secretary General of the U.N.

"He didn't seem too worried, until El Farrar began to widen his sphere of influence. Now, he's biting his nails down to the quick. Word is, he's tried to reason with El Farrar, to no avail."

"Any idea of just how big El Farrar's ambition is?" Ben asked.

Mike nodded. "He's telling his followers, which includes just about every fundamentalist Muslim in the Middle East, that he plans to take over the USA, then Europe, and eventually the entire world."

Harley Reno laughed out loud. "At least he doesn't think small."

"Surely he can't be that naive," Ben remarked.

Mike glanced at Ben. "No, he doesn't think he can storm the countries involved. He knows his army is too small for that, and must know the other countries in the U.N. wouldn't allow that. However, he has a huge terrorist network of fanatical members devoted to his ideals. My guess is he plans to institute a pogrom against the USA by infiltrating terrorists into the country a few at a time, and at some later date, set them loose to use terrorist tactics to destabilize the government up there."

Ben pursed his lips. "And with the growing resentment of many of the citizens against Claire Osterman and her welfare state, he'd find plenty of converts to his cause."

Mike nodded. "You got it, Boss."

"Well," Ben said, "continue to monitor the situation and keep me apprised of any new developments."

"Yes, sir."

"Now, back to the more mundane," Ben said. He turned his attention to his team seated before him. "Now that we don't have any active hostilities facing us, it is imperative that we don't let the men and women in our Armed Forces get stale. I want the training exercises increased so that if push comes to shove and we have to intervene anywhere in the world, we'll be ready."

Ben glanced at Mike. "And with this new information from Mike, we'd better be doing some extra training in desert-warfare tactics."

Harley Reno nodded. "Well, our last little outing down in Mexico certainly gave our forces some experience in fighting in the desert."

Ben smiled. "Good, then use the men with experience down there to help train the ones who didn't serve in the desert."

He stood up. "That's all for now," he said.

His team got to their feet and began to file out.

Jersey gave Coop a little shove from behind. "Oh, Coop," she said, "I'll see you out on the obstacle course right after lunch."

He grinned over his shoulder at her. "I think maybe I'll go get one last physical therapy session before my workout."

"Good. I'll go with you," Jersey said, a malicious gleam in her eye. "I want to give the Swede the good news that your arm is all better now."

Coop's face fell. "You don't have to do that, Jerse."

"No problem," she said. "Glad to help out."

TWO

Abdullah El Farrar's eyes blazed with fury as he glared at the sweating young man in front of him. "You have endangered our holy mission with your reckless disregard of the Prophet's admonition against drinking spirits," he said as he paced around the small room. Whirling suddenly, he backhanded the man, knocking him to the ground. Farrar straddled him and ground the point of a stiletto against his throat. "Can you give me one good reason not to cut out your throat and feed it to the jackals?"

With some difficulty the man rasped, "It will not happen again . . . I promise."

The others in the room watched intently, afraid to avert their eyes and draw Farrar's murderous attention to them. The man cringed, sweat running from his face, as Farrar slipped the point of the stiletto under his shirt. With an abrupt motion he sliced the shirt open, causing the man to cry out in fear. Farrar gently stroked the razor-sharp stiletto against his chest, leaving a thin line dripping blood.

"I shall spare your life but leave you with this mark of shame, lest you forget and again partake of the infidels' poison. Now get out of my sight before I decide to cut out your tongue which the alcohol loosens!"

The man scrambled to his feet, his face flaming in embarrassment, and fled from the room. As the others also began to file out, Farrar said, "Mustafa, remain. We need to talk."

Mustafa Kareem, his second in command, inclined his head in obedience and remained seated. Farrar poured them both fruit juice over ice, then shook his head in resignation. "If we didn't need every man, I would have gutted that camel dung and been done with him."

"You did right, my brother. All of the men have begun to be infected with the infidels' ways. The lesson was sorely needed and adroitly applied." Kareem inclined his head in admiration. "They will all think twice before causing the mission danger in the future."

"We need action, Mustafa. The men grow soft with the waiting." Farrar picked up a newspaper and waved it in the air. "I think this will give the men something to do to alleviate their boredom." Throwing the paper down on the table, he spat on it. The headline read: PRESIDENT CLAIRE OSTERMAN TO APPEAR AT SOCIALIST/DEMOCRATIC FUND-RAISER.

Kareem tilted his head to read the story. "I agree, but there will be much security around such an important gathering. We will need to plan carefully if we are to succeed."

"You're right as usual." Farrar took his stiletto from the table and wiped the blood from the tip with the newspaper, then slipped it into a scabbard behind his neck. "From now on, the men are not to leave the house. Pick up some women and young boys and bring them to the house for the gratification of the men. After a few days, dispose of them in ways which will not implicate us. By then, I will have planned our strike and the need for caution will be over. Our followers in the motherland have been most generous with funds to help us bring the infidels to their knees . . . I would hate to disappoint them."

As Mustafa left to carry out his orders, Farrar turned to the case of AK-47 assault rifles in the corner and began cleaning and inspecting each one. He spoke softly to himself. "Yes, Allah, we badly need to strike back at the infidels to regain our respect among our brothers in the Middle East, and I need to do this to avenge my family."

Known only as the Desert Fox to the United Nations intelligence service, Farrar had been number one on their "hit list" for the past seven years. Three agents had been killed trying to assassinate him, and he currently carried the "kill on sight" designation for intelligence agencies in four countries. Although aware of this, Farrar didn't dwell on it since he was a true believer in the rightness of his cause and of the Prophet's personal protection for him and his people.

Unknown to the intelligence forces of the United Nations, he and a handpicked band of assassins had made their way to the United States of America for the express purpose of assassinating Claire Osterman and softening up the country for its eventual takeover by his forces.

His band of terrorists were hiding out in a poor section of Indianapolis, preparing for the first strike against the United States, knowing it had been terribly weakened by its unsuccessful war against the SUSA of the previous year. If this attack were to go well, Farrar knew he would have little trouble attracting men of influence to back him and his cause.

Claire Osterman glanced up and smiled at her bodyguard, Herb Knoff, as he handed her a cup of coffee in her office. She was surrounded by her team of advisors, which she called her "cabinet."

Harlan Millard, ostensibly Claire's second in command, sat across the room, nervously biting on a thumbnail as he watched Claire with an expression much like a canary watching a cat.

General Maxwell Goddard, who'd recently assumed command of the United States' Armed Forces after General Bradley Stevens, Jr., had failed in the last war against the SUSA and Ben Raines, rolled a thick, black cigar around in his mouth, not daring to light it in Claire's presence. He was tall and thin, and not averse to speaking his mind when he thought Claire was going to do something stupid, but he was generally slow to speak and weighed his words carefully, like a skinflint whose every utterance cost him money.

Wallace W. Cox, her Minister of Finance, sat peering at her through glasses as thick as Coke-bottle bottoms, nibbling at the ends of his scraggly mustache, wondering if she were going to blame him for the sorry state of the country's treasury as she usually did.

Gerald Boykin, her Ministry of Defense and liaison with the U.N., looked bored. The meeting had been called to discuss the upcoming presidential election, and he thought it would have little to do with him. He covered a wide yawn with the back of his hand, and tried desperately to keep his eyelids from drooping as he semi-dozed on the couch.

Clifford Ainsworth, her Minister of Propaganda, sat in a corner in a wrinkled seersucker suit, holes dotting the front of it from cigarette ashes. When he thought no one was looking, he poured dark, amber liquid from a silver flask into his coffee. His head was splitting from a long night at a bar and he needed a bit of the hair of the dog.

"Now," Claire said brightly after sampling her coffee, "does anyone have any great ideas for propaganda for the upcoming election?"

Harlan Millard shook his head. "I just don't know why you're so worried, Claire," he said in his typical whining tone of voice. "After all, we control the voting booths and the counting computers and the press. Anyone who dares to run against you won't have a chance of winning."

Claire's smile faded a bit and her eyes grew hard. "That's not necessarily true, Harlan," she said, her voice hard. "There is talk the United Nations has been asked to intervene in our election." She cut her eyes to Gerald Boykin, who suddenly began to sweat a bit. "If that's true, and Gerry over there can't block it, we may find it harder to steal votes as we did in the last two elections."

General Goddard cleared his throat and took the cigar out of his mouth.

"Yes, Max?" Claire asked. "You have something you want to add?"

"I wouldn't worry overly much about the U.N., Madam President," he growled in a deep voice.

"Why is that, General?"

He shrugged. "The U.N. can decree and fuss all it wants to, but the simple fact is they haven't the troops to back up any orders they give."

"That's true, Max dear, but if they think I stole the election, they could simply not recognize my government. Though it wouldn't be fatal to us, it would severely hamper us in any efforts to trade with other countries."

"Not to mention the havoc it would cause if they cut our allowance of foreign oil and gasoline," Cox said. "At current levels of usage, there wouldn't be an automobile running in two weeks."

Claire spread her hands. "There, you see? We're all in agreement that we must put the best face possible on this upcoming election, just to avoid any messy complications with the U.N."

She stood up and leaned on her desk. "Now, do any of you have any suggestions for the speech I'm going to give next week at the fund-raiser?"

Harlan Millard shook his head, his face a mask of worry. "I don't think it wise for you to speak in public yet, Claire."

"Why not?"

"It's too soon after our defeat at the hands of Ben Raines," he said. "There are still a lot of people who blame you for getting us into a war that caused such hardship and misery."

Claire's eyes flashed. "Are you saying it was my fault we lost?"

"No, no, of course not, Claire," Harlan stammered. "But with so many of our citizens dying from the plague our allies released on the SUSA, there are some people who are not thinking correctly who are bound to blame you." He pulled a handkerchief out of his pocket and swiped it across his face. "I just don't want you to take any chances, that's all."

General Goddard nodded. "I agree with Harlan, Claire. Emotions are still running high out in the country. Perhaps it would be better if the Army took over security for your dinner speech."

Herb Knoff, who besides being Claire's bodyguard and part-time lover, oversaw the security provided by the Secret Service agents assigned to protect Claire's life, bristled.

"I don't think that's necessary, General," he said coldly. "My men are perfectly capable of providing for the president's security during her speech."

The general gave a tiny smile, as if he doubted that very much, but he nodded. "All right, Herb, but don't forget I offered our help."

"Oh, I won't forget, Max," Herb said scornfully, "you can bet on that."

"Now, gentlemen," Claire said, "let's don't argue. The important thing is for us to get the right message across to the voters."

"I think you ought to go with the usual," Gerald Boykin said. "Put the blame for everything on Ben Raines and those SUSA assholes."

"But Claire," Harlan argued, "we can't do that. Raines and his medical people are the ones who developed the vaccine and his medical teams are over here working as hard as they can to save United States citizens' lives."

Claire pursed her lips. "For once, you are probably right, Harlan. I think it wise to hold off on attacking Raines, at least until his doctors and nurses have finished their work here."

"There's always the U.N.," General Goddard said slowly.

"The U.N.?" Claire asked.

"Sure. How about trying to lay the blame on them for not keeping a closer eye on Bottger and Perro Loco? After all, you can argue, if the U.N. had prevented them from building up their forces in the first place, there never would have been a war."

"That's a brilliant idea, Max," Claire said.

"And the added benefit," Boykin said, suddenly coming awake, "is if we stir the people up against the U.N., the U.N. will be less likely to intervene in our election."

"And even if they do, no one will listen to what they say," Claire added, rubbing her hands together, a broad smile on her face.

She turned her gaze to Ainsworth, her smile fading. He was leaning back in his chair, his eyes closed and his forehead wrinkled in pain.

"Are you all right, Cliff?" she asked, though there was no real warmth in her voice.

"Got a bitch of a headache, Claire," he answered shortly.

"I just wondered," she said, "since you haven't bothered to join in our discussion."

Ainsworth opened one eye. "I'll print whatever you tell me to, as usual, Claire. Just don't expect me to come up with all the lies on my own."

Claire gritted her teeth. Ainsworth was a drunk and an insubordinate son of a bitch, but he could write news stories that could make a cynic cry. As such, he was much too valuable to her to let him get under her skin.

"Well, try to pay attention, Cliff. We have some ideas for you to pursue in tomorrow's editorials and news stories."

He nodded, then winced as the pain shot through his temples like a hot ice pick.

"I heard. You want me to do a hatchet job on the United Nations . . . blame everything from the plague to high taxes on their incompetence."

"That about sums it up," Claire said.

Three

Mike Post had his driver slow the HumVee he was riding in as it pulled alongside Ben Raines, who was jogging slowly down the street with Jodie, his malamute dog, by his side.

"Hey, Ben," Mike called out of the passenger-side window. "You want to pull over? I've got some new intel I need to discuss with you."

Ben grinned and shook his head. "Naw, but I'll slow down until you can climb out and join me."

Mike sighed. Ben's penchant for pushing himself ever harder since his fortieth birthday was well known. Ben was determined to fight old age every step of the way. Word had it he was succeeding remarkably well, being able to outperform most of his troops who were less than half his age.

Mike nodded at his briefcase on the seat next to him. "Please see that my case gets back to my office, and notify the medical corps if I'm not back in half an hour. They may need to send an ambulance," he said to the driver.

"You want some advice?" the young man drawled in the thick accent of a Texan.

"Sure," Mike said as he pulled the door open.

"Don't try to keep up with the general," the sergeant said, grinning lopsidedly. "Just go at your own pace and look like you're in pain. Maybe he'll have mercy on you and slow down."

"Thanks," Mike said sarcastically as he jumped down to the pavement.

Ben was jogging in place, until Mike got next to him; then he started down the street again, not waiting to see if Mike was coming.

Jodie, impatient to run full out, bounded ahead with a joyful bark, diverting off the street briefly to scare the living daylights out of a nearby squirrel.

"What's so important you risk breaking into a sweat to tell me?" Ben asked, breathing easily though his fatigues were damp with sweat.

"Things are getting worse in the USA," Mike said between puffs. "There's widespread starvation among the more rural population, the government has no money for even the most basic essential services, and there are shortages of almost everything throughout the country."

Ben gave a short laugh. "Hah. When will the eggheads who advocate socialistic types of government ever admit it just doesn't work? People, especially Americans, just won't put up with giving all their hard-earned money to others who refuse to work out of pure laziness."

Mike nodded, his breath beginning to come harder now. "That's not all," he gasped.

Ben glanced to the side, grinned, and slowed his pace to not much more than a fast walk.

"I think I'll issue orders that senior officers start attending physical-training exercises again," Ben said. "I can see that my staff is getting seriously out of shape."

Mike rolled his eyes, but the pain in his side prevented him from answering.

"Well, what else did you have?" Ben asked.

"We have information that a band of terrorists has crossed into the U.S. from Canada."

"Do we know who?"

"Remember what I said about the situation in Iraq the other day?"

"Yeah."

"It seems this Abdullah El Farrar has decided to attempt a takeover of the USA as his first big target. I have it on good authority he intends to assassinate Claire Osterman and then try to move in during the resultant chaos."

Ben slowed to a walk, his eyes narrowed. "The man must be insane. From what you say, he has no real army, just a ragtag bunch of misfits and extremists who are pissed off at the world."

"Maybe he's not as crazy as we think," Mike said, bending over and putting his hands on his knees and taking deep breaths.

"How so?" Ben asked.

"I have further information that the Armies of both Iraq and Iran haven't been paid for several months now. There is talk that Farrar is using some of his family's old oil money they had stashed in Switzerland to bribe the Armies' higher officers to break allegiance with Iraq and Iran and come under his command."

"Are you talking about a coup?"

Mike nodded. "If that happens, and Farrar can manage to get the religious leaders to endorse his regime, he'll be the de facto new leader of two of the most extreme countries in the Middle East, Iran and Iraq."

Ben stroked his chin. "And he'll have some control over a third of the world's oil fields."

"Not something to look forward to, is it?"

"What do you recommend we do about it?"

"First, I'd send a team of antiterrorists into the USA to give Claire some help. If he can be stopped there, the Army officers back home won't be too anxious to let him take over their Armies, no matter how much money he has."

Ben pursed his lips. "Claire won't be eager to accept our help. She'll think we're trying to take her government over."

"Well," Mike said, straightening up and breathing more

normally now, "you asked what I recommended, and that's it. How you do it is up to you."

"Perhaps we could send our team in disguised as medical personnel, using the plague treatments as a cover for their being in the country."

"Are you going to tell Claire what we've uncovered as far as the terrorists coming after her?" Mike asked.

Ben nodded. "Yes. Like you say, better the devil you know than one you don't. I kinda like having Claire president of the U.S. I know what to expect. If she were to be killed or otherwise ousted from power, there's no telling who would take her place."

"And then we'd have to worry about the domino effect her assassination would have on the situation back in Iran and Iraq," Mike added.

"Yeah," Ben agreed. "As far as that goes, I want you to get on the horn to Jean-François Chapelle at the U.N. and tell him what you've heard. It might be prudent for the U.N. to put some troops in place in the oil fields to prevent any mischief from Farrar's followers."

"Will do," Mike said.

Ben slapped him on the back. "Good. And now that you've rested, we'll do doubletime back to the office."

"Oh, shit," Mike groaned to Ben's back as he began to jog after him.

That evening, Ben gathered his team to eat with him in the officers' mess.

Coop looked around at the variety and quantity of food and whistled softly. "Man, I never realized you officers had it so good."

Ben smirked. "It's a small consolation for having to put up with insubordinate junior officers and enlisted men who continually fail to obey orders and make our lives miserable."

Coop assumed a hurt expression. "I can't imagine who you're referring to, General Raines, sir!" he said, snapping to attention.

"Oh, for Christ's sake, knock it off, Coop," Ben said with a chuckle.

"Yeah," Jersey said, shaking her head, "the only orders you follow are the ones leading to food."

Harley Reno, accompanied by Anna, Ben's adopted daughter and the latest love of his life, took a seat at the end of the table.

"I don't know about you guys," Reno said to the rest of the group, "but I get awfully nervous when men with stripes start offering me extra-special food. It usually means we're gonna get some news that might otherwise ruin our appetites."

Hammer Hammerlick nodded his agreement as he took a seat on the other side of Anna. "Never known it to fail," he said.

"Aw, you boys are just too suspicious," Coop said with an easy smile. "Nothin's going on in the world right now. Ben's just being nice to us 'cause we did so good in the last little fracas. Isn't that right, Ben?"

"Not exactly," Ben said, a serious look on his face.

"Uh-oh, now the ax drops right on our necks," Jersey said, glaring at Coop as if it was his fault.

Beth, the statistician, and Corrie, the radio tech, both took their seats, their eyes fixed on Ben.

"You want to eat first, or hear the assignment first?" Ben asked the team.

"Hell, give us the bad news first," Coop said. "I never could eat when I was worried about something."

"Since when?" Jersey asked, her eyebrows raised. "I've never seen you lose your appetite, not even when you were up to your neck in slime in that jungle a few years back."

"All right, maybe that's so, but I don't enjoy it as much when I'm worried."

"Go on, Ben," Reno said. "Give it to us straight."

Ben nodded and began to fill them in on the situation in the U.S., with Claire in danger from an assassination attempt by El Farrar and his men.

"You really think they'll be able to get to her?" Reno asked. "I'd bet as paranoid as Osterman is, especially after her own cabinet tried to kill her, she's got a pretty good detail of men in place to protect her."

Ben grinned. "The best protection in the world can't stop an assassin who's willing to die to kill his target," he said. "We only have to look at history to bear that out."

"So, you're gonna send us in to help protect the woman who's declared war on us several times?" Coop asked.

"In short, yes," Ben answered.

"Will she cooperate with our efforts?" Jersey asked. "After all, I cut a notch out of her ear last time we met. She might just hold a grudge."

"She's not going to know you all are helping out," Ben said. "You're going in undercover."

"Come again?" Reno said.

"Your mission is not to protect Osterman exactly," Ben said. "It's more to find the assassins and either kill them or run them out of the country before they can get to the president."

"You think that's possible?" Hammerlick asked.

"It shouldn't be all that difficult," Ben said. "The kill team will have to be in Indianapolis, and will almost certainly be made up of Middle Eastern types. They should be pretty easy to ferret out."

"If it's so easy, why not just give the information to the FPPS and let them do the work?" Coop asked.

"Because Mike Post thinks El Farrar may have some inside connections working with him to get rid of Claire Osterman, and we don't know who in her government we can trust."

"So, what's our cover going to be?" Beth asked.

"You'll go in as one of our medical teams. That'll give you reason to be roaming around the city of Indianapolis, knocking on doors and asking questions. You can fake an outbreak of the plague virus there, and I'm sure most of the citizens will cooperate with you in your search for the assassins."

Coop nodded, "Yeah, we can say these Middle Eastern types have been identified as carrying the virus. That way anyone who's seen them will be sure to let us know."

"That sounds good," Ben said. "I'm going to have Dr. Buck work with you for a while to get you ready to pose as a medical team. That way you'll know how you're supposed to act."

Coop laughed out loud. "Acting like a doctor will be easy . . . just walk around with a golf putter in my hand with my lips pursed, nodding wisely and saying h-m-m-m occasionally as if I am in deep thought."

Jersey socked him in the arm. "I'll be sure and tell Dr. Buck what you said, Coop. And I'll make sure he remembers it the next time we need our shots."

Coop's face paled at the mention of shots, one of his most terrible fears. "All right, I take it back," he said, glancing at her out of the corners of his eyes.

Jersey grinned and winked at Ben. "Nope, it's too late for that, Coop." She looked up at Ben. "What is Dr. Buck's extension number, Ben? I need to give him a call as soon as the meeting's over."

"Jersey, I'm warning you," Coop said. "You know I was just kidding around."

"Tell you what, Coop," Jersey said, turning slightly to face him. "My Uzi's getting pretty grungy with all this target practice we've been doing lately. You give it a good cleaning for me, and I might just forget to give Dr. Buck a call."

Coop leaned back in his chair with a sigh. "OK, you win. I'll do it tonight after mess."

Harley Reno asked, "When are you planning on sending us in, Ben?"

"Day after tomorrow. That'll give you time to get a heads-up from the doctor and get your equipment together for the insertion."

Harley looked around at his team members. "Better dig in, guys. From what I hear about the U.S., this may be our last chance to eat real meat for a while."

Four

The insertion of the team went without incident. They were flown into Indianapolis on one of the scheduled flights from the SUSA to the USA. Armed guards of the Federal Prevention and Protective Service, the black-shirted men known as FFPS who'd taken over the old FBI functions after the war, stood watch to make sure only medical personnel were allowed on or off the airplanes.

Harley and the others carried their weapons in their black doctor's bags or in shoulder holsters under their white coats.

Everyone had a Beretta Model 93R on their persons. The handgun fired a 9mm Parabellum bullet, had a twenty-round magazine, and could fire singly or in three-shot bursts. When it was fired on full automatic, a small lever dropped down in front of the trigger for the left hand to hold onto.

In the doctor bags were mini-Uzis, which could fire up to 640 rounds per minute and were small enough to be held like a pistol, though both hands were needed if fired on full auto.

In some large trunks labeled medical equipment, Harley had stashed a few of the shotguns he preferred for close-in fighting, the SPAS Model 12. The Special Purpose Automatic Shotgun had a seven-shot tubular magazine, weighed only four kilograms, and on full automatic could fire at the rate of 240 rounds per minute.

As the men unloaded their equipment, Coop muttered, "I hope those FPPS guys don't try to look inside these crates."

Harley grinned. "They won't. On the manifest, I listed the contents as being vials of plague viruses needed to make more vaccine. I bet they stay well away from us until we're outta sight."

Sure enough, the black-shirted guards glanced nervously at the team until they were in one of the SUSA HumVees that'd been sent to use as ground transport for the medical teams.

Coop got behind the wheel of the big vehicle while everyone else piled in the back. "Where to now, Boss?" he asked of Harley, who was the team's designated leader on this mission.

Harley pulled a sheet of paper out of his breast pocket. "Ben's got us set up with a suite of rooms at the Indianapolis Hilton, right on Main Street downtown."

"The Hilton, huh?" Coop asked as he began to drive. "That sounds nice. I wonder if they have room service."

As they drove through downtown Indianapolis, the team could hardly believe their eyes. It was like driving through a Third World country. There were many people actually begging on the streets, dressed in rags, dirty and thin to the point of emaciation.

"Jesus," Corrie said with feeling. "Some of those people look like they haven't eaten in weeks."

Hammer Hammerlick nodded. "They probably haven't, Corrie. From the news reports, there is widespread famine all across the country."

"I thought we and the U.N. had sent in tons of food and other goods," Anna said.

Hammer looked over his shoulder at her. "We have, Anna, but if it's like anything else in this country, most of that went to the higher-ups in the government, or to friends of the rich and powerful."

"So, I guess the socialist/democratic form of government is like all the others, in spite of their rhetoric about everyone being equal?" she asked.

Harley Reno glanced at her, his eyes warm. "You don't repeal the laws of nature by passing man-made laws, Anna. Man is an animal just like the lion or tiger in the jungle. When push comes to shove, he'll take what he can in whatever way he can in order to survive."

"Yeah," Coop said in disgust, "I'll bet Claire Osterman and her group of sycophants haven't lost any weight lately."

He turned the HumVee around a corner, and in front of them was the Indianapolis Hilton, a twenty-story ramshackle building that had obviously seen better days.

After he parked and they unloaded their own bags and trunks of equipment, there being no bellboys around, they went up to the front desk.

A seedy-looking man in a tattered black coat stepped to the counter.

"Can I help you?" he asked.

"We're part of the medical team from the SUSA," Harley said, putting the paper Ben had given him on the countertop.

"Ah, yes," the man said. "I'm Wilford Riley, the manager of the Hilton."

He turned, grabbed a handful of keys off a board behind him, and placed them on the counter. "Your rooms are on the tenth floor." He hesitated. "In fact, you have the entire floor to yourselves."

"Business not too hot, huh?" Coop asked.

Riley glanced at him. "Not since the . . . war. No one seems to have any money for traveling anymore."

"How about room service?" Coop asked.

Riley laughed quickly, then caught himself. "I'm afraid room service has been discontinued due to the shortage of food lately."

He looked around, as if to see if anyone were listening, then leaned across the counter. "However, if you have sufficient funds, cash I mean, I'm sure you can get just about anything you want."

"You mean on the black market?" Anna asked.

Riley held up his hands, a look of horror on his face. "Oh, no. Certainly not! Engaging in the black market is a capital offense, madam."

"Then what do you mean?" Coop asked.

"It's just that there are certain stores and restaurants, owned by prominent people, that still have plenty of goods. The prices are extremely high, of course, but"—he spread his arms wide—"that should pose no problem for you people from the SUSA."

Harley took the keys and they walked toward the elevators. "By prominent people, I'll bet you dollars to doughnuts he meant Claire Osterman and her government cronies."

From behind them, Riley called out, "I'm afraid you'll have to take the stairs. The elevators have been shut down due to scarcity of electricity."

"Great," Jersey said, hoisting a forty-pound crate onto her shoulders. "Ten flights of stairs."

"Look at it this way," Coop said, following her up the stairs. "It's a great way to get your legs in shape."

Jersey glanced back over her shoulder. "And just what's wrong with the shape of my legs now?"

Harley shook his head and smiled. "Uh-oh, Coop. You know there's no way to answer that without getting into major trouble."

"Don't I know it!" Coop agreed.

On their floor, the team spread out and each took a different room, leaving a large two-bedroom suite in the center of the floor to use as their conference room.

Once they'd all unpacked their gear, they met in the conference room. Harley Reno paced the room as he talked, while the others took seats on chairs and couches spread around the room.

"First, we need to set some ground rules for our search for El Farrar and his men," he said.

"Besides shoot first and ask questions later, what do we need to know?" Coop asked, a lazy grin on his face.

"Rule number one," Harley continued, unfazed by Coop's joking, "is never to go out alone. I want us all to travel in groups of at least two."

When everyone nodded, he continued. "I also want us all to carry our cell phones at all times, and to immediately report any suspicious activities or persons to Corrie, who will be our liaison among the team. That way, if you get into trouble, we'll know where you are and can come running if needed."

"Will we need to talk in code?" Jersey asked. "I know cell phones aren't particularly secure."

Corrie took the question. "Not with these, Jersey. They're keyed to the satellites that the U.S. doesn't have access codes to. However, just to be safe, I'd use a little common sense in what we say. We just don't know what technology this Desert Fox has up his sleeve."

"Third rule, always go armed," said Harley. "We don't think Farrar knows we're after him, but like Corrie says, we also don't know if he's got any spies in the SUSA that may have gotten wind of our mission, so be careful."

"If we see him or some of his cohorts, are we to take immediate action?" Coop asked. "Or just report back and keep them under surveillance?"

"I'll leave that up to you. If we could capture one of his men alive, we might be able to interrogate him to find out more about their plans and capabilities, but if we do that, Farrar will suspect someone's on his trail and may go deeper undercover."

"Do we have any photographs of him or any of his key officers?" Beth asked.

Harley shook his head. "Not since he was much younger, so they won't do us much good. We do think most if not all of his men are of Middle Eastern descent, so they are probably dark-skinned with black or dark brown hair."

"Blondes need not apply in his army, huh?" Jersey said.

"Not from what Intel tells us," Harley replied, "but we do think part of his mission here is to recruit disaffected U.S. citizens, especially military or FPPS personnel, to his cause. If he plans to invade the U.S., he's gonna need some spies on the inside in order for his campaign to do any good."

"From what I've seen of the situation over here," Coop said, "it shouldn't be too hard for him to find people willing to join his forces if it means getting rid of President Osterman."

"That's Intel's take on it too, Coop."

Harley pinned a map of Indianapolis on the wall next to where he stood. He put a box of different colored pushpins on a table in front of the map. "We'll mark all the areas we search with a blue pin if we find nothing suspicious. Areas we're not sure of will be marked with a yellow pin. If we find definite evidence of Farrar or any of his men, we'll mark those areas with red pins."

"While we're busy looking for this asshole, are we going to try and do anything to protect Osterman?" Jersey asked.

Harley shook his head. "No, that's been ruled out. Ben had Mike Post contact her security team and tell them he had information that Farrar was a possible threat and asked if they needed any help. Of course they said no, they could handle it."

"So, what's our first move?" Beth asked.

"First, we're gonna scout out our immediate neighborhood and find some decent places to eat," Harley said, "and make sure there's nothing nearby we need to worry about."

"Speaking of possible threats, are we gonna post guards while we sleep?" Corrie asked.

"Of course," Harley said. "Remember, gang, this is a hot zone, even if it looks a lot like home. We have to consider everyone a potential hostile, so when we leave our quarters, we're always going to have someone here to guard our stuff. I don't want a nosy maid to discover our weapons or gear."

Coop glanced around at the shabby suite. "I don't think we have to worry about any maids in the near future," he said with a grin. "This place doesn't look like it's been cleaned since the big war."

"I'm not worried about cleaners," Harley said, "but about looters. Remember, everyone thinks the SUSA people are all rich, so our quarters would be a natural place for thieves to hit looking for goods to steal."

"If I'm so rich, how come I never have any money?" Coop asked.

" 'Cause you spend it all on wine, women, and song!" Jersey said.

"That's a lie!" Coop retorted. "I never sing."

Five

Beth said she wasn't particularly hungry, so she'd stand the first watch in their hotel rooms while the rest of the team went searching for a nearby restaurant where they could eat.

Less than two blocks from the Hilton they found an eating establishment called Marinaro's.

"I could use some good Italian food," Coop said, pointing at the restaurant's sign.

"I've never seen you turn down food of any kind," Jersey said, "though Italian is all right with me."

Harley Reno shrugged. "Italian it is then."

They entered the doors and stood in a group, looking around at the room. There were about fifteen tables, all covered with the requisite red checkered tablecloths, with old bottles of wine fitted with candles as centerpieces.

A short, rather fat man with a dark handlebar mustache and graying black hair hustled up to greet them.

"Welcome to Marinaro's," he said with a thick Italian accent.

Harley glanced around, noticing only one other table was occupied, by a well-to-do-appearing man and woman.

"Not too busy tonight, huh?" Harley asked.

The man shrugged. "Well, you know, with the recent cutbacks in salaries and such, not too many people can afford to eat out."

He adjusted the apron around his waist and gave the team an appraising look. "I am Marinaro, the owner of this restaurant."

He looked over his shoulder at the window to the kitchen, visible against a back wall. "I am also the head waiter, cook, and dishwasher," he said with a small smile.

"Table for six, please," Harley said.

Marinaro pursed his lips. "We have no tables for six, but I can push two together if that suits you."

"That's fine."

"We'll look at your menus while you get the tables ready," Coop said, licking his lips.

Marinaro raised his eyebrows. "Oh, we have no menus. Our selections of late have been . . . rather limited due to the shortage of food in the city."

"Oh?" Harley said.

"Yes. But tonight, we are serving spaghetti and meat sauce, with garlic bread and salad."

Harley looked around at the team, all of whom nodded their agreement.

"That'll be all right," Harley said. "Do you have any wine to go with that?" he asked the owner as the man pushed chairs and tables together in the center of the room.

Marinaro gave another shrug. "Only a rather pedantic Chianti, I'm afraid."

"Bring us three bottles of that and some water, please," Harley asked.

"Aren't you going to ask how much the meals will cost?" Marinaro asked, a worried look on his face.

Harley stared at him for a moment, then pulled a wallet from his pocket and opened it to show the man a thick bundle of bills inside.

"I'm sure you'll be reasonable," he said.

Marinaro's eyes widened at the sight of so much money; then he grinned widely. "Certainly, sir," he said, and hustled off toward the kitchen.

* * *

As they ate their salads, which consisted of rather anemic and wilted iceberg lettuce with slices of almost spoiled tomatoes and some small pieces of cucumber, Jersey turned to Harley.

"Do you think it wise to show him how much money we have?"

Harley leaned across the table and whispered. "Yes. I want him to know we are rich. It may help loosen his tongue when I ask him some questions about the area."

After Marinaro delivered the main course of spaghetti with a sauce that was mainly tomato sauce with very little actual meat in it, Harley asked him to join them for a glass of wine.

"Thank you, sir. Don't mind if I do," Marinaro said, after glancing at the front of the restaurant to make sure there were no other customers.

As the owner poured himself a glass of Chianti, Harley said, "We're a medical team, sent here from the SUSA to help with inoculations against the plague."

Marinaro nodded. "I suspected as much. There are very few citizens who have the amount of money you do, and even fewer who are willing to spend it on eating out."

"I was wondering," Harley said, leaning back in his chair and sipping his wine, "if you might be able to help us."

Marinaro smacked his lips over his wine and stared at Harley, a slightly suspicious glint in his eyes. "In what way?"

"We have heard that there are some Arabs who have recently come to the U.S. who might have been exposed to the plague and who haven't been inoculated yet."

Marinaro shrugged. "I don't know. As you can imagine, I get very few Arabic customers here."

"Would you be able to help us locate the part of town favored by foreign visitors?" Harley asked.

"Wouldn't it be better to ask the government?" Marinaro asked.

Harley smiled. "I'm afraid the government people spend very little time in the center city," he said, spreading his arms. "They seem to know as little as we do about the various neighborhoods."

Marinaro nodded. "That's true. The bastards refuse to spend any of our tax dollars here in the city where we need it. Instead, they do all their shopping and eating on the Army base, where they don't have to pay taxes on their goods."

"So," Jersey said, smiling sweetly at the man. "Could you help us?"

Marinaro poured himself another glass of wine and thought for a moment. "Most of our foreign visitors, especially those who are not citizens, settle on the west side of town. It is a very poor section, even worse than the center city, and the rents are cheap and no one asks too many questions or requires papers showing citizenship."

"Is it safe to go there and search for persons needing their shots?" Corrie asked.

Marinaro shrugged. "As safe as any other place . . . which is to say, not safe at all if you flash your money around. The people of Indianapolis have been hit very hard by the recent cutbacks due to the war. Hunger will make savages of the most law-abiding citizen at times," he said apologetically.

Harley asked what the charges for the meal were, and Marinaro told him, a worried look on his face as if he thought Harley might complain.

Harley grinned and gave him his money, adding a twenty-percent tip.

Marinaro's face lit up in a wide smile. "Thank you, sir. You are most generous."

"We are going to be here for some time, and the hotel has no facilities for eating," Harley said. He peeled off a few more bills. "If you would be so kind as to restock your kitchen, we would like to make this our main dining facility for the duration of our stay."

Marinaro counted the money and nodded rapidly. "With this, I will get you some veal and some beef for meatballs. You will eat like kings while you are here."

"Good," Harley said, "but if you would, please keep it quiet. We don't want to be bothered by beggars or thieves while we go about our business."

Marinaro grinned and put his finger against his lips. "It will be our little secret."

In a well-used apartment building on the city's west side, Abdullah El Farrar was meeting with his second in command, Mustafa Kareem.

"Mustafa," Farrar asked, sipping orange juice at a kitchen table, "have you been able to find out the arrangements for President Osterman's upcoming speech?"

"Yes," the big man answered quickly. "I found a member of her advisory staff who enjoys the company of young men. Akim was much to his liking, it seems, and was able to get him to talk without much difficulty."

Farrar nodded and gestured for Mustafa to continue.

"I have located the caterer that is to provide waiters and serving staff for the dinner next week. I already have two of our group hired by them. When the time comes for the delivery, we will have little trouble stopping the trucks on their way and substituting our men for all of the other waiters and cook staff."

"Then all is in readiness?" Farrar asked.

Kareem nodded. "It should pose no problem when it comes time to exact our vengeance for what has been done to our families."

Farrar nodded, his gaze wandering to look out the window as he recalled his first meeting with Kareem. . . .

* * *

The desert sun baked the streets of Baghdad, and the heat waves dancing upward through the sand haze in the air made the whole world seem to quiver. The teenagers playing in the streets seemed as insubstantial as ghosts outlined by the 110-degree glare in the haze. They were playing their usual game of taunting the U.N. soldiers, calling them names and throwing garbage and rocks at them as they rode by in their SUSA-supplied jeeps.

Farrar, although a couple of years younger than the others, joined in and gleefully hurled a rock in the general direction of one of the jeeps. He was fully as surprised and scared as the soldiers riding in the jeep were when the rock struck the front windshield and shattered it. The jeep screeched to a halt and the soldier in the passenger seat jumped out, and began to chase the suddenly scattering boys.

As he rounded a corner at full tilt, Farrar felt himself grabbed by the scruff of the neck and lifted off the ground. Screaming, shouting, and flailing out with his arms and legs, he was silenced by a ringing blow to the side of his head. With the world suddenly darkened, and as things began to shrink and swell in his vision, Farrar saw the grinning soldier draw back his fist for another blow to his face. He closed his eyes, waiting for the inevitable.

Out of nowhere, a tall skinny teenager barreled into the soldier, knocking both him and Farrar to the ground. Farrar lay in the garbage in the alley, trying to clear his still-spinning head. The boy and the soldier rolled over and over, each struggling for an advantage over the other.

Finally, due to his superior size and strength, the soldier ended up on top, his hands locked in a death grip around the boy's throat. Sweating with rage and exertion, his face a mask of hate, the soldier squeezed harder and harder until the young man's face began to turn a shade of blue so dark it was almost black.

In a panicked frenzy Farrar began to paw through the trash looking for anything he could use as a weapon. His hands locked on the neck of a discarded wine bottle. He scrambled to his feet and rushed toward the pair on the ground. Putting all of his weight behind the blow, he struck the soldier in the forehead, shattering the bottle and knocking the man to the ground. He stood over the fallen soldier and overcome with hatred, stuck the jagged neck of the bottle into his throat. With a squeal like a gut-shot pig, the young man grabbed his neck and rolled on the ground, crimson blood pumping from between his fingers, his eyes bright with terror and pain.

Farrar pulled the young boy to his feet by the front of his shirt, then led his new friend through the alleyways as if the devil himself were after them. Later, after circling for hours to lose any possible tails, the boys approached Farrar's house.

The boy, who had introduced himself as Mustafa Kareem, grabbed Farrar and pulled him back into the alley just as he was about to run across the street to his house.

"Look, Abdul, the U.N. security forces!" said Kareem, pointing to the black four-door sedan pulling up in front of Farrar's house. There was no doubt that the two men in Western style suits were indeed members of the dreaded secret police of the U.N. No one else so dressed would have business with Farrar's father, who insisted that anyone entering his house dress in the customary Arab fashion.

As one of the richest families in Iraq due to their extensive oil holdings, Farrar's family could do just about anything they wanted.

"Do you think the soldiers recognized you?" Kareem asked Farrar.

Farrar shrugged his small shoulders. "I do not know," he said, "but if they think my father will care that I killed a U.N. scum soldier, they are very much mistaken."

"Do you think he will stand up to the U.N. security forces?" Kareem asked, his face a mask of worry.

Farrar was confident. "My father is not afraid of anything,

least of all these U.N. men who scurry around trying to curry favor with him."

Twenty minutes later, Farrar saw his father, mother, and younger brother dragged screaming out of the house and thrown into the rear seat of the car. It was all Kareem could do to convince Farrar that there was nothing he could do to help them.

Farrar knew that even though his family would probably not be harmed, his life of privilege was over. The young boy stood in the alley, tears coursing down his cheeks as his world crumbled around him. In less than a day, he'd gone from one of the richest people in the world, to a hunted fugitive in his own land. He looked down at the soldier's blood that covered his hands, and swore that it would not be the last blood that he would shed to avenge his family.

"Come on, let's see if they've gotten to your house yet," said Farrar, brushing away the tears.

"Yes, we must hurry if we're to be in time to warn my family."

As it turned out, they weren't in time. Kareem's family, not as influential as Farrar's, was never seen again. The two young fugitives were to be for many years the only family for each other. Farrar's family's oil holdings and company were taken over by the U.N. after the great war just as everyone else's had, and the oil distributed to whatever country needed it the most, regardless of ability to pay.

Farrar, however, retained access to his family's huge bank accounts in Switzerland, and would from that day on use the money to finance his quest for revenge against the rest of the world for his family's shame and degradation at the hands of the U.N. infidels.

Six

Claire Osterman buzzed Herb Knoff to come into her office. She was in the process of writing her speech for her upcoming talk to the influential men and women who were supposed to help her win the next presidential election.

Herb stepped into the room and immediately went to the coffee machine in the corner of the office.

"You ready for a refill?" he asked, holding the coffeepot in his hand.

Claire glanced at her half-empty cup on her desk. "Sure," she said, in a fairly good mood this morning, for a change.

Herb emptied the cold coffee out of her cup into a sink, and refilled it with steaming-hot brew.

"How's the speech coming?" he asked, looking over her shoulder as he sipped from his own cup.

She grinned. "Good, I think. The problem is to tell these nabobs what they want to hear, not necessarily what's going to happen."

He laughed. "That's easy," he said. "All you have to do is tell them under your new Administration, things will go on as they always have. That is, the rich will get richer and the poor will stay the same."

"That'll sure make these jerks happy," Claire agreed, looking back at her speech. "The lower the government's treasury has gotten, the more they've been able to sock away."

Herb shrugged. "Can't be helped, my dear," he said. "The movers and shakers in every government since the dawn of time have always profited from their support of the ruling classes. It's just the way it is."

Claire leaned back. "You know, Herb. When I first took office, I was naive enough to think I could actually do something for the poor and downtrodden . . . actually make a difference in their lives for the better. That was the whole premise of the socialist/democratic movement."

Herb sat down across from her, shaking his head. "And then you found out what every leader has discovered since history has been recorded. The poor and downtrodden are that way for a reason. For the most part, they're too lazy or stupid to prepare themselves to make a living in the modern world."

Claire nodded. "And the sad part is, they expect the government to provide everything they need without them having to work or sacrifice for it at all."

He gave her a sarcastic look. "Maybe they think that way because their leaders keep telling them there is such a thing as a free lunch."

She gave him a sharp glance. "Are you referring to me?" she asked archly.

He smiled back at her. "Of course, dear. But I don't blame you . . . that's what you have to say nowadays to get elected in the first place."

She relaxed again. "I sometimes think Jefferson was right."

"Thomas Jefferson?" Herb asked.

"Yeah. When the Founding Fathers were discussing the Constitution, he recommended that only landowners and the wealthy should have the vote. He distrusted the masses, thinking they would be too easily led by their emotions."

Herb laughed. "I wouldn't put that in your speech, Claire. It sounds an awful lot like the drivel Ben Raines preaches about personal responsibility being a prerequisite for voting."

"Jesus, do I sound that bad?" she asked, a wry grin on her face. "The last thing I want to do is sound like Ben Raines."

"Well, the good thing is all the arrangements have been made for the dinner Friday night."

"You've got the caterers lined up and there'll be plenty of food?"

"Yeah, and that took some doing, let me tell you. I actually had to go to the black market to get the stuff we needed."

She frowned. "Are things really that bad?"

"Claire," he said, "you need to get out more. There is practically no food to be had anywhere in the country. Those that have it, the farmers and growers, are hoarding it and selling it piecemeal on the black market. The food stores' shelves are practically bare. If it wasn't for the U.N. and SUSA and the food they're sending over, there wouldn't be anything for the average citizen to eat."

"That's just it," Claire said, an angry look on her face. "I thought the food they're sending was ample for our needs."

"It would be, Claire, except that the people in charge of distribution are the very ones you'll be talking to Friday, and they, like the farmers, are finding it much more profitable to sell the donated goods on the black market instead of putting them in the stores to sell at the regulated prices."

"So these bastards are getting rich by selling food given to us free by the U.N. and SUSA?"

"That's about the size of it."

"Well, we'll see about that!" she said.

Herb held up his hand. "Hold on, Claire, don't go off half-cocked. Wait until we've won the election; then you can clamp down on these black marketers as hard as you want. But for right now, they're the ones with the power to get you reelected, so don't do or say anything to rock the boat."

"Don't worry, Herb," Claire said with a sly smile. "I'll

tell them what they want to hear, but as soon as the election is over, they're going to rue the day they stole from the government."

"That'a girl," Herb said, grinning.

She leaned forward across her desk. "I want you to begin to put together a list of these black marketers, and as soon as I'm ready, we'll have the FPPS take a close look at their tax returns and maybe even confiscate some bank accounts in the bargain."

"Hell, if you do that, the treasury might even show a profit next year."

The team split up into groups of two to search the city for the Arab terrorists. Coop and Jersey, Harley and Anna, Hammer and Beth, with Corrie staying at the hotel to monitor the cell phone communications and to guard their gear.

Each team member was dressed in the typical garb of medical people, white coats over white pants or skirts, and each carried "doctor" bags that contained their Uzis. Their handguns were worn in shoulder holsters for easy access in case of an unexpected confrontation.

By noon, Coop and Jersey had covered most of the four-square-block area they'd been assigned by Harley.

Coop rubbed his stomach as they left the building they'd just searched. "I'm so hungry I could eat a horse." He moaned, as if in pain.

Jersey gave him a look. "You're always hungry, Coop, and horse meat is probably just what we have been eating since we've been here."

"How 'bout we head on over to Marinaro's and see if he can fix us up a meatball sub?"

"You really are going to live dangerously, aren't you?" she asked, smiling.

"Hey, eating horse, or whatever it is, is better than starving to death."

"Yeah, well, that may be true, but we've got one more building to cover before we break for lunch."

Coop looked at their list. The address was right up the street. It was what appeared to be an old apartment building, with four apartments on each floor, and about ten floors for them to cover.

"Jesus, Jerse, that's gonna take all day," he complained.

"Standing here and griping about it won't make us finish any sooner."

Coop grabbed her arm before she could walk off. "Hey, at least let's get a cup of coffee at that diner over there," he said, pointing across the street to a small cafe.

"All right," she replied, "but only a ten-minute break, then it's back to work."

"You got it," he said as they crossed the street.

The diner seemed typical for what they'd seen of downtown Indianapolis. There was a long counter with stools covered with stained and torn plastic, and several booths with formica tables lining the front windows. Coop took a corner booth, where he had a good view of the street and the people coming and going along the sidewalk, as was protocol when in a hot zone.

Jersey picked up a menu, then rubbed her fingers together, grimacing. "Now I know what they mean when they say 'greasy spoon restaurant.' "

Coop gave an uncertain half grin. "Well, the coffee's probably safe anyway."

A waitress approached, her dress as grease-stained as the menu. "Yeah, whatta ya have?"

Coop raised his eyebrows and looked at Jersey. She held up the menu to the waitress. "A cup of hot tea, please."

"And a cup of coffee," added Coop.

A few minutes later, the waitress plopped the cups down, slopping the coffee and water into the saucers, and sauntered off. Coop shook his head and placed napkins in the saucers to absorb the liquid, then looked around for some sugar.

Finding none on the table, he motioned for the waitress to come back.

"Yeah?" she asked, her hip cocked.

"We'd like some sugar."

She looked surprised. "Sugar? It's gonna cost you extra."

Coop sighed, forcing himself to stay seated and not jump up and strangle the rude woman. "All right, just bring it," he said through tight lips.

After a moment, the waitress returned and placed two single packets of sugar on the table. "That'll be two bucks extra," she said, and walked off.

As Coop handed one packet to Jersey and was in the process of adding the other to his coffee, he stiffened and looked down at the table.

Keeping his voice low, he whispered, "Don't look around, but two characters just walked in who may be what we're looking for."

Jersey sat up a little straighter and let her hand rest on her black bag on the seat next to her. She didn't turn around, but kept her eyes on Coop, following his lead.

He leaned back and took a drink of his coffee, then began to talk about the weather and other innocuous subjects while watching the men out of the corner of his eye.

Using broken English, the two men ordered some doughnuts, and left with a paper sack full of the pastries. Coop noticed they paid the exorbitant fee with crisp, new fifty-dollar bills.

After the men left the diner and walked down the street, Coop threw a couple of five-dollar bills down on the table and he and Jersey hurried out the door.

At the first corner, they crossed the street so that they could follow the men without being observed.

As they walked, they paused frequently and looked into store windows, pretending to window-shop. After the men turned into the building they had been about to search, Coop turned down a side street and pulled Jersey out of sight into a small alley.

"Get on the cell phone and tell Corrie we may need backup ASAP!" he said.

In the building, Abdullah El Farrar and Mustafa Kareem were discussing their plans for the attack on Claire Osterman when they heard a loud cheer and much raucous laughing from the room next door. Kareem excused himself and went to investigate. He returned a few moments later and smiled. "How like children the men are. They sent out for doughnuts and are fascinated over them, chewing and rolling their eyes as if Allah himself had sent them the food."

"We must let them have their fun while they can," Farrar said, his eyes clouded. "I fear they will be sorely tested in the next few weeks, and assuredly many of them will be called home to sit at Allah's side."

After taking out a thin, black cigar and lighting it, he continued. "It is strange how this country which provides so much bounty for the body provides so little sustenance for the spirit. The Americans seem to feel that their wealth is their due and that no price will be exacted in order for them to keep it. Even the present time of few resources seems to sap their will to try and regain their old strength."

"I agree with you, brother," said Kareem, "but it would be dangerous to forget the lesson of the great war. The Americans will fight, and fight fiercely, if they feel their way of life is threatened."

"You're right, Kareem, but the other side of the coin is that the citizens are divided into many sub-groups. Unless all of the sub-groups are threatened equally, it is extremely hard for the American politicians to get a consensus of opinion for any meaningful action. It therefore behooves us to pick our targets with extreme care." He went to stand before the window, looking out with his hands in his pockets. "As long as our actions are seen to threaten only the rich and powerful, and not the average citizen, we are virtually assured that the response will be weak and uncoordinated."

"So, that is why you have decided to attack the American president when she is speaking before an audience of the upper echelon of their citizens?" asked Kareem.

He turned. "Yes, we are going to hit the most influential woman in America while she is with the richest of the rich. That way, the ordinary citizens will not feel threatened and rise up against us."

"At least, not until our forces that are on their way here arrive on their shores," Kareem said.

"By that time, it will be too late for the Americans," Farrar said. "Our army will sweep across the country like a whirlwind, destroying everything and everyone before it."

Downstairs, after calling for backup, Coop and Jersey slipped through the front door of the apartment building.

They stood in the foyer, their backs against a wall, and pulled out their Uzis as they peered up the stairs.

"We better be careful, Coop," Jersey said. "These men may not be terrorists after all, just a couple of Arabs living here."

He shook his head. "Did you see that stack of new money they had?" he asked. "No one dressed as they were would have that much money on them, and if they did, they certainly wouldn't show it in public like that. Not if they knew this country at all."

"You're probably right, but . . ." Jersey began, just as a man carrying a Kalashnikov machine gun over his shoulder walked by on the landing to the second floor.

Coop nodded at the man. "Satisfied now?" he asked.

Jersey jacked a shell into the firing chamber of her Uzi and nodded.

Coop put his finger to his lips and started up the stairs,

keeping his back to the wall. At the top, he peeked around a corner, then jerked his head back.

He laid his Uzi down on the floor and took his K-Bar assault knife from a scabbard under his coat.

As a small, thin, dark-skinned man with a rifle in his hands walked around the corner, Coop slipped his left arm around the man's neck and pulled his face tight against his chest as he slipped his knife up under the man's ribs and into his heart. The muffled groan was barely louder than a gasp. Coop lowered him to the floor and whispered down the stairway to Jersey, "Scramble, the party's heating up fast."

Less than a minute later, Jersey skipped up the stairs, her Uzi cocked and ready. Coop started to say something to her as another youth leaned over the stairwell above them on the third floor, saying, "Amal?"

His eyes widened when he saw them, and he began to shout as he reached toward his shoulder holster.

Jersey didn't hesitate. She leveled her Uzi at him and loosed a burst of five rounds, cutting him down. Coop bounded up the stairs, screaming for Jersey to cover her ears as he lobbed a stun grenade down the hallway. Several doors opened and men began to emerge like ants from a disturbed anthill just as the grenade went off.

The shock wave from the blast threw Coop backward down the stairs into Jersey, and they both ended up in a tangle at the foot of the stairs.

"Jesus!" said Coop, looking astonished when he realized he couldn't hear himself talk. He felt himself shoved aside and saw Jersey's lips move, but couldn't hear what she was saying.

The floor where he had been lying disintegrated in a hail of bullets and splinters as Jersey began to spray upward with the Uzi on full automatic, the gun bucking and jumping in her hands.

Coop jerked his Beretta from its holster under his arm,

and rolled over in time to see a man dance under the impact of the bullets and then topple backward out of sight.

Coop struggled to his feet once again, and scrambled back up the stairs just as another man appeared, blood running from his nose and ears, and opened up with a Kalashnikov machine gun. Coop crouched and put three shots in the man's chest, horrified as he saw Jersey picked up and thrown back against the wall as bullets tore into her chest, shredding her jacket.

Coop screamed incoherently and threw another stun grenade, then followed with a tear-gas canister. He didn't wait for the explosion, but ran back down the stairs and took Jersey in his arms, covering her body with his.

The door burst open and Harley and Anna, followed closely by Hammer and Beth, entered, their hands full of weapons.

Coop pointed up the stairs and shouted, "Terrorists, up the stairs—automatic weapons and probably grenades!"

Harley and Anna squatted, covering the stairway, while Beth and Hammer ran partway up, taking positions where they could cover the advance of the others.

In a matter of seconds Harley and Anna proceeded rapidly up the stairs. Harley threw himself to the floor as a burst of automatic fire boomed ahead of him, while Anna began to fire as she ran to his side.

The noise was incredible, and soon the stink of cordite was joined by the irritation of the tear gas as visibility steadily decreased to zero. Coop felt Jersey's neck for a pulse, and was astonished to find one.

He picked her up in his arms and staggered out the door and down the street, out of the way of any stray bullets. As he laid her down, he was grabbed from behind, his arms pinned, and he was thrown up against the brick wall of the building.

"Let's see some ID—fast!" said a man holding a pistol to

Coop's head. He was dressed all in black, and Coop knew immediately the man was with the FPPS.

"Okay, okay, but first get an ambulance for the lady," gasped Coop as he reached in and pulled out his wallet.

The man looked down and muttered, "One's on the way, should be here any minute." He quickly scanned Coop's ID, then lowered his gun and released Coop's arms.

"Want to tell me what the hell's going on here, and what a medical team's doing firing off automatic weapons and getting shot in my city?"

Before Coop could answer, the ambulance arrived and the paramedics rushed to Jersey's side. Coop squatted down as the paramedic asked what her injuries were.

"She took several hits from a Kalashnikov in the chest and a blow to the back of the head. She's been unconscious for about ten minutes."

The paramedic took Jersey's pulse and blood pressure and looked up with a frown on his face. "I don't understand it. Her pulse is steady and her pressure's fine."

He tore her jacket open to examine her wounds and found a Kevlar vest, with five 9mm bullets embedded in it, but no blood. He whistled softly. "The wonders of modern science. Boy, is she lucky. Couple of inches higher and she'd be history."

He ran his hands lightly through her hair, examining the back of her head. "Oh, here's the problem. She's got a knot on her head the size of an egg. That accounts for the unconsciousness."

As he and his assistant lifted Jersey up on the stretcher, he told the FPPS officers that he was going to have to take her to the hospital for tests to see if she had a skull fracture.

Coop turned to the FPPS man and said, "You have my ID . . . can I ride to the hospital with her? I'll wait there for you and answer any questions you might have."

The officer shook his head, "Damn right you will. Bulletproof vests, automatic weapons, hand grenades . . . you've got a lot of explaining to do, mister."

Just then, Harley and the rest of Coop's team walked out of the door of the building, Uzis slung over their shoulders.

The FPPS man shook his head. "Oh, shit, not more of you?"

Harley walked up to the man, holding out his ID. "I'll explain it all to you later, sir, but for now could you call for some more men? The terrorists ran out of the back of the building."

"Terrorists?" the FPPS man asked.

"Yeah, they plan to kill the president," Harley said, causing the FPPS man's eyes to widen and his face to pale in the light from the flames consuming the building down the street.

Seven

Abdullah El Farrar and Mustafa Kareem led their men out of the back door of the apartment building, and across an alleyway and around a corner to a second building he had rented for just such an occasion.

Farrar, long hunted by the forces of the U.N., was no stranger to having to change locations at a moment's notice. He always had a bolt-hole nearby to go to ground in, stocked with extra weapons and ammunition.

As the men spread out, covering various windows in case of pursuit, Farrar and Kareem sat and made plans for the future.

"How many men did we lose in the attack?" Farrar asked.

"Three dead, two wounded slightly," Kareem answered quickly.

"Then we are still in good shape to go through with the assault on the president?"

"Yes. We should have no problem in that regard."

"But you are worried about something else?"

"Yes. How did the authorities know of our presence here? And how did they find us?"

Farrar shrugged. "Mustafa, we have over fifty thousand troops and mercenaries on the way here by various means. It is impossible to keep such an undertaking secret, with so many people aware of it."

"But, my leader, how did they locate us here in the city?" Kareem asked, his face a mask of worry.

"Perhaps it was mere luck," Farrar answered. "After all, our men have been allowed to go out among the Americans often. It might be they were seen, or acted in some way as to bring attention to themselves."

Kareem nodded, considering the possibility.

"In that regard, inform the men they are no longer to venture out of the building . . . at least, not until after our attack later this week."

"Yes, sir," Kareem said, rising to give the men the message and to take care of the wounded.

The FPPS men loaded the rest of the team into a van and followed the ambulance to St. Martin's Hospital in downtown Indianapolis. Coop rode in the back of the carrier with Jersey, holding her hand as the ambulance sped through the streets.

Jersey's eyes flickered once, then opened and stared around the interior of the ambulance. After a moment, they drifted down to look at Coop's hand in hers.

She gave a wry grin. "Don't get any ideas, Romeo," she croaked through dry lips. "Just 'cause I'm unconscious doesn't mean you can take advantage of me."

Coop gave a derisive laugh. "That'll be the day," he said. "From what I hear from your many man friends, you make love like you're unconscious most of the time anyway."

Jersey's eyes flashed. "Bullshit! Number one, none of the men I know would stoop to talking with someone like you, and number two, if they said that they'd be lying through their teeth."

The attendant leaned over and took Jersey's blood pressure. "You'd better let her rest," he said, a slight grin on his face. "You're driving her blood pressure through the roof."

* * *

Later, after the doctor on duty had cleared Jersey, letting her go with a warning to take it easy for a few days, she and Coop joined the others in a conference room at FPPS headquarters on the Benjamin Harrison Army base on the outskirts of town.

When they entered, Harley gave them a sly wink and went back to talking to the lead investigator, who was sitting at the head of a long conference table surrounded by several other agents.

"As I was saying, Mr. Pearson," Harley said, "we were in the process of scouting the building for people who needed inoculations against the plague, when some men carrying automatic weapons tried to take us prisoner."

Pearson looked skeptical. "And, of course you and your team were unarmed at the time?"

"Certainly," Harley said with a straight face. "We're a medical team, not commandos."

"And in spite of that, you were able to take the weapons away from these men and defend yourselves . . . and in the process kill three of the terrorists?"

"That's about the size of it," Harley said, leaning back in his chair and trying to look innocent.

Pearson leaned forward, his elbows on the table. "I take it then that you and your team have had previous military experience."

"Of course," Harley said. "As you may or may not know, Mr. Pearson, everyone in the SUSA serves in the military. It is part of our duty as citizens to help defend the country when needed."

Pearson nodded, but it was clear from his manner he didn't believe a word of what Harley was saying. "We have had a warning from your country that your intelligence people have heard terrorists have threatened to assassinate President Osterman. Do you think these are the men who were sent to do that?"

Harley shrugged. "I have no idea, sir," he said. "All I

know is we stumbled across a group of Arab types who were extremely well-armed and who seemed to have no hesitation in using their weapons. However, if that is what my country told you, I'd sure believe it."

"After all the trouble between our countries, why would Ben Raines try to help President Osterman?" Pearson asked.

"Sir, I know Ben Raines personally," Harley said, "and I've heard him say on numerous occasions he hopes President Osterman wins your upcoming election. He feels she is just what your country needs in the coming years."

Pearson grinned and chuckled, shaking his head. "Mr. Reno, if that is your name, I think you are as full of shit as a Christmas goose."

When Harley started to protest, Pearson held up his hand. "However, as far as I can tell, your men and women did nothing wrong other than try to defend yourselves. You are free to go . . . but I warn you, the FPPS is going to be keeping a sharp eye on you and your activities."

Harley stood up. "I would expect nothing less, Mr. Pearson. Thank you for your consideration."

Pearson gave a wry grin. "And thank you for what you're doing to help our citizens in our fight against the plague," he said, and then he turned and left the room.

When they got back to the hotel room, the team gathered in the conference suite.

"I guess we'll spend another couple of days here; then we might as well pack it up and head back home," Harley said.

"You're just going to let those terrorists get away?" Coop protested.

"We don't have a lot of choice, Coop," Harley explained. "With the FPPS sticking to us like fleas on a hound dog, we won't be able to do much more looking. Besides, they've been warned and they've seen the evidence that terrorists are in the area and are heavily armed. If they can't manage to protect their president, we sure as hell can't do it for them."

"Well, I for one am ready to get back to the SUSA and some good food. I'm wasting away on this diet of poorly cooked pasta without any real meat," Jersey said.

Coop glanced at her. "Hell, Jerse, you can afford to lose the weight. What about me? I'm losing muscle mass."

"Muscle mass my ass!" Jersey said. "All you're at risk of losing is that potbelly you call a stomach."

Coop looked at his abdomen, sucking it in as he looked back up. "What potbelly?"

Eight

Herb Knoff knocked, and entered President Claire Osterman's private apartment off her office without waiting for a reply.

He smiled and spread his arms at the sight of her in front of a mirror, checking her new dress out, turning and staring at herself over her shoulder like a model on a catwalk.

"Claire, you look wonderful," he said, walking across the room to embrace her.

She stared at him, her eyes soft. "You really think so, Herb?" she asked, as coquettish as a schoolgirl.

"Yeah," he replied, standing back and looking her up and down. "Beautiful, yet sophisticated, just right for the speech you're giving to the fat cats tonight."

She nodded and turned back to the mirror, smacking her lips as she applied a fresh coat of lipstick. "What about that terrorist threat the SUSA wired us about? Do you have any new information?"

He sat in a corner chair and crossed his legs. "Some, but not much. Seems an SUSA medical team ran into a nest of Arab-type men with machine guns. There was a fight and three of the Arabs were killed, but the rest escaped out a back door."

She turned and looked at him, her eyes narrowed. "What about the medical team?" she asked.

He shrugged. "One slightly injured, the others came out all right."

She pursed her lips. "Don't you think that's kinda suspicious, Herb?" she asked.

He looked surprised. "Why?"

She sighed. She liked Herb, and she loved having sex with him, but he wasn't exactly the brightest bulb in the chandelier. "Look at it this way, Herb. A team of medical people stumbles onto what is probably a highly trained terrorist cell. A firefight ensues, and three of the terrorists are killed and not one of the medical team is seriously injured." She raised her eyebrows and spread her arms. "Doesn't that make you the tiniest bit suspicious about the medical team?"

He sat up straight in his chair, an alarmed look on his face. "You think the medical team is in cahoots with the terrorists?" he asked.

She shook her head. "No, dummy," she said, but not unkindly. "I think the medical team is something more than a medical team." She rubbed her chin as she thought. "I think perhaps they were sent here to find the terrorists by Ben Raines."

"Why would he do that?" Herb asked.

She smiled. "Why, to protect me, of course. I think Ben wants me to win the upcoming election."

"Huh?" Herb grunted.

"Yes," Claire continued, turning to preen before the mirror again. "Old Ben and I, we have a history."

As she arrived at the hotel picked for her speech, President Claire Osterman was not happy and felt no need to hide her unhappiness behind social niceties. "Goddammit, Herb, you're going to have more security men in the audience than dinner guests."

Herb Knoff, her bodyguard and head of security, shrugged apologetically at Claire and the two FPPS men with her. "I know, Claire, but the FPPS hasn't been able to find those terrorists that surfaced last week and you're a logical target tonight."

Claire pursed her lips in a pout. She didn't for a minute think that some rag-head terrorists would try to attack her dinner party, not with the FPPS and Secret Service men all over the place. However, it wouldn't hurt her election chances for the people to think she was so dangerous a candidate that the terrorists wanted her eliminated. She sat with her chin resting on her thumb and her index finger on her cheek, thinking how she might turn the FPPS's overreaction to her benefit. When the makeup lady appeared with the towel to cover the neck of her new dress, she made her decision. Swiveling in her desk chair, she looked at Bill Stanton, the head of the FPPS contingent working with Herb to ensure her protection. "Okay, here's the deal. You can add the extra men, but they are to be deployed at the direction of Mr. Knoff here."

As Stanton opened his mouth to protest, the president held her hand up. "No, that's the only way we'll play it." She turned to Herb Knoff. "Herb, put all the men you want around the building and in the halls outside. I want no more than one man at each doorway on the inside. In addition, I'd like you, Mr. Stanton, to be present when Herb gives an interview with the media."

As she stretched her neck so the makeup lady could position the towel around her neck, she cut her eyes over to Stanton. "I want the media to know of the terrorist threat and of my determination not to be intimidated by them. Okay?"

Stanton tried, not entirely successfully, to keep his anger at being used in such a manner out of his face. "Of course, Madam President, if that's how you want it."

Claire turned her attention to her makeup, dismissing the men curtly. "That's not only how I want it, that's how it's going to be."

* * *

The applause following President Claire Osterman's speech was not just polite, it was thunderous. Of course, after paying a thousand dollars per plate at the Socialist/Democratic fund-raiser, and being served two minuscule chicken breasts and some asparagus and rice, the folks needed something to cheer about.

Osterman gave it to them with a rousing speech on the need for courage in government in dealing with terrorists, as well as the need for workers to be more effective in making the products the country needed, and which most of the audience happened to sell. To hear her speak, she would be ready to bomb Libya, Iran, and Syria if the terrorists so much as poked their heads up on this side of the Atlantic. In an American city, with Americans who would never, ever be called to do any actual fighting as the audience, this was like gospel music to an evangelist.

As the people on either side of her at the head banquet table were congratulating her on a fine speech, the busboys and waiters from the catering company began to clear the tables.

In the midst of people milling around and getting ready to leave, a shout rang out. "Allah be praised!"

There followed in short order, first gunshots, and then screams as the busboys whipped out AK-47's from their carts and began to spray the room with murderous fire. Food, drinks, and blood filled the air, mingling with the stink of cordite and fear as people began to jerk and dance under the impact of the bullets.

The table in front of Claire Osterman seemed to explode as several of the guns were trained on her and her companions.

Herb Knoff, in an act of heroism he never understood, dove over the table, knocking Claire back out of the line of fire and saving her life.

Knoff took three 9mm parabellum shells in the back in the process, but managed to cover the president with his body.

The screaming, terrified crowd all tried to get out of the room at the same time, preventing the security forces in the halls outside the dining room from entering the room and bringing their guns to bear on the terrorists for several minutes.

Finally, as the crowd began to hit the floor, the security men started to take out the terrorists, one by one.

Abdullah El Farrar, seeing the end was imminent, lobbed a smoke grenade into the melee and slipped out a side door. He ran through the kitchen and out the back door into the alley behind the building.

Mustafa Kareem was waiting in a van with the motor running, and raced down the alley as soon as Farrar was inside.

Inside, the hastily summoned ambulance crews were doing all they could to keep the death toll at a minimum, but the total kept climbing. At final count there were thirty-one dead, over one hundred wounded, and another hundred suffering from shock and smoke inhalation.

President Claire Osterman, the primary target, had two wounds, one in the arm and another in the shoulder. Her press secretary made sure the news cameras filmed images of her being carried to the ambulance, lying on a stretcher and covered with blood.

In the ambulance, Bill Stanton, sitting next to her with a 9mm automatic in his hand, asked with some bitterness if she regretted her decision not to have the security men in the hall during the dinner, since it had cost over thirty people their lives.

She grinned through her pain and shook her head. "Of course not, Bill," she said. "After all, my wounds are probably worth over a million votes each."

Herb Knoff survived the attack. When the paramedic was starting his IV in the ambulance, Herb asked him if he would call the president and let her know that he was all right, but that he might be late getting back to the office.

Both because of the newness of terrorism to America and because of the wealth and importance of many of the victims, the media had a field day. The FPPS, the Secret Service, and the Indianapolis Police Force were all portrayed as bungling idiots, to one degree or another.

E. William Stanton did not in the least appreciate this, and in some injudicious press releases reminded the press that the FPPS had tried to warn the Secret Service and the president about the terrorists and that they evidently had not listened.

Unfortunately for Bill Stanton, when President Osterman heard his remarks on TV, she flew into a rage. Stanton was reduced in rank and assigned to foot patrol in the inner city of Indianapolis, a job only slightly higher in prestige than a street sweeper, but much more dangerous.

Herb Knoff, on the other hand, was treated to the best medical care the government's money could buy. The surgery to remove the bullets from his back was successful, and it was determined he would have no serious side effects, other than a slight limp.

Claire had fresh flowers delivered to his hospital room every day.

Nine

Abdullah El Farrar and Mustafa Kareem did not bother to return to their hideout after the failed attack on Claire Osterman. With the few men who escaped the firefight at the hall loaded in the back of their van, Mustafa Kareem pointed the car to the northeast and traveled as fast as the speed limit allowed.

As they moved down the interstate highway, swerving from side to side to avoid the potholes that hadn't been repaired in years due to lack of money in the U.S. treasury, Kareem glanced sideways at Farrar.

"Where are we supposed to meet the incoming troops, my brother?"

"Portland, Maine," Farrar said. "The troops have been gathering on five hundred acres just outside of Yarmouth, Nova Scotia, that I purchased through intermediaries last year. By now, there should be over fifty thousand troops and five transport vessels waiting for my order to invade the U.S."

Kareem nodded thoughtfully. "And you think that will be enough?"

Farrar looked at him, his eyes hard. "For this phase, yes," Farrar answered. "When these troops hit the American Northeast, which has been sparsely populated since the destruction of the big war several years ago, all of President

Osterman's attention will be drawn that way. As soon as she commits a sizeable portion of her army to the Northeast, my men on the West Coast will land near Seattle. We will then have the country in a vast pincer movement that she will be hard-pressed to defend against."

"But we will still be vastly outnumbered, my leader," Kareem protested, wondering if Farrar was making a mistake in moving so soon.

"That will matter little, Mustafa," Farrar answered, "since we will not be fighting a conventional war. Our men will not march against Osterman's Army, but will spread out in small groups, no more than fifteen or twenty men, and will move through the countryside, spreading death and destruction by hitting and running . . . hitting and running."

The Desert Fox smiled at his companion. "When the civilian casualties begin to mount up, Osterman will be forced to sue for peace with me, and then I will tell her my conditions."

"That is what I do not understand, Abdullah," Kareem said. "I know you intend to offer her a government with both you and her in control, but how can you seriously contemplate sharing leadership with a female?"

Farrar's smile turned to an evil grin. "She will not long survive the agreement, Mustafa," he said. "I fear someone will assassinate her soon after she agrees to share her power with me."

Now Kareem returned the smile. Perhaps Farrar's plan was no so farfetched after all.

Claire walked into Herb's hospital room, a large cup of espresso coffee in her right hand and with her left arm still in a sling.

Herb looked up and grinned. "Oh, thank God!" he said. "I think there must be a law against caffeine in hospitals.

The stuff they call coffee around here is so weak you can see through it."

Claire handed him the cup and leaned over and kissed him on the cheek. "How are you doing, Herb?" she asked.

He took a deep draught of the dark, steaming liquid and sighed deeply. "Better now," he said, shifting his shoulders as Claire fluffed the pillows behind his back.

"The doctors say you'll be able to be released in a few days. Evidently the bullets missed all your important organs."

He gave her a look. "Missing me already, huh?" he said.

She looked around to make sure no one was listening, and then she nodded. "My bed is very lonesome without you to share it."

He winced as he changed position again. "Well, as for that," he said, "it may be a while before I'm back up to speed on the lovemaking department."

She leaned forward and gently stroked his thigh with her good hand. "Don't worry about that, Herb. I won't mind doing all the work for a while, until you get your strength back, that is."

He looked down at her hand. "If you keep that up, I may get stronger faster than you think."

"I can't wait to show you how much I appreciate your saving my life at the dinner," Claire said.

Herb's face got serious. "I don't know what came over me," he said. "I must care about you a lot more than I thought."

"The feeling is mutual, Herb," she said, moving her hand higher, until his face blushed and he leaned his head back with a deep sigh and began to move his hips against her.

Mike Post knocked and entered Ben Raines's office without waiting for a reply.

Ben glanced up from his desk and leaned back, stretching

his arms over his head and shaking his head to get the kinks out. "Hi, come on in, Mike."

"Good morning, Ben."

"Glad you dropped by," Ben said, looking back down at the mass of papers on his desk. "I'm getting awfully tired of flying this desk. I hope you have some news that might mean action."

Mike nodded. "I certainly do. Remember that memo we got about the attempt on Claire Osterman's life last week?"

"Yeah."

"Well, my contact in Canada just radioed me that some Arab types have purchased several hundred acres in two different locations up there."

Ben raised his eyebrows. "Why would they do that?" he asked.

"Wait until you hear where they are," Mike said. "The first is near Yarmouth in Nova Scotia near the coast of Maine, and the second location is on Vancouver Island near the west coast of Washington."

"You think they're gonna use those places as staging areas to gather troops for an eventual invasion of the U.S.?" Ben asked, a skeptical look on his face.

Mike took a seat opposite Ben's desk and began to fiddle with his pipe. "That'd be my first guess."

Ben shook his head. "I can't believe this Desert Fox or whatever his name is would have that many troops or that much war matériel to think he could mount a successful invasion of the U.S."

Mike stared at Ben through clouds of smoke that smelled faintly of cherry blossoms. "I don't think you appreciate the situation in the Middle East, Ben."

Ben leaned back and steepled his fingers in front of his face, resting his chin on his fingertips. "Enlighten me then," he said.

"The entire region's economy was centered on the oil fields in Saudi Arabia, Iraq, Iran, Kuwait, and some other smaller states in the region. After the big war, the U.N. took over running the oil fields so the oil could be distributed evenly across the world."

Ben nodded. "I know that, Mike, but the people were compensated for the loss of oil revenues, weren't they?"

Mike shook his head. "Not nearly as much as before the war, and the money was spread out among all the population of the region, not with the majority going to the few ruling families as it had previously."

"So, you're telling me we have a few pissed-off royal families and a lot of angry common people to deal with."

"More than a lot," Mike said, "several million at the very least, most of whom are accomplished guerrilla warriors."

"But what about the war matériel they'd need for such an undertaking?" Ben asked. "Where would they get the tanks, ships, airplanes, bombs, and all the stuff necessary to wage war?"

Mike shook his head. "It's my guess that several of the old elite families have banded together, pooled the money they'd stashed in Swiss banks, and put it in support of this Desert Fox, Abdullah El Farrar, in hopes he can do enough damage to make the U.N. relent and give them back control of the oil fields."

"So, you think he's got plenty of experienced troops, enough money to buy whatever equipment he needs, and the will to try and take over the U.S.?"

Mike nodded, exhaling smoke from his nostrils. "I do."

Ben leaned forward, his elbows on his desk, and stared at Mike. "And what would you suggest we here do about it?"

Mike shrugged and shook his head. "I'm just a lowly intelligence-gatherer," he said with a wry smile. "Planning strategy is up to you higher-paid generals."

Ben's shoulders slumped. "And unless President Osterman asks for our help, we're in no position to do anything to prevent this El Farrar from carrying out his plans."

"That's about the size of it, General," Mike said, his face suddenly sober.

"Mike, I want you to get in touch with whomever you can in the U.S. that might show some sense and let them know what we think is going on."

Mike laughed out loud. "And just who might that be, Ben? I've tried a couple of times to let Osterman's government people know what this Arab has in mind, but they would rather bury their heads in the sand than do anything about it."

Ben pursed his lips. "Perhaps I could set up a telephone link with Claire and tell her personally. She's usually paranoid enough to take precautions, even if she doesn't quite believe our motives are pure."

"Why are you so concerned with what happens to Claire Osterman?" Mike asked.

"Because a stable government to our north is to be desired, even if it is run by a megalomaniac like Claire," Ben said. "Hell, almost twenty percent of our budget this year is going to help the U.S. keep its head above water and provide essential services to its citizens. Can you imagine what would happen if this Arab zealot manages to create even more chaos up there?"

Mike nodded. "It would probably mean another war between us."

"Correct," Ben said, "and that is something we just don't need right now."

Ten

It took Abdullah El Farrar and Mustafa Kareem and their men a little over three days to travel from Indianapolis to the port city of Yarmouth in the province of Nova Scotia. Crossing the border between Canada and the U.S. was uneventful . . . the guards didn't even bother to check the back of the van, just waved them through.

Once in Yarmouth, they traveled an additional ten miles to the compound where Farrar had his men gathered for the incursion into the U.S. Hastily built Quonset huts housed twenty thousand men, who'd been brought to the island on large transports and off-loaded at night using smaller boats so as not to alert the Canadian authorities to their presence.

Osama bin Araman, Farrar's leader of his troops, met them in a large office on the edge of the camp. He served them Turkish coffee in tiny cups along with dates and other Arab delicacies.

Farrar smacked his lips over the strong, bitter brew, and then he stared into Araman's eyes. "Are the men prepared to do battle, Osama?" he asked.

Araman nodded. "Yes, my leader. I have been conducting daily training exercises in terrorist tactics, explaining to them how to pick appropriate targets for their bombs and grenades."

"Have you divided them up into teams of fifteen to twenty men as I ordered?"

"Yes, and I have with each team at least one man who can speak passable English."

"Good," Farrar said, slipping a date between his teeth and chewing it as he spoke. "Then all is in readiness."

Araman nodded again. "We can have the men loaded onto the transport ship within ten hours, and the trip across the ocean to Portland, Maine, will take only another six or seven, depending on the weather."

He pulled out a map and spread it out on the table. "As you can see, my brother, there are no good east-to-west roads in Maine, so we will have to travel south along the interstate until we pass through Boston to Worcester. From there, the men can spread out both west toward Syracuse and south toward New York and Philadelphia. Once they have dispersed, there are many roads for the men to take and then they will be unstoppable."

Farrar studied the map. "Why not just take the men by ship all the way down the coast to New York City and land there?" Farrar asked.

Araman shrugged. "It is possible, of course, but our ship would have to pass the Navy base at Bridgeport, Connecticut, Abdullah, and I fear that would be unwise. If one of the U.S. navy ships spotted us, they could call in an air strike from the nearby Air Force base at Dover, Delaware. I feel it would be much more dangerous that way, but if you prefer . . ."

Farrar shook his head. "No, Osama. I chose you to lead my eastern contingent of troops for your expertise and knowledge of these matters, so I will let you decide the course to take."

Araman inclined his head in a slight bow of thanks. "As you wish, my leader."

"How do you propose to land twenty thousand men in Portland and then transport them several hundred miles down the coast without alerting the U.S. authorities?" Mustafa Kareem asked as he perused the map over Farrar's shoulders.

"That would be impossible," Araman answered. "My plan is to have several teams begin their terrorism in the city of Portland, attacking the governmental offices and local police stations in a coordinated manner. In the ensuing chaos, as the city burns and explodes under our attack, the rest of the men will hardly be noticed as they head southward."

"So, by the time the U.S. government responds and sends troops to quell the disturbances in Portland, our men will be safely on their way into the interior of the country."

Araman nodded, smiling craftily. "Yes, and after they separate into hundreds of smaller groups, each going their separate ways, they will be almost impossible to stop," he said, spreading his arms wide.

Farrar slammed his hand down on the map, a smile of admiration on his face. "You have planned our attack well indeed, Osama," he said.

"Thank you, my brother," Araman said, dipping his head modestly at the compliment.

Farrar stood up. "Mustafa and I must rest for now," he said. "Let us plan to leave tomorrow night, so that we may land in Portland around midnight."

"Excellent," Araman said. "Come, I will show you to your quarters."

Claire was sitting on the edge of the bed she'd prepared for Herb Knoff in her quarters when her secretary rang saying she had a phone call from Ben Raines on the long-distance line.

"You want me to have it transferred in here so you can listen in?" she asked.

He shook his head. "No, thanks. I think I'll take a nap. I'm kinda tired."

She leaned over and kissed him on the forehead, as one might a child. "See you in a little while," she said.

"Don't let him talk you into anything you'll regret," Herb advised before turning over and pulling the covers up to his neck.

Claire walked into her office next door and sat down at her desk. She took a deep breath, wondering what Ben Raines had to say to her, and then she picked up the phone.

"Hello, this is President Osterman," she said into the receiver, her tone frosty and official.

"No need to be so formal, Claire," Raines said. "It's me, Ben."

"Ben Raines, the perpetual thorn in my side," Claire responded. "How are you?"

"I'm doing all right, for an old man," Raines said.

"Dare I hope this call is your way of telling me you've contracted a fatal illness of some sort?" Claire asked.

"No. In fact, it's more in the way of a warning to you that a fatal illness to you and your presidency may be growing just around the corner."

"Are you threatening me?" Claire asked, surprise in her voice.

Raines had the temerity to laugh out loud at her suggestion. "No, of course not, Claire. I'm just calling with some friendly advice."

"Since when have we been friends?"

"Since now," Raines replied. "My Intel officer has some information you might be interested in."

"More bogeymen hiding out to do me in?" she asked with a sneer in her voice.

"Well, if I'm not mistaken, we were right on the money about the attack that was planned during your speech, weren't we?"

"Yes, I have to give you that," she replied grudgingly.

"We have some new information from our friends in Canada that may be of interest to you."

Claire bit her lip; he was getting her interest now. "And just what is that?" she asked, leaning forward at the desk.

"We've received information that various Arab types have acquired substantial plots of land in Nova Scotia off your East Coast and Vancouver Island off your West Coast."

Claire didn't speak for a few moments as she digested this latest information.

"Are you still there, Claire?" Ben asked, wondering if the line had been disconnected.

"Yes, but I'm wondering why they would do that," she said, biting a fingernail.

"You've never been slow on the uptake before, Claire. My guess would be they're gonna use those lands as staging areas for an upcoming invasion of the United States."

"They wouldn't dare!" she exclaimed.

"It's not such a far stretch, after a failed assassination attempt against the head of a country, to attempt to invade it later," Ben reasoned. "In fact, it is my conclusion that the attempt to kill you was a prelude to just such an attempt."

Claire nodded slowly, though there was no one in her office to see it. "Yes," she said slowly, "I can see your reasoning, Ben. But what I can't see is why you would bother to give me a heads-up on it."

"Claire, I know we've had our differences in the past, but I've always believed in the proverb 'Better the devil you know than the one you don't.' "

She gave a low chuckle. "In other words, you'd rather deal with this devil than some Arab devils who might take us over, right?"

Ben returned the laugh. "Exactly. That's why we've agreed to help you rebuild your country after our last little . . . disagreement. A stable, prosperous country to our north is something we think will in the long run be better for both you and us."

"In that spirit of cooperation, do you have any suggestions as to how I should deal with this latest development?"

"You don't need me to tell you how to defend your country, Claire. You've been quite a capable leader in the past, and I see no reason to doubt your ability to deal with some rag-heads with aspirations of global aggression now."

Claire laughed again. "Thanks for the vote of confidence, Ben. I'd better ring off now. I've got to have a serious talk with some of my military personnel."

"Good luck, Claire."

"I'll let you know what we find out, Ben."

"And if I hear anything further, I'll be sure and keep you in the loop, Claire. After all, stability on this continent is something we can all agree is in our best interests."

"By the way, any idea who is behind this move?" she asked before hanging up.

"A man by the name of Abdullah El Farrar, otherwise known as the Desert Fox."

Eleven

The small port city of Yarmouth was practically deserted at ten in the evening when Osama bin Araman led his twenty thousand troops through the outskirts of town to board the transport ship anchored offshore.

By midnight, the troops were on board and the ship was steaming southward toward Portland, Maine.

At three in the morning, the ship anchored at the mouth of the Portland harbor. Fifteen rubber Zodiac boats fitted with electric motors were lowered over the side and filled with black-clad assault troops, all carrying Uzis with silencers on their barrels.

There was only the slightest buzzing sound as the boats made their way toward the shore, two miles away.

Captain Jerry Pike was busy preparing his forty-foot deep-sea-fishing boat for departure when the Zodiac bumped up against his starboard side, causing the vessel to dip and tilt slightly.

"What the hell?" Pike mumbled, stepping over a pile of fishing nets and looking to the right.

A bearded man carrying a short black rifle peered over the gunwale.

"Who the hell are you?" Pike asked, stepping backward.

"Nobody," the man answered in guttural English, and fired his weapon.

A slight puffing sound was washed away on the evening wind as three closely spaced holes appeared in Pike's chest, blowing him backward to land sprawled atop his nets.

Several more men in black clothes swarmed over his boat and down the gangplank toward the dock, to move swiftly and silently toward the row of other boats lined up along the wharf.

Within an hour, over a hundred deep-sea-fishing boats had been taken over and were on their way out to the transport ship to bring in the rest of Araman's troops, the bodies of their captains left floating and bobbing on the waves of their wakes in the predawn darkness.

It was still an hour before dawn when the troops arrived at the docks and separated into their teams of twenty men each. Araman had gone over maps of the city of Portland with the leaders of each of the groups, and they all had specific orders of what to hit and how to do it.

Omar Sharak led his men down the street toward the closest police station, three blocks from the docks. Since it was still the middle of the midnight-to-eight shift, the station house was practically deserted.

Sharak stepped through the front door and walked rapidly toward the front desk, where the desk sergeant sat snoring softly.

He never awoke as Sharak put a bullet through his forehead, snapping him backward off his chair.

Sharak's men spread out through the station, and several muted shots could be heard as officers were killed where they stood or sat.

Once the station was under control, Sharak methodically destroyed all the communications equipment, and then opened the locked and bolted doors to the weapons lockers.

He took weapons he thought might be useful, including a stash of smoke and flash-bang grenades and canisters of tear gas.

Once he'd taken what he might need, he piled the rest of the weapons and ammunition in the center of the floor, poured gasoline over it, and tossed a match onto it as he and his men ran for the door.

Minutes later, it sounded like the Fourth of July as hundreds of cases of cartridges went off with a resounding bang, sending flames and smoke billowing upward and setting the entire building on fire.

There were four radio stations and three television stations in the city of Portland. Araman had targeted all seven, intending to stop any word of the assault on the city from being spread over the airwaves.

Muhammed Khaled Issa led his small band of troops into the studios of WZTV, Channel 6 in Portland. Due to the early hour, there was no receptionist on duty, only an aging black security guard who was sitting behind the desk in the lobby sipping on a cup of coffee and chewing a bagel.

"What the hell?" he began, rising to his feet and reaching for the ancient pistol in a holster on his right hip when he saw the band of terrorists coming through the door.

Issa raised his silenced Uzi and shot the guard in the face, knocking him backward over his desk chair.

Issa spoke to his men over his shoulder as he raced up the corridor. "Leave no one alive and smash all the equipment and cameras," he growled in a low, deadly whisper.

His men split up into teams of two as they spread out through the corridors, kicking office doors open and spraying whoever was there with molten lead from their Uzis. They grinned and joked among themselves like small children playing an innocent game of soldier as they killed over fifteen people in a matter of minutes.

Issa himself stood before the large control room, filled with millions of dollars' worth of communications gear, and laughed as he hosed the wall down with his Uzi on full automatic.

The monitor screen on a far wall showed a handsome man with brown blown-dry hair sitting next to a pretty lady with blond hair pulled up in a chignon, both anchoring the morning edition of the news.

Suddenly, the woman's eyes flitted to the side, widening as she stared in horror at something off camera. The man stopped in mid-sentence, his mouth hanging open.

Just as the screen turned dark and started to fade, their bodies could be seen dancing and twisting in their chairs under the onslaught of hundreds of 9mm bullets, blood blossoming on the front of their expensive designer clothes and splattering onto the camera lens before the picture faded to black.

Engineer Tom Ferguson leaned out the window of the big diesel engine on the Portland-to-Boston express train, and checked to see if the brakeman was giving the go ahead. When he saw the lantern waving back and forth, he pulled the throttle lever toward him and the engine began to ease forward slowly.

Just as it was building up to ten miles an hour, the early morning darkness was lit up by a huge explosion on the tracks just ahead of the express.

Ferguson cursed and pushed the throttle all the way to full stop, and simultaneously took his foot off the dead-man's brake to stop the train as fast as he could.

Little by little the big engine slowed, but it was not fast enough. Ferguson screamed and jumped out the side door just as the wheels of the engine ran over the steel rails in front of it that were twisted like so many strands of spaghetti.

Ferguson hit the ground, rolled twice, and came to his feet

just in time to see the engine topple toward him. He screamed again and held out his arms, as if by sheer force of will he could hold the fifty-ton heap of metal off him.

One by one, the cars behind the engine ran off the tracks and fell onto their sides, the shrill screaming of the passengers a counterpoint to the breaking of glass and the screech of tortured metal as it bent and twisted into a crumpled mass of wreckage.

As the passengers began to crawl and walk out of the cars, Jamal Ahmed Fadl and his men stood in a row alongside the tracks, following them with the barrels of their Uzis.

The passengers, when they saw what confronted them, all stopped and raised their hands.

Fadl screamed a few words in Arabic and the soldiers began to spray the prisoners with murderous fire, killing men, women, and children where they stood.

There are three major exits leading from Portland to I-95, the Maine Turnpike. Two of these were dynamited into rubble so as to be impassable by any type of vehicle, effectively sealing Portland off from access from the south. The third was barricaded with twenty men standing guard to keep anyone from approaching or leaving Portland via the freeway.

Portland International Airport is small as such airports go. It has only two main runways long enough for jet aircraft to land on.

Wadih El Amal and his men got to the airport just after the six A.M. flight to Newark Airport took off. Without bothering to go through the airport concourse, he and his men shot down the security guards and ran out onto the runway. The landing lights of an incoming plane could be seen in the distance.

Amal had his men shoot out the tires of the three airplanes waiting to load passengers, and then he had them drive several of the long baggage trains out onto the runways. While he was doing this, three other of his men ran up the stairs to the control tower and burst through the door.

A security guard managed to kill one of the men before the other two assassinated everyone in the room, blowing out the huge glass windows of the tower in the process.

"Why waste explosives when you can shut the runway down using a landing plane?" he asked his men, laughing at his own joke as he pointed to where the baggage trains blocked the runways.

Minutes later, a 727 American Airways jet drifted slowly lower toward the runway. The pilot was trying frantically to raise the control tower when his copilot screamed, "Pull up . . . pull up, for God's sake!"

The pilot glanced down, and barely had time to curse as the front of the jet hit a tractor and baggage train and disintegrated around him.

The fireball as the jet erupted in flames rushed toward the airport concourse building a hundred yards away at over a hundred miles an hour.

In an ironic twist, the fireball from the exploding jet incinerated Wadih El Amal and all of his men just as it did the 276 people in the building.

The runway was left with a twenty-foot-deep crater surrounded by wreckage and twisted, shattered corpses covering over two acres.

In the inner city of Portland, people erupted from their homes like ants from a disturbed anthill as rumors of an invading Army spread like wildfire. The absence of any local television or radio stations on the air and the lack of response to any calls to the police stations only added to the confusion.

Many of the men and women were carrying guns, rifles, shotguns, and pistols as they roamed the streets. Unfortunately, many more innocent natives were shot by the vigilantes than the few terrorists who were found and killed.

As dawn began to break, Osama bin Araman recalled his squads by radio to the rendezvous point he'd shown them on the map. They met at a local Army National Guard station, where over fifty deuce-and-a-half-ton trucks and innumerable HumVees were lined up waiting for his men.

As they arrived at the station, the leaders were given their orders, and they grabbed trucks and HumVees and headed south along I-95 toward Worcester, Massachusetts, where they would then scatter out westward and southward to spread more havoc across the country.

Twelve

After her phone call from Ben Raines, Claire Osterman called an emergency meeting with her cabinet and military advisors. Once they'd been seated and served coffee and pastries, she got right to the point.

"Gentlemen," she said, sitting on the corner of her desk, "I've just had a very disturbing call from Ben Raines."

Gerald Boykin, her Minister of Defense, looked up from his prune danish. "He called you direct?" he asked.

She nodded. "He did. He said he had some disturbing intel he wanted to share with me." She stood up and carried her coffee cup with her as she went around to sit in her desk chair.

"He said his sources in Canada had information a man named Abdullah El Farrar had leased several hundred acres of land in Nova Scotia and on Vancouver Island."

Boykin sat straight up in his chair, a look of alarm on his face. "Farrar, the man known as the Desert Fox?" he asked, glancing around at the other men.

"Yes," Claire answered. "I see you are at least aware of his name, Gerry."

Boykin nodded. "We've been keeping an eye on him for the past six or seven months. His family was one of the richest in the Middle East, until the U.N. took their oil fields away from them for redistribution to other nations."

"From what I hear," Claire interrupted, "he's now set on some holy war to regain his lands . . . and his riches."

Boykin nodded in agreement. "Yes, that's our take on it. Seems he's taken a lot of his family's money out of Swiss banks and is using it to raise a ragtag Army of sorts. So far, there's been no indication he's gotten far enough along to be of concern to us."

Claire shook her head, a look of disgust on her face. "Well, you'd better kick your Intel officers in the butt, Gerry, 'cause Ben Raines thinks Farrar is using these locations as a staging area to gather troops for an invasion of the U.S."

All of the men in the room began to talk at once. The general consensus was the bastard wouldn't dare.

As the argument grew in intensity, Claire held up her hand. "Enough!" she exclaimed, her irritation showing.

"General Goddard," she said, addressing Maxwell Goddard, the man she'd assigned to lead her Army after Bradley Stevens' failure in the last war.

"Yes, ma'am?" he answered.

"I want you to send some units to both coasts to check these allegations by Raines out. If this son of a bitch is even thinking about invading us, I want you to send some planes or whatever to those locations and blast him into the next world."

Goddard bit his lip. "That might be rather tricky, Madam President."

She narrowed her eyes and leaned forward, her elbows on the desk. "And just why is that?"

He shrugged. "Well, to begin with, the Canadian government might look askance at our bombing their country."

"Fuck them!" she almost yelled, slamming her hand down on her desk and standing up. "If they're harboring a hostile Army, then they deserve whatever they get."

"Yes, ma'am," Goddard said hastily and rose.

"And General," she added.

"Yes?"

"Don't spare the horses," she said. "Send your best troops with plenty of firepower to do the job."

"Yes, ma'am," he said, putting on his hat and almost running from the room.

After he left, Gerald Boykin spoke. "Claire, do you think you can believe what Ben Raines said? After all, he's not usually considered one of our friends."

"Yeah," Clifford Ainsworth, her Minister of Propaganda, said, "perhaps he's just doing this to make you look foolish right before our elections."

Claire gave a secretive smile, as if she knew something the rest of the men didn't. "No, Ben assured me he wants me to win this election. He said he feels that I am the leader our country needs right now."

She waved them out. "Now, get out there and beat the bushes. I want to know everything there is to know about this rag-head named Farrar."

Two hours later, General Maxwell Goddard stood in front of Claire's desk, his face blotched and red, sweat beading on his forehead.

Claire studied him as she chewed on the end of a pencil, noting his worried look.

"I assume the news you've brought me is not good, General?" she asked.

"No, ma'am. Before I could get any troops under way to Maine and Washington State, we began to get news of a serious problem in both areas."

"What kind of problem, General?"

Goddard licked his lips and twisted the hat he held in his hands. "It seems there *was* an invasion in both areas last night and early this morning. Troops, evidently from the areas you mentioned, were transported into the ports of both cities and began a widespread attack on the populace there."

"Goddamnit!" she exclaimed. "Why weren't we prepared for this?"

Goddard shrugged and held out his hands. "Madam President, most of our troops and intel are concentrated on our southern borders, because of our concerns with the SUSA and Ben Raines. We never expected trouble from the north, since our relations with Canada have always been peaceful."

She snapped her pencil in half and threw the pieces across the room. "And what are you going to do about this invasion, General?"

He held out his hands in a placating manner. "Don't worry, Madam President. From what I can gather, the number of troops was not exceptional, probably less than twenty or thirty thousand in each location. I've moved several battalions into both areas, and we should have the invaders under control in a matter of days."

He wiped his brow with his sleeve. "And I've sent several squadrons of attack helicopters as well as observer planes to aid in the defense. Hopefully, they'll be bottled up soon and we can proceed to destroy them at our leisure."

A knock sounded on the door and the rest of her ministers filed in, all carrying stacks of papers in their arms.

"We've heard what's going on, Claire," Gerald Boykin said. "We've managed to get quite a bit of intel on Farrar and his followers."

She waved Goddard to take a seat and she leaned back in her chair. "Good. Give it to me."

After they'd filled her in on Farrar's background and history, and that of the men known to be following him, she shook her head.

"This man has managed to survive years of being targeted by the U.N. security forces, and in that time has even built up a sizable Army of men who are willing to go into combat and die for him."

Boykin nodded, not sure where she was going with this.

"So," she continued, "we know one thing for certain. The man is no fool."

"No, ma'am," Boykin said.

"Then, why on earth would he try to invade and take over a country of two hundred million with only fifty thousand or so troops?"

"Perhaps he is a megalomaniac, Claire," General Goddard said.

"No, I think we're missing something, General." She looked around at her advisors. "I have a feeling defeating this man is not going to be as easy as you all think."

"You think he's got something up his sleeve?" Boykin asked, glancing at General Goddard.

"I don't know what it could be," the general said. "So far, all they've used is small arms, no heavy guns, no air support, nothing to indicate they are going to be able to give us too much trouble."

"That's if he fights as you think he's going to," Claire said through pursed lips.

"How else can he fight?" the general asked.

"What if instead of keeping his men together and moving as a unit, they separate and spread out across the country, turning this into a guerrilla war?"

The general shrugged. "What would that gain him?" he asked. "Sooner or later, his men would be picked off, one by one. They might be able to do some damage here and there, but as far as being a serious threat to the country, I just don't see what good that would do them."

Clifford Ainsworth cleared his throat. "I have an idea," he said tentatively.

"Speak up, Cliff," Claire said with irritation.

"Well, as Minister of Propaganda, it's my business to keep a close check on the mood of the country."

"We know that . . . get on with what you have to say," Claire interrupted.

"It's just that, since our last war, with the cutbacks in essential services and consumer goods, the mood in much of the country is not too favorable to the government."

Claire bristled. "Don't those fools know it takes money to wage a war?" she argued.

Ainsworth held up his hands, his face paling at her anger. "Claire, don't kill the messenger here," he pleaded. "I'm just telling you how it is."

"All right, go on."

"Perhaps this Farrar expects to tap into this discontent and to get some new recruits to his Army . . . sort of a civil uprising in support of his cause."

Goddard stroked his chin. "That *is* the only way a guerrilla war would make any sense."

"Do you think he'll find any sizable support out there?" Claire asked through tight lips.

Ainsworth shrugged, not wanting to tell Claire just how hated she was by a great many of the people she ruled over. "I don't know, but it's certainly possible," he said in a low voice, as if speaking the unthinkable any louder might make it more likely.

"Okay then," Claire said. "We're going to have to fight this battle on two fronts. One, General, you're going to have to go all out to kill these bastards as fast as you can."

When the general nodded rapidly, she continued. "Two, Ainsworth, you're going to have to step up our propaganda efforts, especially as regards this Farrar and his men. I want you to put out everything negative you can about the Arabs . . . their religion, how they treat women, the fact they don't allow liquor . . . in short, I want a full-scale attack on everything Muslim or Arabic."

"But, Claire," Boykin argued, "what about our native Arabs and Middle Eastern types? Won't this put them at risk of attack by the citizens—like the Japanese in World War II?"

She glared at him. "So what? We're at war here, gentlemen. We don't have time to play nice or by any set of so-called rules. I want us to put everything we've got into this, and I want it fast."

Thirteen

Abdullah El Farrar and Mustafa Kareem sped down I-95 heading south. They were traveling in advance of the convoy of terrorists using the same road, and were headed for a meeting with the man who was going to put them in contact with various U.S. dissidents who were organized around a single idea—to get rid of the regime of President Claire Osterman by whatever means necessary.

John Waters was the head of the FFA cell on the East Coast—the Freedom Fighters of America—and was a right-wing zealot whose ambition to be a leader in the U.S. knew no bounds. Standing a shade over six feet tall, he was lean to the point of being gaunt, and sported a thick black beard covering his entire face. His head was bald and his face was angular and hard, with eyes as black as coal and as hard as stones.

Though he was a fundamentalist firebreather when it came to religion, he saw no problem in using El Farrar and his men to help achieve his ends. He told his followers, "Sometimes you have to get in bed with demons to defeat the devil."

He fully intended, once Farrar had helped him overthrow Osterman, to be able to easily wrest control of the country from the rag-heads. In truth, he didn't credit Arabs in general and Farrar in particular with any great military sense. "After all," he often said, "millions of Arabs couldn't even defeat tiny Israel even though they outgunned and outmanned them a hundred to one."

When Farrar and Kareem got to U.S. 90, they took a right and proceeded to Albany, New York, where Waters had his headquarters on a farm outside of the city.

Waters stepped out on the porch and greeted his new friends when they pulled up outside the rambling eighteenth-century farmhouse. They'd been in contact for over six months planning for this meeting, though they'd never met in person.

"Mr. Farrar, Mr. Kareem," Waters said, grinning and sticking out his hand when they got out of the car.

Farrar and Kareem inclined their heads and shook his hand as they glanced around at the farm and its surroundings.

"Come on in and we'll get started," Waters said, leading them into the house.

They gathered in the kitchen, where Waters's wife served them all coffee and fruit juice before she left them alone to talk business.

"It is good to meet you in person after all our discussions in the past," Farrar said.

Waters nodded. "Yes, it is good to finally start the process of freeing my country from the oppressive regime of President Osterman. I've been planning and waiting for this moment for more years than I care to think about."

"It should not be long now, Mr. Waters," Mustafa Kareem said in a serious voice. "At this moment, our troops are making their way across the country, hitting the targets you so generously pointed out to us."

Waters took a sheet of paper from his jacket pocket and handed it across the table to Farrar. "Here is a list of my people and their locations in the Northeast. They're waiting to make contact with your people at your convenience."

Farrar handed the paper to Kareem without reading it.

"We will inform our leaders of their names and locations," Farrar said, "so they may join forces."

"How are you gonna do that?" Waters asked. "Osterman'll be monitoring all the radio transmissions as soon as she hears about the invasion."

Kareem took a small cell phone from his pocket and flipped it open. "We have coded cell phones that cannot be monitored or intercepted by her security forces. Each of our commanders in the field has his own number, so we are able to keep in constant contact without fear of interception."

"You were kinda sketchy in our previous conversations about your plan of attack," Waters said. "You want to fill me in now?"

Farrar drained his coffee and looked at the cup approvingly. "This is very fine coffee. Could I have another cup, please?"

"Sure," Waters said, standing up and taking the cup to the maker on a counter in the corner. "I bought a Turkish brand, knowing you probably liked it stronger than our local brews."

"As for our plan of attack," Farrar said as Waters handed him his cup back, "it is very simple. I have divided my men up into hundreds of small groups of fifteen or twenty, each of whom will be acting independently in concert with the men of your organization."

Waters smiled. "Will there be a language problem? I'm afraid very few of my people speak Arabic."

Farrar shook his head. "No. We have made certain that at least one or two men in each group speak passable English, which our schools have been teaching for over fifty years."

"That's great," Waters said, leaning back in his chair. "Each of the men on that list I gave you has specific targets in his area that need to be taken out."

"And these targets, they are important to President Osterman?" Kareem asked.

"Yes. For the most part, they're power plants, bridges on

roads her troops will need to use, and police stations and Army outposts. When we destroy them, it will not only make retaliation by Osterman's troops next to impossible, it will also cause widespread dissatisfaction among the populace of the region, helping us to find recruits who will agree to fight with us against her government."

Farrar looked at Kareem and grinned. "You seem to have thought this out very well, Mr. Waters," he said.

"As I told you, I've been planning this for a very long time. When you contacted me with your offer of assistance, it was like a dream come true."

Farrar held up his cup in a toast. "Then let us drink to all of our dreams coming true, Mr. Waters, for I too have been waiting for a very long time for this day."

Osama bin Araman halted the convoy of HumVees and transport trucks just past Worcester, Massachusetts. After speaking on the phone with Mustafa Kareem and getting the list of contacts with the Freedom Fighters of America, he gave the leaders of each of the teams their contact persons and the locations where they could meet with them.

Once all the preparations were made, he saluted the men and they divided up, each taking different roads to the west and south to meet with their contacts and continue their reign of terror against the United States.

The leader of the Vancouver Island contingent of Farrar's terrorist army, Achmed Sharif, held a similar meeting with Samuel Jensen in Olympia, Washington, after their invasion of the state met with very little resistance.

"Mr. Sharif," Jensen said as they stood alongside U.S. Highway 5 just south of the city, "here is a list of men and women who are committed to the destruction of the Osterman regime. They have agreed to work with your men any way they can to insure the defeat of President Osterman."

Sharif didn't have much use for traitors, even if they were on his side, and he especially didn't like the fact this Jensen man hadn't had the courage to meet them at his own home, but had insisted they meet at a roadside park along the highway. Sharif had always found traitors of any stripe to be cowards, and Jensen's actions merely confirmed this for him, but he tried to keep his feelings from showing.

"Thank you, Mr. Jensen," Sharif said, taking the list. "I will give this to my team members and we will be on our way."

"What are your plans now, Mr. Sharif?" Jensen asked, looking over his shoulder as if he were afraid someone might see them together.

Having no intention of giving any useful intel to such a man, Sharif just shrugged. "We will spread out over the countryside and begin to do what our leader brought us here to do, Mr. Jensen."

Before Jensen could ask any more questions, Sharif gave a curt nod and began to move away toward his command HumVee, which they'd "liberated" from the Olympia National Guard base just up the road.

"Uh . . . good luck," Jensen called before he scurried back to his five-year-old Chevy pickup truck and raced away into the night.

Sharif snorted through his nose and handed the paper to his second in command. "Give these names to our team leaders and assign them each a place to go and a man to meet. We must be on our way before the U.S. Army has time to respond to our invasion."

His second in command nodded vigorously, and ran back along the road to the row of trucks and vehicles they'd stolen to transport them across country. His teams were going to move southward down the coast through Oregon and California and eastward across Idaho and Wyoming. The country they would be moving through was ideal for their plans— heavily wooded, mountainous, and remote, with few major roads that could be used for the transport of a defending Army. Sharif had plans for those roads, which would be great places to set ambushes against anyone trying to stand in their way.

He lit a cigarette and glanced back over his shoulder as he waited for his men to move out, admiring the way the flames from Olympia lit up the night sky and turned it orange and red and yellow. It reminded him of the sunsets over their camp in Iraq where they'd trained for the past six years.

In Portland, Oregon, Mohamed Omar and his FFA contact, Billy Wesson, crouched near the Police Headquarters Building in the downtown area. It was ten-thirty at night, and the evening shift was just coming in to make their reports and the late-night shift was arriving to go on duty.

"This'll be the best time to hit 'em," Wesson said, peering through a Star-Lite night-vision scope at the building. "There's always a lotta confusion at the shift-change time."

As Omar raised his hand to start the attack, Wesson whispered, "Did you tell your men to go easy on the explosives?"

Omar nodded. "Yes, for as you say, there will be many weapons and boxes of ammunition we may use when the attack is over."

"God damn right!" Wesson said, nodding his head vigorously. "That there building is the center for the SWAT teams of the city, an' they've got a ton of good shit to have in a fight."

Omar turned his head to hide his expression of distaste at the crudity of this infidel's language. He and his men had been warned by Achmed Sharif they would have to deal with many unpleasant individuals in their war against the white unbelievers, but Omar hadn't realized just how bad it would be until this moment.

He whistled shrilly and stood up from behind the car he was hiding behind, his AK-47 automatic rifle to his shoulder.

All at once, the darkness of the night was lit up by twenty-five men firing automatic weapons at the police station. Windows and doors shattered under the onslaught, and crowds of policemen caught outside were mowed down in seconds, their bodies dancing and jumping under the impact of hundreds of 9mm bullets.

Screaming like banshees, half of Omar's men rushed into the front doors of the building, while the remainder gave them covering fire, blasting out the windows on the first, second, and third floors of the building to keep the men inside from forming any kind of resistance.

Flashes of light and booming echoes could be heard as flash-bang and concussion grenades were set off by the intruders.

"Follow me, Mr. Wesson," Omar said as he sprinted across the street toward the station.

"But . . ." Wesson began to say, not having intended to take such a personal part in the attack. He'd figured to let the Arabs take all the chances.

Omar slowed when he noticed Wesson was not coming with him. He stopped and turned, his eyes narrowed at the American, who was still crouched behind the car.

Omar cursed in Arabic and resisted the urge to kill the infidel on the spot. He knew they might have further use of his local knowledge later, so he turned and continued his run toward the battle still going on in the police building.

Kicking the shattered remnants of the front door out of his way, Omar ran into the lobby of the police building. He whirled, his AK-47 cradled in his arms as a door off to his right banged open and three men dressed in blue rushed out, pistols in their hands.

Omar shouted and pulled the trigger of the Kalashnikov, grinning at the wonderful feel of it bucking and jumping and exploding in his hands.

The three cops were riddled with bullets without being able to get off a single shot, their bodies whirling and toppling lifelessly into a jumbled pile of blood and excrement as they died.

Minutes later, all sounds except the occasional single shot of a wounded policeman being finished off ceased, and an eerie quiet descended over the building.

Omar didn't waste any time, for he knew there were still cops out on the street who would soon be responding to the carnage he'd engineered. He barked orders to his men, and they shot the locks off the weapons room door and began to haul away the heavy SWAT armament and bullet-proof vests and ammunition and explosives as fast as they could.

His men outside pulled up alongside the curb near the entrance in their stolen military vehicles, and helped to load the stolen equipment on them.

In less than twenty minutes from start to finish, Omar and his men had killed over 120 police officers, ransacked the building, and stolen almost a ton of weapons and high explosives from the building.

They'd disappeared into the night mere minutes before squad cars from around the city screeched to a halt in front of the building, coming to see what had disrupted radio communications with headquarters.

The first men to enter the building stumbled back outside, some in shock, others bending over to vomit in the gutter at the sight of what they'd seen inside.

Within minutes after that, a Lieutenant Johnson was on a landline phone to Oregon State Troopers headquarters on the other side of the city, telling them what had happened and asking for help.

Fourteen

In the eastern U.S., Omar Sharak had met up with his FFA contact, John Duke, at a rest stop on U.S. Highway 90 near the city of Albany, New York.

After Sharak had made the introductions to the other fifteen men in his team, Duke pulled him aside. "We've gotta get going, Omar," he said.

"What target do you have in mind for us, Mr. Duke?" Sharak asked.

"Call me John . . . if we're gonna be working together, it'll make things easier," Duke advised.

"All right, John," Sharak said, though the familiarity with an infidel made him just a bit nervous. In Sharak's mind, it was all right to use the infidel traitors to kill their countrymen, but any sort of friendship with the unbelievers was out of the question.

"We're gonna head due west along 90," Duke said, pointing down the highway. "We're gonna take out the Falls."

"The Falls?" Sharak asked, not having any idea what the American was talking about.

"Yeah, Niagara Falls."

"You mean the big waterfall on the border with Canada?" Sharak asked, wondering how this would hurt the Americans.

"No, not the waterfall," Duke said, somewhat exasperated.

"The power plant that uses the water to make electricity for the entire state."

"Oh," Sharak said, nodding his head. "That I understand. To disrupt the power plants is one of our most important missions here."

"Good," Duke said, glancing over his shoulder to make sure no one had seen the convoy of three HumVees stopped there. "Let's get a move on. We should get there just before dawn."

Omar Sharak and John Duke, riding in the lead HumVee, pulled up in the parking lot of the Niagara Falls Power Plant at five-thirty in the morning. The lot only had about fifteen cars parked in it, since the late shift was the lightest manned of all the shifts due to the low demand for electricity at that time of night.

Sharak looked around at the huge expanse of parking space. "Why is there such a large space for cars?" he asked.

Duke glanced around, surprised at the question. "Oh, that's 'cause of the tourists."

"Tourists?"

"Yeah. During the day, the plant is opened up for tourists to take guided tours . . . though in the last few years there've been precious few people who could afford to go on tours since that bitch Osterman has ruined the economy."

Sharak shook his head, amazed at the stupidity of the Americans. In his country, such a valuable building would be guarded around the clock, and no one who was not authorized would ever be allowed inside.

"How should we mount the attack?" Sharak asked.

Duke shrugged. "Why, I'd send your men in right through the front door," he answered.

"Won't there be guards?" Sharak asked.

Duke laughed. "Guards? Hell, no. Just send your men in,

kill all the workers, and then we'll blow up the turbines with a few grenades. Should be duck soup."

Sharak didn't understand the reference to duck soup, but he got the general drift of what Duke was saying. He spoke rapidly in a low tone to his men, and they took off for the front door to the power plant at a dead run.

Bruce Watson, senior engineer on the night shift, had just stepped out of the door to have a cigarette, cursing the rules that made the building "Smoke Free."

"God damn," he said as he bent his head to light his butt. "Ain't smokers got the same rights as everybody else?" he grumbled to himself.

As he raised his head and blew a cloud of smoke from his nostrils, he saw a group of fifteen or twenty men running toward him across the parking lot, and they all seemed to be carrying rifles in their arms.

"Shit!" Watson said, throwing his butt on the ground and running back inside the door. He stopped long enough to throw the dead bolt, and then he took off across the lobby toward the corridor leading to his office.

He heard the pounding on the door as he jerked open his office door. He bent over his desk, picked up the phone, and dialled 911.

A sleepy female voice answered, "Nine-one-one . . . What is your emergency?"

"There's a goddamned bunch of terrorists attacking the power plant," Watson screamed into the phone. "Get the goddamned police out here fast!"

"How many men?" the female asked, her voice still bored.

"Fifteen or twenty, an' they're armed to the teeth!" Watson said hurriedly before slamming down the phone. He knew he didn't have long before the men would gain entrance to the plant.

He ran to his door, and was about to open it when he heard

the sound of screams and gunfire echo throughout the building.

"Oh, shit!" he cursed again. He was out of time.

He whirled around, rushed to the back of his office, and opened his closet door. He bent over and shoved some boxes around, rearranging them, and then he got down behind them and pulled an old overcoat off a hanger and laid it over himself after he closed the closet door. With any luck, he thought, they won't find me here.

Minutes later, he heard his office door being kicked open, and he held his breath. Light flooded the closet as the door was opened.

Watson could see a pair of Army boots standing in the doorway from under the edge of the overcoat, and he gave a silent prayer while he waited for the impact of a stream of bullets.

After what seemed an eternity, the boots turned and walked away, leaving the closet door open.

Watson took a shallow breath, but didn't move. He intended to stay right where he was until the police came, however long it took.

Sharak and Duke walked around the power plant, checking the bodies of the workers to make sure they were all dead.

Once they'd determined there were no witnesses left alive, Duke showed Sharak's men where to place their explosive charges so they'd do the most damage.

"We want to put the turbines out of business," he explained, "but not completely ruin them."

"Why not?" Sharak asked.

"Because once we take over running the country," Duke said, referring to the Freedom Fighters of America, "we don't want to have to spend all the country's resources on rebuilding what we've torn down."

"Oh," Sharak said, though personally he thought blowing

this terrible country of unbelievers back into the Stone Age was probably a good idea.

Duke showed the men how to position the charges so only the big belts that ran the generators would be destroyed. Something easy enough to fix, but that would put the plant out of business for at least a few weeks. Weeks that would give the FFA and the Arabs time to do enough damage to the country to make Osterman give up her position as president, or so Duke thought.

Just as they set the timers for ten minutes, enough time for them to get free of the building, shots rang out from the doorway to the turbine room and three of Sharak's men fell, twisting under the impact of hot lead.

"Put your hands up and come out one at a time! This is the police!" a voice yelled from the doorway.

Sharak ducked behind a turbine, raised his AK-47, and let go with a stream of bullets, yelling in Arabic at his men to do the same.

As the police and the Arabs exchanged gunfire, Duke looked worriedly over his shoulder at the charges placed just a few feet away from them.

"Hey, Omar," he said, pulling on Sharak's shoulder. "Them charges are gonna go off any minute now. We got to get outta here or turn 'em off."

Sharak laughed, sweat pouring off his forehead and running down his face. "Look there, John Duke," he said, inclining his head toward the doorway, which was filled with policemen pointing guns into the turbine room. "There is no way out of here."

"Then, we have to give ourselves up," Duke said, sweat pouring off his face too.

"You don't understand, John," Sharak said, not unkindly. "We will be martyrs to the cause . . . we will have everything we want when Allah takes us home."

"Martyrs?" Duke shouted, backing away from Sharak. "I ain't gonna be no goddamned martyr!"

He ran out from behind the turbine, his hands in the air, yelling, "Don't shoot! Don't shoot! I give up!"

Sharak shook his head sadly. Cowards, these Americans, so afraid to die. He raised his AK-47, centered the sights between Duke's shoulder blades, and let go with a short burst, blowing the traitor forward onto his hands and knees.

Duke, still alive, tried to crawl forward, but collapsed after only six yards. He moaned, coughed, and spewed blood from between pale lips, and died on the cold concrete.

Sharak glanced at his wrist watch, saw the time was at hand, and stood up. He held his automatic rifle at waist level, screamed, "Allah be merciful!" and rushed the door, firing as he went.

The astonished policemen saw the Arabs all come out from behind cover and rush their position.

"Jesus!" the lieutenant in charge whispered as he pointed his M-16 and pulled the trigger.

Men were bowled over and cut down like flies as the police unloaded on the rushing Arabs. Two policemen were hit and went down in the melee.

Just as the last of the Arab attackers was hit and knocked to the floor, six tremendous explosions occurred almost simultaneously, sending a giant fireball across the room and through the door, incinerating four more policemen and severely burning three others.

The force of the explosions caused the roof of the turbine room to cave in, covering the huge electric turbines with two tons of concrete and Sheetrock.

The lieutenant, blown over backward and flung across the room by the blast, got to his feet in time to look out of the window. There was nothing but darkness as far as the eye could see.

"God damn!" he muttered. "They've killed the electricity all over the state."

After he saw to his men as best he could, he went to the nearest phone and dialed headquarters.

"This is Lieutenant Waler," he said tiredly into the phone. "Send some ambulances out to the power plant; we've got officers down."

"Hey, Lieutenant," the female communications officer said, "did you know all the lights in town are out?"

He gave a low laugh. "Yeah, I kinda figured they might be. After you get the ambulances on the way, get the chief on the horn for me."

"He's not going to like being waked up," she said.

"That's not all he's not gonna like," Waler said. He hung up the phone. I sure hope the chief's still taking his ulcer medicine, he thought wryly.

Fifteen

Claire Osterman called an emergency meeting of her cabinet in response to reports coming in from both the Northwest and Northeast of multiple attacks on cities, defense installations, and power plants and roads.

Her Defense Minister, Gerald Boykin, was sweating under her intense glare.

"All right, Gerry," Claire said in a low, ominous tone of voice as she stared at him over the rim of her coffee cup. "Tell me just what the hell is going on and why we haven't been able to do anything about it."

"Uh, Madam President," he began, his voice croaking, "it appears we've been invaded in both the Northwest and Northeast borders by a substantial number of troops of Middle Eastern origin."

Claire sighed and drained the last of her coffee in one gulp. "I *know* that, Gerry," she said, exasperation in her voice. "We've known that for over twenty-four hours. My question is, what exactly are our Armed Forces doing about it?"

Boykin spread his hands, looking to his left and right at Wallace Cox, Minister of Finance, and Clifford Ainsworth, Minister of Propaganda, as if searching for help. Neither man appeared ready to step to his defense, so he continued.

"I've asked General Maxwell Goddard to come here this

morning to give you a briefing, but so far, he hasn't shown up yet."

Claire shook her head. "You and the general are supposed to work in concert, Gerry. Why don't you fill me in while we wait for the esteemed general to arrive?"

Boykin sleeved sweat off his brow. "All I know is he sent some air-assault troops into both areas by helicopter late last night . . . Rangers, I believe."

Just as he finished talking, the door opened and in walked General Goddard, his tie loose and his shirt collar open, with sweat stains under his arms. He looked harried, as if he hadn't had much sleep in the last twenty-four hours.

"Good morning, Madam President," he said, and nodded at the other people in the room.

"Ah, the ever-late General Goddard," Claire said with some sarcasm.

The general bristled at her tone. "I'm late to the meeting because I haven't left the radio for more than five minutes in the last twelve hours," he said crossly.

Claire held up a placating hand. "I know, General. Now, would you please give us some idea of just what is going on in my country?"

He took a seat and opened his briefcase on his lap. He withdrew a sheaf of papers and studied them as he spoke. "As you know, over twenty thousand foreign troops have invaded our country from Vancouver Island in the west and Nova Scotia in the east."

Claire nodded. "I'm aware of that, General, but that doesn't seem to be such a large amount that our Army couldn't handle them."

He pursed his lips and shook his head. "Under ordinary circumstances, we would be able to overrun them without any problem whatsoever," he said.

Claire's eyebrows raised. "So, we're talking about extraordinary circumstances, I presume?" she asked.

Goddard nodded. "Yes, ma'am. Instead of marching together in a straight line as most armies do, these invaders have evidently divided up into hundreds or thousands of smaller bands and spread out across the country in an almost random manner. They are all skilled terrorists and are targeting centers of government and police stations as well as important Army National Guard facilities and power plants and road bridges."

"With what purpose in mind?" Claire asked. "They will cause some minor problems, but surely not anything we can't eventually overcome with the proper Army response."

Goddard shook his head. "That might be the case were they acting alone, Claire, but they've managed to get substantial help from some local dissidents."

"What?" Claire asked, her face flushing red.

"Yes. It appears members of some splinter groups are aiding and abetting the invaders. The FFA seems to be playing an important part in helping the invaders with both their choice of targets and with routes that will make them almost impossible to interdict with conventional forces."

"The FFA?" Claire asked, turning her attention to Ainsworth.

The Minister of Propaganda frowned. "Yes, ma'am. They call themselves the Freedom Fighters of America, and they oppose just about everything we stand for."

"Go on," Claire said, leaning back in her chair and steepling her fingers under her chin.

"They are far-right-wing zealots who oppose any government interference in their lives. They think people should be left alone to fend for themselves without any aid from the government."

"They sound like the citizens of the SUSA," Claire observed, glancing around to see if the ministers agreed with her.

Ainsworth nodded slowly. "In many aspects, they do agree with the tenets under which Ben Raines formed the SUSA; only these people are even more adamantly against government intervention in their lives. They refuse to pay taxes, they hoard arms and weapons and explosives, and live in communes out in the boondocks where they've formed heavily defended areas."

Claire leaned forward and slammed her hand down on her desk. "And why haven't these traitors been rousted out and imprisoned before now?" she asked angrily.

Goddard shrugged. "It's been a matter of priorities, Claire. As Cliff says, the areas where they live are isolated and heavily defended. It would take a major effort to take them out, and for the past few years, the military and the police have been more concerned with the wars we've been in and maintaining order in a populace that has grown increasingly rebellious as our standard of living has fallen."

"What do you mean?" Claire asked, her face flaming red at the implied criticism of her policies.

"Well . . ." Gerald Boykin began, and then hesitated.

"Go on," Claire demanded, staring intently at him.

"Over the past few years, the citizens have gotten tired of everything they need to live being in short supply. They've become surly and argumentative with local authorities, and there have even been riots in some localities when food and sundry supplies have gotten low," he said, dropping his eyes to the floor, unable to meet Claire's stern gaze.

"And you're saying this is my fault?" she asked, a dangerous tone in her voice.

"Of course not, Claire," Goddard interrupted. "We are on your side, and as your ministers, we've backed you up on every decision you've made about trying to defeat the SUSA. It's just that our efforts have strained the economy to its bursting point and the people are ready to rebel. The constant shortages followed by this damn plague that's killed thousands of civilians has caused them to be less than respectful of any governmental officers."

"So, what does all this mean?" she asked, relaxing a little at Goddard's conciliatory tone.

"I'm afraid, if the invaders keep going, they're gonna find a large number of citizens willing to join them in their quest to overthrow the government," Cox said. "The number of malcontents among the citizens is at an all-time high, and if the terrorists succeed in cutting even more essential services out, such as electricity and roads, then the people are going to want a change."

"And you think the average citizen is dumb enough to think these rag-heads will be able to do more for them than we can?" she asked scornfully.

Goddard smirked. "Claire, the average citizen is a mushroom . . . kept in the dark and fed bullshit. Don't expect them to make rational decisions based on logic. All they know is their electricity is off, they can't get food at the stores 'cause the roads and bridges are destroyed, and these FFA guys will be promising them the moon. A lot of them are bound to fall for these lies and join up with the terrorists."

Claire nodded slowly, seeing his point. "All right, I get the picture. Now, just what do you men propose we do to counter this invasion?"

"I'm sending all the Rangers I have out into the field to combat these infiltrators," Goddard said, "but I'll soon be running out of men."

"What about the Regular Army?" Claire asked.

He shook his head. "No good. Those soldiers are trained to fight a regular war, with huge masses of troops going up against other huge masses of troops. As for guerrilla warfare, which is what we are engaged in here, they don't have a clue. They'd probably do more harm than good."

"So this Army that's costing the government a fortune is useless when we need it?" she asked scornfully.

Goddard shook his head. "No, it's not useless. In fact, I am spreading the Regular Army units out and posting them as guards along major roads and around important facilities for electricity and communications. But as for going out in the field and rousting out these terrorists, only the Rangers are trained for that kind of fighting."

"So, what do you suggest?" Claire asked, her face looking defeated for the first time they could remember.

Goddard glanced at the other ministers, who all nodded at him as if they'd already discussed this eventuality.

"I think it's time to give Ben Raines a call," Goddard said.

"Ben Raines?"

"Yes. You said he offered to help when he gave us the warning about these terrorists, and he has a large contingent of troops that are trained for just this kind of war."

"Rangers?" Claire asked.

Goddard shook his head. "No, I believe Raines calls them Scouts, and from what my officers tell me from the times they've faced them in combat, they're even deadlier than our Rangers in guerrilla warfare."

Claire turned in her chair and glanced out the window. "Damn, I hate to go begging on hands and knees to Raines. The son of a bitch will give me a horselaugh."

"I don't think so, Claire," Boykin said. "After all, Raines said he supports your continued presence as president of the United States, and it would do him no good at all to have a bunch of Middle Eastern terrorists in control on his northern border."

"I agree, Claire," Ainsworth said. "Raines will welcome the chance to keep some stability here."

Claire looked over at Herb Knoff, who had been sitting silently throughout the meeting. He smiled slightly and nodded his head in agreement.

"Okay, I'll think about it," she said, turning back to her desk and standing, indicating the meeting was over.

As the men stood up, Goddard stepped closer to her desk. "Don't think about it too long, Claire. We may not have much longer to get a handle on this before it's too late. Once the people begin to join the FFA, the cat will be out of the bag and very hard to put back in."

"You think we're that close to losing the support of the people?" she asked.

Goddard held up his hand with his index finger and thumb a half inch apart. "Very close, Claire, very close."

Sixteen

"Hello, Claire," Ben said into the speakerphone, adjusting the volume a little so Mike Post, his Chief of Intel, could hear the conversation from where he sat across the room.

"Hello, Ben," Claire Osterman replied.

"How are things going?" Ben asked, wondering just why she'd called him.

"Not so well, Ben," she replied, her voice sounding tired and worn out. "You were right about the possible invasion of the U.S. by the Arabs."

"Oh?" Ben asked, but Mike had already filled him in on the current status of the invasion and how the invaders were systematically moving southward, destroying vital U.S. infrastructure as they went.

"Yeah, and we're having a bit of a problem controlling them," Claire said.

"What's the problem?" Ben asked. "My information is there are only twenty or thirty thousand invaders so far. Your Army should be able to easily handle that number of terrorists, especially if you have the help of your citizens in the fight."

A sigh could be heard through the speaker. "Well, as you know, Ben, our citizens have always believed strongly in gun control, and therefore not many of the people in my country have access to firearms."

Ben grinned at Mike Post and shook his head. This was

indeed one of the many differences between the SUSA and the U.S. The bleeding heart liberals of the U.S. with their wrongheaded notion that guns were all bad had long ago decreed that no one other than the government should own or have access to firearms.

The SUSA, under Ben Raines's leadership, had always felt just the opposite. Ben believed a well-armed populace was the nation's surest defense against tyranny, and virtually everyone in the SUSA owned guns and knew how to use them. Any invasion of the SUSA would be short-lived, with the invading troops being fought by everyone in the country as well as the Army.

"We've had this discussion before, Claire, about the importance to a nation's defense of its citizens being armed, but even now I don't expect to change your mind."

"I didn't call you up to argue philosophy, Ben," Claire said, an edge in her voice.

"That brings up an interesting point, Claire," Ben said. "Just why did you call me?"

"We may need your help," Claire said, her voice croaking a bit, as if asking her old enemy for aid was difficult to articulate.

"Oh?" Ben asked.

"Yes. The terrorists have separated into hundreds of small groups of men who are all moving independently of each other, and thus our Army is virtually helpless against them. General Goddard has decided to send in our Rangers in helicopters to see if they can stop the terrorists' advance, but he says the Rangers will be severely outnumbered."

"So, the terrorists have resorted to a sort of guerrilla warfare, huh?" Ben asked.

"Yes, those were Goddard's exact words."

Ben shook his head, frowning. "Claire, I wouldn't want to try and tell your general how to run his war, but I don't think helicopters are the best bet against this kind of attack."

There was silence for a moment, and Ben wondered if the

general was sitting in the room with Claire listening to their conversation.

"Why not?" she asked after a few moments.

"Helicopters are fine for attacking large concentrations of men and equipment and for inserting troops into combat zones," Ben said, "but they are fairly slow and make very tempting targets for men spread out in wooded areas, and are virtually worthless in urban areas. I'm afraid your general is going to lose a lot of very valuable troops if he insists on using the helicopters against guerrilla warriors."

Another silence, finally broken by a question. "What would you advise?"

"If it were me, Claire, I'd use the latest intel to find out where the pockets of invaders were and HALO-drop small teams of Rangers, or Scouts as we call them, into the areas just ahead of the invaders. That way, the defenders could get set up and ambush or take out the invaders before they knew they were under attack."

"That's an interesting game plan, Ben, but my general says we just don't have enough Rangers to do it that way."

"Are you asking me for help, Claire?" Ben asked gently.

"Would you consider . . . uh . . . lending us some of your Scouts to help eradicate this threat to my country?" Claire asked, a slight note of desperation in her voice.

"No, Claire," Ben said, his voice firm. "I won't 'lend' you any of my troops. But," he added before she could respond, "I will send some of my troops to help get rid of the terrorists if they can act independently and under the command of our own leaders."

"I don't know if General Goddard will agree to having troops here that aren't under his command," Claire said.

Ben shrugged and leaned back in his chair, his hands behind his head. "It's your call, Claire, but it's the only way you're gonna get any troops from us."

"Let me get back to you on that, Ben," Claire said.

"Don't wait too long, Claire. The more spread out the

guerrillas get, the harder it will be to take them out, and the more damage they'll be able to do."

"That's exactly what General Goddard advised," Claire said, a note of humor in her voice for the first time.

As Claire was speaking to Ben Raines on the phone, General Goddard was meeting with his Ranger commanders at his headquarters. Present were Colonel Blackie Johnson, Major Ralph Jackson, Colonel Randy Morrow, and Colonel Jimmy Doolittle.

Goddard was sitting at his desk, with his men arranged on chairs around his office.

"All right, men, here's the plan," Goddard said. "We'll send in your teams of Rangers in Chinook helicopters to areas where the terrorists are active. Since we're short on men, we'll try to take out the most advanced teams of invaders first and then backtrack toward the ones not so far along."

"General," Colonel Johnson said, his voice a slow Southern drawl, "those Chinooks are gonna be mighty temptin' targets for those Arabs." He pronounced Arabs like A-rabs. " 'Specially if they've got their hands on any TOWs or anti-titank rockets."

Colonel Randy Morrow nodded his agreement. "Blackie's right, General," he said. "Those damned Chinooks are slower'n Christmas. My men are gonna be like sittin' ducks up there."

Goddard held up his hand. "Wait a minute, gentlemen. I plan to have some Apaches and Cobras and Defenders along to give your men air support."

Lieutenant Ralph Jackson, the only black man among the group, shook his head. "That's great, General, if the terrorists oblige by standing around all bunched up. But if they've got any brains at all, they're gonna be spread out where the attack helicopters won't be worth a bucket of spit."

"The attack helicopters are just to occupy the attention of

the terrorists," Goddard said, "while the Chinooks let your men off ahead of the invaders' area. Then, while the attack helicopters are harrying the hostiles, your men can advance on foot and take them out."

Colonel Jimmy Doolittle shook his head. "I sure hope your intel is accurate on the location of these bandits," he said. " 'Cause if it's wrong, my men are gonna be in a world of hurt."

Goddard sighed deeply. "I need you men to work with me on this," he said. "We don't have a whole lot of choice in the matter. These terrorists are systematically destroying half the countryside while we sit here arguing over how to go about defeating them."

He stood up. "If you have any better suggestions, make them now; otherwise get your men together and let's go kick some ass!"

The officers glanced at each other, shrugged, and got to their feet.

"I guess you're right, General," Blackie Johnson said, "but I have a feelin' we're gonna need a lot of body bags 'fore this little fracas is over."

The big Chinook helicopter shuddered and jumped in turbulent air as it headed for Erie, Pennsylvania. Colonel Blackie Johnson sat on metal benches along the walls with twenty of his Ranger troops.

As they rode, the men were constantly checking their equipment. Each man was outfitted with an M-16 carbine, the short-barreled model; a Colt .45-caliber automatic pistol; and a K-Bar assault knife. The equipment was relatively outdated, but the U.S. defense budget couldn't afford the better, but more expensive, Uzis and Berettas used by the Scouts of the SUSA.

The latest intel relayed to Johnson said a band of terrorists were in the area and expected to hit the dock facilities at Erie on Lake Erie that were used to import goods and food from Canada. If the docks were destroyed, it would be a major setback for the people of the Northeast as it would severely hamper their ability to get food and other supplies for some time.

A McDonnel-Douglas OH-6 Defender attack helicopter was flying on the Chinook's port side, while on the starboard side an Apache was leading the way toward the rendezvous with the invaders.

"Lock and load, gentlemen," Johnson yelled, trying to make his voice heard over the roar of the Chinook's big double engines.

The plan was to off-load the troops between the towns of Ashtabula and Erie, and to have them advance in the jeeps that were slung under the helicopter, while the Apache and Defender kept the invaders busy.

At least that was the plan. But Colonel Johnson, ever the realist, knew such battles rarely went as planned.

The Chinook began to settle along a lake-side road as the Apache and Defender flew in wide circles to keep watch while the troops and matériel were unloaded.

As the Chinook lowered toward the ground, Johnson looked out the window to the north and could see huge, billowing dark clouds of smoke some five miles away where the town of Erie would be.

"Damn," he said to himself, "it looks like we're too late to save the docks. Fuckin' intel, wrong as usual," he told himself.

Intel had said the terrorists were at least twenty miles to the north of the town, and wouldn't be in a position to hit the docks for another twelve hours.

"Sons of bitches must be movin' pretty fast," Johnson muttered as he got to his feet in preparation for leaving the chopper.

A booming explosion, followed by a bright light off to the

left, caught his eye. He glanced over his shoulder out the window in time to see the Apache go up in a red fireball.

"God damn!" he yelled, knowing the attackers were lying in wait for them below.

"Hit the ground!" he hollered, diving out the cargo door of the Chinook and rolling as he hit the dirt.

Off to the right, the Defender made a sharp turn and lowered its nose as it dove at the ground just ahead of them, its 20mm cannon firing at unseen troops on the ground.

Johnson got up on his knees in time to see a bright orange streak of light head directly at the Defender, followed seconds later by another fireball as it exploded into fist-sized pieces of molten metal.

"Shit!" he screamed as he and his men began to come under withering automatic-weapons fire.

He recognized the distinctive sound of the AK-47's that were being used against them—one of the most fearsome attack weapons ever made.

Half his men were cut down before they could exit the chopper, while the rest lay on their bellies and returned fire blindly at flashes of gunfire ahead of them.

Johnson threw his M-16 to his shoulder and pulled the trigger, just as a slug tore into his left shoulder, spinning him around to land facedown on hard-packed dirt.

There was no immediate pain, but he knew that would come later, after the shock wore off. He tried to get to his feet, but his left arm hung useless at his side, so he just rolled over onto his back and pulled his .45 from its holster.

He could see black-clad figures rushing toward them out of the darkness, and he tried to cock the pistol, but his left hand wouldn't cooperate. He finally managed to cock the weapon by putting the butt against his chest and using his right arm.

A man screaming something in Arabic appeared twenty yards ahead and ran toward him, firing his rifle.

Johnson gritted his teeth in a savage grin and raised his

Colt. "Take that you bastard," he growled, pulling the trigger as fast as he could.

The big pistol bucked and jumped in his hand, and the Arab shuddered under the impact and was thrown backward with his arms outflung in death.

From his left, Johnson heard the stutter of another AK-47, and felt as if he'd been kicked by a mule as seven slugs tore into his chest and abdomen.

As blood welled up between his lips, he lay his head back and said, "Fuckin' intel."

And then all was quiet.

After a few moments, shadowy, black-clad figures emerged from their hiding places among the trees and shrubs nearby.

They walked slowly among the dead and dying Rangers, occasionally firing a single shot to put an end to suffering, looting and stripping each body of weapons and ammunition before moving on to the next one.

Jamal Ahmed Fadl, the leader of this particular Arab team, walked with his second in command over to stand in front of the Chinook helicopter. He could see the pilot and copilot's bodies through the bullet-shattered Plexiglas, slumped over their controls, the rotors still moving slowly around as the big twin engines idled roughly.

Fadl inclined his head toward the chopper's cargo doorway. "Go and see if there is anything worth taking inside," he said in Arabic, "then torch it."

"Yes, sir," his man said, and moved quickly off to do as he'd been told.

Fadl turned to watch his men strip the bodies and nodded. "All in all, a good night's work," he muttered to the night air.

Seventeen

Mike Post knocked on Ben Raines's door once and entered without waiting for a reply. Ben was in the corner pouring himself a cup of coffee.

"Hey, Mike," he said, holding up the carafe, "want some?"

"Only if it's better than what they've got in the mess hall," Mike answered, sitting in the chair in front of Ben's desk and placing his briefcase on his lap.

"Guaranteed," Ben said, and poured another cup.

While Mike got his case opened and a sheaf of papers arranged on Ben's desk, Ben handed him his coffee and walked around to sit in his desk chair.

"So, what's the latest news from Intel?" Ben asked.

"I just got a call from General Goddard."

"Oh?"

"Yeah. Evidently his best Rangers went up against the terrorists last night and didn't fare too well."

"What happened?"

"Seems the general's intel is not so good. Half the time the invaders weren't where they were supposed to be, and the other half of the time they were lying in wait for the Rangers when they arrived."

"He sent them in by chopper, didn't he?" Ben asked, though he knew the answer. Men like General Goddard were far too conservative to think outside the limits of their rather limited imaginations. They were much too prone to do things the way they'd always been done, and that was one reason Ben had such good luck in defeating such men in combat.

"Uh-huh," Mike said, nodding his head. "Big Chinooks with Apaches and Defenders to run interference."

Ben shook his head. "I can't believe he was that stupid. The men he was going after could hear those choppers coming a mile off. Even if the intel had the right area, there was no chance to get his men in secretly."

Ben slammed his hand down on his desk. "Shit!" he said. "Those men were doomed from the get-go with that kind of a plan of attack."

Ben hated to see good fighting men, no matter the side they were on, wasted by incompetent commanders. It went against his grain.

"What did Goddard want, other than to tell us his problems?" Ben asked.

"He wants to talk to you personally," Mike said. "I think he's anxious to work out some kind of compromise on the chain-of-command issue so he can get some of our Scouts over there to help save his ass."

Ben's lips compressed into a thin line, a sure sign he was angry. "Okay, get him on the phone," he ordered.

Mike glanced at Ben and took a deep breath. He wouldn't want to be in Goddard's shoes when he talked to Ben, that was for sure.

Mike picked up the phone on Ben's desk and spoke briefly into it. After he hung it up, he said, "Sally's gonna ring through when the general's on the line."

A few minutes later, the phone on Ben's desk buzzed. Ben reached over and picked it up.

"General Raines," he said, his voice curt so as to let General Goddard know who was in charge.

"Hello, General Raines, this is General Maxwell Goddard," the voice on the other end said.

Ben reached down and pressed a button, activating the speakerphone. "I'm gonna put you on the speaker, General," Ben said, "so my Chief of Intel, Mike Post, can hear the conversation."

"Good," Goddard said, "I'd like us both to have his input on the situation."

"Me too," Ben said. "Well, Max, it's your nickel. What can we do for you?"

"Has Mike filled you in on the situation here, Ben?" Goddard asked.

"Yeah. How many men did you lose last night?" Ben asked.

After a short hesitation, Goddard answered in a low voice, "Over a hundred, along with three commanders."

"And how many terrorists did your men manage to take out on their missions?"

Another hesitation. "Uh, about fifty, give or take a few."

"That's not a very good ratio, Max," Ben said wryly.

"I know," Goddard said. "Our intel was badly mistaken on both the whereabouts and strength of the opposition. Due in part to the cooperation with the terrorists of some of our own citizens."

"You talking about the FFA guys?" Ben asked.

"Yes. The traitors have aligned themselves with these invaders in hopes of eventually taking over the reins of government from President Osterman."

"So I hear," Ben said. "Now, you've explained your problems, Max. What is it you want from us?"

"President Osterman said she'd discussed with you the possibility of your sending some of your Scouts over here to help us eradicate these bastards," Goddard said, a tentative note in his voice.

"Yes, we discussed it," Ben said, "along with my requirements for the assistance."

"You mean about the men not being under my command?" Goddard asked.

"Yes."

"Ben, you know that'd be very difficult to set up," Goddard said. "It would be extremely difficult to coordinate a good plan of attack without unified leadership of the troops."

"Just how coordinated was your plan of attack last night, General Goddard?" Ben asked, his voice dripping with sarcasm and scorn.

"What do you mean?" Goddard asked huffily.

"General, I'll be frank with you," Ben said, leaning forward so his face was closer to the speaker. "Your operation last night was a complete cluster-fuck!"

"What?"

"You heard me, Max. If you were under my command and had planned such a terrible operation, I would've had you court-martialed and probably shot at dawn."

"I don't have to listen to this shit!" Goddard said, his voice rising to a high pitch.

"No, you don't," Ben said quietly, "but you'd damned well better listen to someone, Max, or you're not only going to get a lot of good men killed, you're gonna lose your country."

"But how was I to know what was going to happen?" Goddard asked, his voice no longer angry but more hushed. "These invaders are just a bunch of rag-heads who don't even know the country."

Ben leaned back and looked at Mike Post, wondering whether it was worth his time to try to explain the fundamental aspects of guerrilla warfare to this man.

"Using the helicopters was a big mistake, Max," Ben said in an even voice, trying to keep the accusation on a professional level.

"How would you have done it then?" Goddard asked.

"I would have inserted my men into the region quietly, either by ground vehicle or by HALO drop, so the enemy wouldn't have known they were there."

"You'd send your men in by high-altitude, low-opening drop at night?" Goddard asked, his voice showing his disbelief.

"Of course," Ben said. "My Scouts are all trained in such maneuvers. Aren't your Rangers?"

"Well, yes," Goddard said. "But that kind of drop is so dangerous, you'd probably lose a high percentage of men in the drop itself."

"In our hands, casualty rates from the drop alone are less than five percent," Ben said. "But how many men did you lose by inserting your Rangers into a hot zone in choppers so loud the enemy could hear them coming half an hour before they got there?" Ben asked.

There was a long hesitation before Goddard answered, "Your point is well taken, Ben."

"Now, regardless of all that," Ben said, "we are still willing to help you out if you want us to."

"How do you propose we work it?" Goddard asked.

"How about this?" Ben asked. "I'll come over with my troops and work out of your headquarters and coordinate our operations with your troops through you. But my men will be under my exclusive command and will answer only to me."

"So, we'd share command of the Army?" Goddard asked, his voice skeptical.

"Not at all," Ben said. "I would only be in charge of my Scouts, and I would keep you well informed of what my plans were. Whatever you decided to do with your men would be entirely up to you, as long as your plans didn't put my men at risk."

"That sounds acceptable," Goddard said. "What would we need to do to set this up?"

"Simply send us a letter from President Osterman stating the terms of the agreement so we'll have something to show the U.N. that we're not invading or interfering with your government, and we can have our men on the way within twenty-four hours and on site within forty-eight."

"You've got a deal, Ben."

"Good. Get the letter drafted and sent and I'll begin to get my men ready. And Max," Ben added.

"Yes?"

"We'll be flying directly into your base at Indianapolis. Get with Mike Post and set up some code words so your anti-aircraft batteries don't get too nervous when we come into your airspace."

"Roger," Goddard said. "And for what it's worth, I'll have the latest intel on the movements of the invaders ready for your perusal upon your arrival."

"Thanks," Ben said, and hung up the phone.

He turned to Mike Post. "Get my team in here as soon as you can."

"Yes, sir!" Post said, getting to his feet.

Eighteen

Ben kicked back in his desk chair and put his feet up on the corner of his desk as Mike walked into his office followed by the rest of Ben's team.

Ben took a close look at Jersey to see if she was fully recovered from her recent head injury.

"How're you doing, Jersey?" he asked.

She grinned, her hand unconsciously moving to the back of her head. "I'm doing great, Boss," she said.

"No nausea or double vision?"

She shook her head. "Nope, not since the first week anyway."

"Good. Now, down to business. I've just gotten off the phone with President Osterman."

"She didn't call to tell you she'd gotten tetanus from her wounds, by any chance, did she?" Coop asked sarcastically.

"No such luck," Ben answered with a grin. "Actually, she called to ask for our help against the terrorists who've invaded her country."

"What, her Army gone on strike?" Harley Reno asked skeptically.

"It's not that," Ben answered. "It's that the terrorists have started a sort of guerrilla war by breaking up into small groups of fifteen or twenty men and spreading out over the countryside."

"How does that keep her Army from going up against them?" Anna asked, glancing at Harley, who was sitting next to her.

He looked at Ben, who nodded. "Go ahead, Harley. Tell her the difference."

"In normal warfare," he said, "you pit huge crowds of soldiers against one another, using all the appliances of modern warfare . . . tanks, ships, aircraft, and even artillery. The men and the generals are used to thinking in certain ways about troop and matériel movements."

"Yeah, I know that. But I still don't see why the Regular Army wouldn't be effective against the guerrillas."

"It's a completely different scenario, Anna," Harley said. "When you're fighting as a guerrilla, you use your enemy's strengths against them."

"Huh?" she asked, confused.

"Well," Harley said, pursing his lips as he thought of a way to explain it to her. "If your enemy is big and you are small, that means he will have to move slow and you can move fast. If he has a lot of troops, they'll have to be supplied with food, ammunition, medical care, and all that. The guerrillas, on the other hand, confiscate the weapons of those they defeat and then use those weapons against the bigger foe, and they live off the land, taking what they need when they need it. They don't have to worry about supply lines or support troops or any of that nonsense."

"So, they can hit and run and by the time the big Army units respond, they've moved on to hit another location," Anna said, nodding her head.

"You got it, babe," Harley said. "Like Ben said, it's a completely different type of warfare, and it takes a specialist to win at it."

"How can you beat something like that?" Beth asked.

Ben leaned forward, his elbows on his desk, and grinned at his team. "Exactly like Harley said, by using the enemy's strengths against them."

"How?" Beth asked again.

"If they're small and mobile, we send troops against them who are smaller and more mobile. We use their tactics against them—we hit them and run, we strike and pull back with small, elite groups that can move and disappear quickly."

"You're talking about Scout units," Coop said.

Ben nodded. "Yep. And they will have the one advantage of being able to call in air strikes when and if the need arises."

"You don't mean you're thinking of sending our Scouts over there to take orders from those idiots that are running Osterman's Army, are you?" Hammer Hammerlick asked incredulously.

"Not for a minute," Ben answered. "I'm gonna go along and I'll be in charge of our men and women, and I'll coordinate our fighting with the Rangers of the U.S. who'll be under Goddard's command."

"You didn't call us in here just to tell us about a fight we're gonna be left out of, did you, Ben?" Jersey asked, her eyebrows arched in a way that made her look very dangerous indeed.

"Of course not, Jersey. I intend for my team to go with me, and to be used as a special strike unit for the most important jobs that come up."

"I don't know if Jersey'll be up to it, Boss," Coop said, a devilish glint in his eye. "She took a pretty nasty blow to the head and the doc says it may have scrambled her brains just a bit."

Jersey turned to glare at Coop. "My ass!" she said. "I would've been all right if you hadn't thrown all your weight down on me. That's what caused my head injury."

"Oh, so that's the thanks I get for saving your hide?" Coop asked, a hurt expression on his face.

"Saving me? Hell, you damned near killed me with your clumsy attack—"

"All right, people," Ben said, trying to hide his grin at the goings-on between Jersey and Cooper.

They settled back in their chairs, refusing to look at each other, as Ben continued. "I want each of you to get fitted out in the typical Scout outfits," he said. "And Harley, you and Hammer get the ordnance together the team's gonna need, including some HALO chutes and gear."

"Damn!" Coop said in a low voice. "I hate HALO drops."

"Puck-puck-puck," Jersey said slowly, mimicking the sound of a chicken.

Less than twelve hours later, Ben had fifteen hundred Scouts geared up and ready to travel. He'd assigned Buddy Raines, his son, to be the commander of the Scout squadron and to act as his second in command for the operation in the United States.

It would be Buddy's job to assemble the Scouts into teams of from five to ten men and women each, and to coordinate communications among the various teams as they were sent out on find-and-destroy missions against the terrorist groups.

In a meeting in his office with Buddy, Mike Post, Dr. Larry Buck, and Harley Reno, who would assume command of Ben's team, Ben explained the procedures to his leaders.

"We'll transport everyone to Indianapolis in a couple of C-130 transport planes, and we'll also bring along a squadron of Ospreys for the drops into hot zones, and a few of our Apaches and Cobras for backup air support that can be called in by the various Scout squads when and if they need it," Ben said.

"Each squad will be given a coded cellular phone as well as a long-range portable radio transceiver to use to keep in touch," Buddy explained. "Corrie has agreed to be in overall charge of communications, with several junior communications officers working under her in case Harley needs her when his team is deployed."

Ben nodded. "What if some of the teams are overrun and their phones or radios are captured?" he asked.

"Neither the phones nor the radios will work unless the proper code sequence is keyed in prior to use," Buddy said. "They'll be useless to anyone except the people who know the correct codes to use."

"What if one of the Scouts is forced to give up the codes?" Mike Post asked.

Harley grinned. "You've obviously never tried to make a Scout talk," he said. "Every one of them would die before talking."

Post nodded. "And as far as medical care in the field?" he asked Dr. Buck.

Larry answered. "I'm taking a large team of surgeons and med-techs along. We'll set up a MASH unit on the Indianapolis base for the use of our troops, and we'll have some special medevac teams ready to travel to hot zones by chopper when they're needed."

"What about supplies?" Post asked.

"We're gonna do like the terrorists," Harley said. "Live off the land, use weapons and ammunition we take from the terrorists, and confiscate whatever else we need from the local economy."

"Okay, if there're no further questions, let's load 'em up and move 'em out," Ben said, getting to his feet.

Nineteen

The twin C-130's lumbered through the skies over the United States, heading toward the airfield at Fort Benjamin Harrison in Indianapolis, Indiana.

Ben Raines, his team, and another few hundred Scouts sat on metal benches lining the wall of the big cargo hold. A handful of Ospreys and Apaches and Cobras were flying in formation with the C-130's, but they would fall behind as they had to make frequent refueling stops, whereas the C-130's could make the trip on one tankful of av-gas.

The noise inside the hold of the C-130 was loud and the ride was bumpy, discouraging much talk among the passengers, but Coop was never able to go very long without some chatter.

He was sitting next to Jersey, which was their usual arrangement. Even though they were almost always at each other's throats, when they were going into hot zones they were also never far apart.

Jersey was, as usual in these circumstances, moving her K-Bar slowly back and forth across a whetstone, honing it to a razor-sharpness.

Coop glanced at her and shook his head. "Jeez, Jerse," he said, "we're just goin' in to kill these motherfuckers, not scalp 'em."

She cut her eyes over to him and laid the blade of her

K-Bar on his thigh, the point near his privates. "Who said anything about scalping them? I've got better plans for them."

"Whoa," Coop said, pushing the knife away, "take it easy there, Geronima."

"Geronima?" she asked, raising her eyebrows.

"Yeah, female for Geronimo," he said, referring to her Apache ancestry.

"Jesus, Coop, you're a very sick puppy," she said, shaking her head back and forth.

"You just say that 'cause you love me and are afraid to admit it," he teased.

"I love you like a blister on my backside, mister," she retorted, and went back to her sharpening.

The convoy landed at Fort Benjamin Harrison in Indianapolis without incident, the choppers hovering on the periphery of the landing field until all of the C-130's made it safely onto the tarmac.

As Ben, followed closely by his team, and then the remaining Scouts in his plane disembarked, they were met by a welcoming committee consisting of President Claire Osterman, General Maxwell Goddard, and several of Claire's cabinet ministers. Herb Knoff was not present because his wounds were not healed well enough for him to make the trip out to the landing field.

Buddy Raines, Ben's second in command, took charge of the Scouts, and had them move immediately to the quarters that had been provided on the base for their use, leaving Ben and his team to greet the greeters.

Claire stepped up to Ben, a half smile on her face. "Hello, Ben," she said, sticking out her hand. "It's been a long time."

"Howdy, Claire," Ben said in his usual informal way. He inclined his head at her left arm, still in a sling from her wounds suffered when the terrorists attempted to assassinate her. "How's the arm?" he asked.

She shrugged. "It's healing," she said quickly.

"Hello, General Raines," Maxwell Goddard said, stepping forward.

He was tall and lean, and his bearing reminded Ben of the character played by Henry Fonda in the old movie *In Harm's Way.*

"Good afternoon, General Goddard," Ben replied, taking his hand and giving it a firm shake.

Claire introduced her ministers, and Ben made the rounds, saying hello to each one, putting a face with the names he'd heard before in intel briefings by Mike Post.

"We have a table set up in the officers' mess if you'd care for some lunch," Claire said.

"Absolutely," Ben replied. "One thing I've learned over the years is to eat at every opportunity, 'cause you never know when you'll get another chance."

"My feelings exactly," Claire agreed, "though lately, I've been cutting down quite a bit."

Ben smiled, noticing her new, svelte figure. "I see you've lost quite a bit of weight, Claire," he said as the group began to move across the landing field toward a line of cars waiting to take them to the base itself. "Was that doctor's orders, or is it the result of your recent wounds?"

She smiled, obviously pleased that he'd noticed. "Actually, it began a couple of years ago, when I was . . . when a plane I was riding in crashed in the countryside. I was marooned without a lot of food for several weeks and the diet was a matter of necessity at that time, but I felt so much better with the weight off, I decided to continue working at it."

"Well," Ben said diplomatically, "it certainly becomes you."

"Thank you," Claire said demurely.

Behind her back, where she couldn't be seen, Jersey

glanced at Coop and made a motion of gagging at the syrupy sweetness of the talk between the two leaders.

Coop tried to keep a straight face, failed, and gave a short laugh.

Claire turned at the sound, spied Jersey, and unconsciously fingered the notch in her ear left by Jersey when she'd had Claire as a prisoner one time in the past.

"Oh," Claire said quickly, "I know you."

"Yes, ma'am," Jersey replied, her face flat with no expression. "We met briefly a while back."

Claire nodded, but didn't speak further of the incident, obviously not wanting to put a damper on the new cooperation between the two countries.

When they got to the officers' mess, Claire hesitated, looking at Ben's team as if she didn't quite know how to tell them they would have to eat in the enlisted men's mess, until Ben told her quietly that his team stayed at his side at all times as a matter of precaution against assassination attempts.

She nodded, her face somewhat grim at the implied statement that he didn't feel safe on her base.

Once all of the participants were seated, and Buddy had joined the group and been introduced, they began to eat.

After the meal, which had been accompanied by only small talk with no important things being discussed, Claire invited Ben and Buddy to join her and General Goddard in her office.

On the way, Ben told his team to get their gear arranged in their quarters while he talked with Claire.

Jersey, who was Ben's self-appointed bodyguard, started to object, until Ben told her he was sure he'd be safe in Claire's office.

"Come on, Jerse," Coop said, taking her by the arm and physically leading her toward their new quarters. "Maybe we can find a room and bunk in together," he explained, a salacious leer on his face.

"That'll be the day," Jersey said, though she grinned as she said it.

In Claire's office, Ben listened as she went over the most recent happenings, including the news that a significant portion of the populace was joining the terrorists and giving them aid and comfort.

"Even a few Army and National Guard units have deserted to join the Freedom Fighters of America contingent in their support of the invaders," she told them.

"You think there's any chance of a widespread movement to join the terrorists?" Ben asked.

She shrugged, glancing at Goddard.

"We just don't know yet, Ben," Goddard said. "Times have been pretty rough since our last . . . hostilities. There've been widespread shortages of food and gasoline and other sundries, so there are quite a few citizens who may feel things will be better for them under a new government led by these Arabs."

"What do you think, Claire?" Ben asked.

"I think that if these terrorists do manage to take over the country, the FFA and all of those who went along with them will be in deep shit," she said firmly. "This El Farrar and his followers aren't in this out of any altruistic motives to help the poor downtrodden people of the United States."

Ben nodded his agreement. "You're right, there, Claire," he said. "Our Intel says he's one of the rich Middle Eastern families who feel they were disenfranchised when the U.N. took over the oil fields. His family evidently went from being one of the richest in the area to just regular citizens."

She raised her eyebrows. "But I understood the oil families were reimbursed by the U.N. for the loss of their oil revenues," she said.

Ben smiled grimly. "Oh, they were, but the levels of re-imbursement, while extremely generous by any normal stan-dards, were still far below what they'd been used to."

"Yeah," Buddy said, a smirk on his face, "I guess going from being billionaires to merely millionaires was quite a step down for them."

"Does your Intel have any idea of just how many troops this Desert Fox may be able to bring into this war?" General Goddard asked Ben. "Our sources are rather vague on that."

"Our best estimate is he has access to well over a hundred thousand, and more will probably jump on the bandwagon and join up if he has some initial success here."

Claire stared at Ben, a worried look on her face. "But surely he won't be able to transport that many troops here. How would he do it without our knowing and being able to intercept them?"

"I'm afraid he has several options," Buddy said. "He can move them in relatively small numbers to Vancouver Island or Nova Scotia and boat them over, or he can load them on huge transport ships and keep them outside the three-mile limit until his terrorists can take over one of the coastal ports, and then bring them in late at night."

"But wouldn't we know about that and be able to attack the transports?" she asked.

Goddard shook his head. "Not if they stayed outside the three-mile limit. If we attacked them there, the U.N. would step in and cut our balls off."

"Max is right," Ben said. "Your only chance to avoid a full-scale war is to crush this terrorist invasion quickly and completely before he has time to make any inroads."

"If you do that," Buddy said, "his support back home will evaporate and the other troops will never be sent, and any other Middle Eastern nations who might be thinking of join-ing in will have second thoughts."

Claire's lips compressed in a tight line. "Then I guess we'd better kick his ass right now," she said.

Ben smiled. This was the ball-busting Claire he was used to dealing with.

"I couldn't agree more," he said.

"As regards that," Goddard said, "just how do you plan to deploy your Scouts?"

Ben leaned back in his chair and nodded at Buddy, giving him the go-ahead to explain.

"We're gonna send them out in five-man groups," he said, leaning forward with his forearms on his thighs. "We'll spread them out all across the country in front of the places where the terrorists have already hit and, hopefully, in their direct line of march."

Claire frowned. "Five-man groups?" she asked. "But our information says the terrorists have at least fifteen to twenty men in their squads, not to mention the FFA fanatics who might have joined them. Won't they be seriously outnumbered?"

Ben grinned. "Not by a long shot, Claire. Every man in a Scout unit is an expert in guerrilla fighting, as well as demolitions, infiltration, and setting up ambushes. Each squad will be in constant communication with home base and able to call in air support at a moment's notice, and each squad will have the latest in firearms, and each squad will have a Thumper along."

"A Thumper?" Claire asked.

"An M-79 grenade launcher," Buddy explained. "So, even though there are lots more invaders than defenders, I think the terrorists are gonna have their hands full dealing with our Scouts."

"How do you plan to deploy them?" Goddard asked. "By helicopter?"

Ben shook his head. "Not usually. That's too noisy, as your Rangers found out last week. It gives the locals too much notice the troops have arrived. I plan to send them in by HALO drop in the middle of the night. That way, they can be on location and dug in before the invaders even know they've arrived."

"HALO drop?" Claire asked.

"High-altitude, low-opening parachute drops," Ben replied. "The terrorists won't even be able to hear the airplanes as they go overhead to drop the Scouts."

"And when the Scouts attack, it will be a complete surprise to the terrorists," Buddy said.

"What about supplying them with ammunition, et cetera?" Goddard asked.

Ben grinned slyly. "Oh, my men are also experts at living off the land. What they can't steal, they'll take from the enemy and use against him later."

"General," Claire said, turning to Goddard. "I want you to coordinate your Ranger deployments with Ben and make sure we box these bastards in and take them out as soon as possible."

"Madam President," Ben said, "one more thing."

"Yes?"

"My Scouts are not going to be taking any prisoners, unless they're needed for intel. Their mission is to destroy the enemy, and they won't have time to baby-sit prisoners."

"You mean even if the enemy gives themselves up?" she asked, her eyes narrow.

"Let me know now if that bothers you, Claire," Ben said, " 'Cause my men ask no quarter and give none."

She thought about it for a moment, then asked, "Even the citizens who might be fighting with the Arabs?"

"They've got to learn a hard lesson," Ben said. "Don't mess with the buzz saw when it's busy cutting wood."

Claire leaned her head back and laughed out loud. "Good," she said. "It'll serve the bastards right for becoming traitors."

"Then we're a go?" Ben asked.

"Absolutely," Claire answered.

Twenty

After the meeting in Claire's office was over, Ben and Buddy huddled with General Maxwell Goddard in his office with a team of his intel specialists.

They poured over maps of the United States that had red pins stuck in them indicating areas already hit by the terrorists, and blue pins in them showing the suspected tracking south of each of the known terrorist units.

"How up-to-date is this intel?" Ben asked a junior officer.

"It's supposed to be accurate up to an hour ago, sir," he answered. He glanced at his superior officer, as if waiting for him to speak, and when he didn't, he added, "But we thought we had accurate intel when we sent our Rangers in a couple of days ago and they got their butts kicked."

Ben and Buddy glanced at Goddard with upraised eyebrows, even though their own intel back in the SUSA had told them as much.

Goddard cleared his throat and put his index finger in his collar and stretched it, as if it were getting tighter by the minute.

"Yeah, that's right, Ben. It seems we badly underestimated just how fast these small groups of men can move when they want to."

"You say a number of your Ranger units were ambushed?"

Buddy asked, stroking his chin with a thoughtful expression on his face.

Goddard nodded. "Yeah. Why?"

"Is there any chance you've got a leak, or maybe even a traitor in your outfit who might've warned some of those units to be on the lookout for the Rangers?"

Goddard, after thinking on it for a moment, shook his head. "Of course it's possible," he conceded, "but I don't think it's likely. For one, all of my men in a position to know the distribution of the Rangers have been with me for a long time, and for another, I don't see how they could get in touch with the invaders to give them the warnings you're talking about."

Ben shook his head. "General, as for the second, they could do it just like I plan to keep in touch with my Scouts . . . through a coded cell phone to the leader, who could then warn the individual units."

He glanced at Buddy and then back at the general. "As for loyalty, that could easily be circumvented in a number of ways."

"What are you talking about?" Goddard asked.

"Well," Ben said, looking upward as he thought, "a close family member of one of your staff officers could have been kidnapped by one of those FFA guys, and as bits and pieces of their body were delivered, it might convince the officer to give them the information they wanted . . . or perhaps a bit of blackmail for a past indiscretion, or even the most prosaic of all . . . money."

Now it was General Goddard's turn to scratch his chin. "I never even considered. . . ."

"That's because you're used to regular warfare, General," Buddy said. "When you're dealing with guerrillas, especially when they have a built-in group like the FFA helping them, anything is possible."

Goddard cut his eyes toward Ben and Buddy. "What do you suggest?"

"There are two ways to go, one quick and one slow," Ben said.

"Go on," Goddard asked.

"The slow way is to give each of your officers slightly different intel and to see which way the enemy responds, which could point to the one giving them the info," Ben said.

"What's the fast way?"

"Tell each of your officers there is a mole in headquarters and they're gonna have to undergo drug-induced questioning the next morning," Ben said.

The general's face fell. "I don't know if I could . . ."

Buddy held up a hand. "Don't worry, General, you won't have to. We'll have each of your officers under surveillance from the time they leave work until they show up here tomorrow."

"What good will that do?" the general asked.

"I have a feeling the guilty one, or ones, will not want to undergo drug interrogation," Ben said, "so they'll either bolt, or if they have a good reason for their treachery, they may even give themselves up."

"Either way," Buddy added, "you probably won't have to do any questioning."

"What if no one runs or gives themselves up?" asked Goddard with a worried expression.

"Then we either have no mole, or he's got bigger balls than I do," Ben said.

Finally, the general agreed to the plan, and all of the senior officers, the only ones who would be in a position to give out the information that was leaked, were called into Goddard's office.

"Gentlemen," he said, "we have discovered there is a mole in our senior staff."

After the excited buzzing from the assembled men died down, he held up his hand. "There is only one sure way to deal with this problem in order to keep any more of our troops from being lost due to compromised battle plans. Tomorrow, at 0700, General Raines here and his men, who are experts at psychological warfare, will take each of the senior staff and do interrogations under chemical guidance."

"What do you mean, chemical guidance?" a man with a name tag on his chest that identified him as Major Benson asked.

"We'll start with sodium Pentothal," Ben said, "and proceed with stronger and stronger drugs until we get a confession."

"Max . . . General Goddard," Benson said, "I really must protest this assault on our loyalty."

"Protest all you want, George," Goddard said, his face firm. "We lost over a hundred of our best-trained Rangers the other night because someone in this room is a traitor, and I don't intend to rest until we find out who was responsible."

When Benson opened his mouth again, Goddard held up his hand. "We know that under certain circumstances," Goddard said, glancing at Ben, "there might be good reasons for the traitor to have done what he did. If that is the case, and he admits to his wrongdoing prior to the interrogation tomorrow morning, we might be inclined to grant him some leniency. But if we have to find out through drugs, he will be summarily court-martialed and shot before the day is over."

A couple of the other men registered some mild disapproval, until Ben stepped forward.

"If any of you men who think we are acting unwisely have any better ideas to ferret out the mole, speak up," he asked, looking around at the group.

When he got no answer, he added, "So, I feel the loss of some of your dignity is worth the saving of hundreds of Rangers' lives, don't you?" he challenged.

Most of the men nodded slowly, while others just dropped their eyes.

"So, we go with the interrogation in the morning. I'll see you then," Ben said, a hint of warning in his voice.

After the men filed out, Goddard shook his head. "Damn, I hated to do that," he said.

"Was it harder than writing all those letters to the families of the men the traitor killed?" Ben asked gently, knowing that of all of his duties that one was the most painful for him.

Goddard stared back at him. "No, when you put it that way, I guess it wasn't."

Twenty-one

Because they were unknown to the senior officers of General Goddard's staff, Ben assigned members of his team to shadow the officers when they left the base after the announcement of the upcoming drug interrogations scheduled for the next morning.

Jersey was assigned to follow Lieutenant Colonel Ralph Madison, the assistant to Goddard's Chief of Intel, while Coop, Beth, Anna, Harley, and Reno shadowed the other members of the senior staff.

Goddard went along with the exercise, but he didn't have high hopes of its success.

Colonel Madison left the base at five-thirty in the afternoon and headed south toward his home in the Oak Hills subdivision. Jersey had a copy of his personnel file, and knew where he lived and that he had a forty-four-year-old wife and two children, a fifteen-year-old son and a thirteen-year-old daughter, both of whom lived at home with their parents.

Jersey, driving a nondescript staff car, had no trouble keeping the colonel in sight, though traffic was light because of the strict rationing of gasoline in the United States since the last war.

He drove at a normal rate of speed, and made no unscheduled stops along the way. Jersey was disappointed. The man was acting perfectly normal, and she'd been hoping for some action to come her way.

When he pulled into the driveway of a ranch-style house on a residential street, she parked several houses down around a corner in front of an empty lot so her car would be out of sight of the house, just in case anyone was watching.

Madison hadn't acted suspiciously on the trip home, though she thought he drove rather slowly for someone heading home to his family. Perhaps he wasn't in any hurry to get there for some unknown reason, she thought.

Jersey hunkered down in the car so she wouldn't be visible from the street and cause the local residents any worries, and waited for darkness to fall.

While waiting, she glanced around, wondering if the residents of such a white-bread sort of neighborhood had any idea of the momentous struggle going on for control of their country. Probably not, she figured, or they'd be up in arms at the idea of some Arabs from halfway around the world possibly being the next leaders of their destiny.

As soon as it was full dark, she got out of the car, checked her Beretta to make sure it was loaded and a shell was chambered so all she'd have to do to fire was to pull the trigger. She stuck the pistol in the waistband of her black jeans and let the tail of her shirt fall to cover the butt so it wouldn't be too obvious to anyone she might meet on the street.

She walked casually down the sidewalk, letting her eyes roam from side to side to make sure no one was paying her any mind, until she came abreast of Madison's house.

It was set back about twenty yards from the street, with a series of low bushes fronting the house and extending around the side of the yard.

She slowed and stretched and yawned, using the movement to cover her checking to see if she was observed. When she saw no one, she crouched and ran silently up to the corner of the house, and squeezed in among the bushes next to a side window.

Moving very slowly, she cautiously raised her head until her eyes were just above the windowsill. Blinds were drawn, but there was a gap of about an inch she could see through.

Jersey's breath caught in her chest at what she saw in the living room of the house.

Madison, his wife, and two children were sitting in a row on the couch, with three men standing before them across a coffee table. The teenage girl had tears in her eyes, and the boy was staring sullenly at the men, a look of hatred and fear on his face.

Madison seemed to be arguing with one of the men, speaking earnestly, waving his hands as if he were desperately trying to convince the man of something.

As Jersey studied the men, she noticed the butt of an automatic pistol sticking out of the belt of one of them, while the other two wore shoulder holsters with pistols in them. She felt sure she'd found the mole.

Jersey eased back out of the bushes and made her way around the house, looking in each of the windows, trying to get a mental picture of the way the house was laid out. She needed to decide whether to intervene on her own or to call for backup.

She thought about it for a moment, wondering if backup could be arranged silently enough not to alert the men in the house. Better not to risk it, she thought, or the entire family might be killed.

As she squatted out of sight near an oleander bush, a small sedan pulled down the street and stopped three houses down from the Madisons'. It had a Domino's Pizza sign attached to the roof, and a young man got out, carrying a large square box.

Before he could get to the front door, of the house three houses down, Jersey sprinted down the sidewalk and called softly to him, "Hey, you."

He stopped and turned around, a quizzical expression on his face.

"Come here a minute," Jersey said, keeping her voice soft so as not to alarm the young man.

"Whatta you want?" he asked suspiciously.

"You want to make twenty bucks?" Jersey asked.

The boy thought about it for a moment, looked around to make sure no one else was with Jersey, and then walked back up to her.

"Sure," he said, his eyes roaming over Jersey's body and his voice becoming a bit more cocky.

Jersey pulled a twenty-dollar bill out of her pocket and held it out in front of the boy.

"Let me borrow that pizza and your hat and car for five minutes," she said.

"What?" he asked, his eyes widening at the craziness of her request.

Jersey smiled her most seductive smile. "I want to play a trick on my boyfriend," she said in a conspiratorial tone of voice. She turned and pointed at the Madisons' house just down the street. "He lives right there, and I want to go up to the door carrying a pizza and give him a surprise."

"But . . . what about these people who ordered this pizza?" the boy asked. "If they complain I could get fired."

"It'll only take a minute, then you can have the pizza back," Jersey said, moving a little closer to the teenager. "And I'd be ever so grateful," she added, raising a hand and patting his cheek.

"Uh . . . I guess it'd be okay. But you got to hurry so the pizza don't get cold."

He handed her the pizza and she gave him the twenty dollars. She reached up, took the paper hat with the Domino's insignia on it off his head, and placed it on her head.

"Wait right here and I'll be right back," she purred, and he grinned.

"All right."

She got in his car, made a U-turn, and drove the three houses down the street to the Madisons' house.

Getting out, she opened the pizza box, put her Beretta on top of the pizza, and laid her K-Bar assault knife next to it.

She took a deep breath and walked up the sidewalk to the front door. Reaching up, she unscrewed the lightbulb in the porch light, and then she rang the bell.

When she'd checked out the house through the windows, she'd noticed the front door opened onto an alcove that couldn't be seen from the living room. With any luck, she'd be able to get one of the men there, and then take out the other two before they became suspicious.

The front door opened a crack and Colonel Madison stuck his face out. "Yes, what can I do for you?" he asked, looking over her shoulder at the pizza delivery car parked in front of his house at the curb.

"I have a pizza delivery," Jersey said in a bored tone of voice.

"We didn't order any pizza," Madison said in an aggravated voice.

"Look, mister," Jersey said, letting a little anger into her voice, "all I know is I was told to bring this pizza to this address."

"What's going on here?" one of the men from the living room asked, stepping into the doorway and shouldering Madison aside.

Jersey noticed he had his hand over the butt of the pistol in his belt.

"Nothing's goin' on, I'm just tryin' to deliver this pizza," Jersey drawled in her best imitation of a Midwestern accent.

The man glanced at Madison suspiciously, and then back at Jersey. "What address were you looking for?" he asked, taking charge of the conversation.

Jersey made a show of trying to read the receipt on the front of the pizza box in the darkness. "Uh . . . I don't know, I can't read it in the dark. Could you turn on the porch light?" she asked, trying her best to look helpless.

The man reached up next to the door and flipped the switch several times, to no avail.

A voice called from inside the house. "Hey, Bud, what's going on out there?"

The man looked back over his shoulder. "Nothin', we just got a lost delivery girl. I'll take care of it."

He turned back to Jersey and stepped back into the alcove. "The porch light's out. Come on in here where you can read the address."

"Gee, thanks, mister," Jersey said, and stepped into the doorway.

As she moved past him, she slipped the box open, grabbed her K-Bar, and as she turned around she buried it in his throat.

His eyes popped open and he reached up to his neck, but the blade had severed his vocal cords so he couldn't cry out.

In one fluid motion, Jersey shoved Madison, who was standing there with his mouth hanging open and his eyes wide, aside and pulled the Beretta out of the box as she dropped the box on the floor.

Three quick steps and she was in the living room, her arms outstretched before her, the Beretta held in both hands moving back and forth, covering both of the men in front of her.

"Don't make a move!" she growled at the two men standing there. When they saw her, and the gun she was pointing at them, they both took an involuntary step back and squared around to face her head-on.

They stared at Jersey for a moment, and then looked back at each other. Finally, both men made the fatal mistake of grabbing for the pistols in their shoulder holsters, one of them diving to the side as he drew his gun.

Jersey didn't hesitate for a second. She squeezed off four quick rounds, two to the chest of each of the men, driving them backward to land spread-eagled on their backs, their eyes still wide open but staring at nothing as scarlet blood pumped out onto the Madisons' beige carpet, turning it an ugly shade of brown.

The acrid smell of cordite hung in the room as Jersey whirled and covered Madison with her pistol, just in case he wanted to get involved. She still wasn't sure of just how committed he was to the Osterman program. He wasn't even looking at her; he was staring at the couch where his wife and children were sitting.

At the sight of the two men being killed, the girl and her mother both screamed and threw their arms around each other, while the teenage boy dove to the floor, covering his head with his hands.

Madison, after a quick look at Jersey, ran to their sides and put his arms around their shoulders, hugging them tight to him.

Jersey, seeing he would be no problem, ran back to the front door to check on the man she'd stabbed. He was sitting on the floor, his back against the wall, his legs outstretched in front of him, as dead as yesterday's news.

As Jersey pulled her K-Bar from his throat and wiped it on his shirt, the pizza boy burst into the doorway.

He took one look around and said, "Aw, shit. Look at that mess."

"What?" Jersey asked.

"You got blood all over the pizza box. Now what am I gonna do?" he asked, making no mention of the dead man on the floor or the shots he'd no doubt heard.

Jersey laughed out loud. It seemed nothing fazed teenagers these days.

She bent over and picked up the box. "Rinse it off with the hose out front," she said.

"But then it'll be all wet," he complained, taking the box from her.

"Hell, tell the customers you got caught in a rainstorm," Jersey offered, pushing him out the door and shutting it in his face.

Twenty-two

While Madison comforted his wife and children, Jersey got on the phone and called the base, asking to be put through to General Raines.

"Yeah, Jersey, what've you got?" Ben asked, knowing Jersey wouldn't've bothered him with a routine report.

"Madison's wife and children were being held hostage by three men, probably FFA members," she answered.

"What's the current status?" Ben asked.

"The three hostiles were terminated with prejudice," she answered, "so we're gonna need a cleanup crew over here at the colonel's house, and maybe some counseling personnel to be with the family while we debrief him."

"Roger," Ben said. "I'll get the general and his Chief of Intel and some help and we'll be right over. Any . . . uh . . . injuries among the family?"

"No, just the hostiles," Jersey said, and hung up the phone.

She stepped into the living room and stood before Colonel Madison.

He glanced up at her, fear in his eyes and on his face.

"You'd better make some coffee," Jersey said to the wife, knowing that getting her back to her normal routine would help to keep her from becoming hysterical. "We're fixing to have some company from the base."

The colonel's wife wiped her eyes and nose, straightened

her shoulders, and smiled wanly at her teenage daughter. "Come on, Janine. You can help me in the kitchen," she said, standing up and taking her daughter by the arm.

Jersey cut her eyes back to the colonel, and he dropped his gaze and stared down at his hands clenched between his knees. "I had to help them," he said, his voice taking on a whining quality as he spoke. "They said they would kill my family."

Jersey shook her head. "Don't tell me your story, mister," she said, absolutely no sympathy in her voice. "Save it for your commander, who's on his way over here."

She hesitated, then couldn't resist adding, "But while you're waiting, you might be thinking up something you can say to the families of the hundreds of men you got killed to save your own family. I'd be interested to hear how you try and justify it myself."

With that, Madison put his hands over his face and began to cry. Jersey, disgusted with his gutless behavior, snapped, "Why don't you go get a couple of sheets or something and put them over the bodies so your son doesn't have to stare at them all night?"

The son was sitting next to his dad, giving Jersey the same insolent, sullen look he'd given their captors a few minutes before.

"Come on, son," Madison said, getting to his feet and heading down the corridor toward the bedrooms.

After the cleanup team had removed the bodies, and while some female psychologists were talking with the wife and kids, Ben, General Goddard, Colonel Joshua Currey, who was his Chief of Intel, and Jersey sat at the kitchen table facing Colonel Ralph Madison.

Ben took the lead in the questioning. "Ralph, we're not going to get into reasons why you did what you did, but we do need to know if you're aware of any of the other officers on the senior staff who may be giving information to the enemy."

Madison began to speak, but his voice broke and he had to cough and clear his throat. "Uh, not to my knowledge, General Raines, but I wasn't given any information, just asked to give them times and dates and locations of intercept teams that were being sent out."

His face screwed up and tears welled in his eyes. "I swear I didn't know they were going to ambush the teams," he groaned. "I thought they would just tell their people to avoid those areas and our men would come home after finding no terrorists where they thought they were."

"Can you give us any information about who your captors' contacts were?" Ben asked.

Madison shook his head. "No. I gave them what I knew about our schedule of flights, and they would go into the other room and talk on their cell phones for a few minutes. I don't even know the phone numbers they called."

Ben glanced at Josh Currey. "Any chance of tracing those numbers and perhaps getting a location?"

Currey shook his head as he glanced at one of the cell phones he was holding, which had been taken off one of the dead men. "Not a chance," he said. "The phones are coded . . . that is, the transmissions are scrambled and don't go through the routine channels most normal cell phones use."

Ben smiled slightly. "Yeah, I know. It's the same technology my people are using to keep in touch with the teams. It's pretty much intercept-proof."

"We can't even use the phones' redial button since it takes a special code to activate the phone," Currey said. "They're completely useless to us."

Ben leaned back in his chair. "Well, I think to make sure no other officers are being blackmailed in a similar fashion, I'd recommend that all of the senior men and their families be moved onto the base until this war is over."

"That's gonna take some doing," Goddard said.

Ben shrugged. "It's the only way I know to protect your men and your information from coercion. That still won't keep someone from selling information to the enemy, but judicious and frequent use of lie detectors and such should keep that sort of treachery to a minimum."

"What do you suggest we do about Colonel Madison here?" Goddard asked Ben, wondering what the SUSA man would say.

Ben looked at Madison, his face a mask. "That depends on how useful he is to your war effort. I'm not much one for punishment for punishment's sake. The man was put in an impossible situation. If he's good at interpreting intel, then I'd continue to use him, after some suitable slap on the wrist like losing some rank and pay. But if this war lasts as long as I think it will, you're gonna have need of all the good men you can find."

Goddard slowly nodded and looked at Madison. "You think you can pull your shit together and get back to work, Ralph?" he asked. Though his words were harsh, his voice was not unkind and his expression was more one of sympathy than censure.

Madison nodded eagerly. "Yes, sir!" he said.

"Good. Then get in there and pack your family up for a trip to the base."

Ben cleared his throat. "Uh, General, I have a suggestion to make if it's all right."

Goddard laughed. "Now, don't go getting shy on me now, Ben," he said.

"Why don't we leave a couple of men here just in case some of the FFA types pay a visit?" he asked. "That way, we might just be able to catch a couple of live ones we can question."

"Good idea, Ben. And I'll have my men in Intel keep these cell phones close in case a call comes in from their boss. Maybe we can fool him enough to set a trap."

"Won't hurt to give it a shot," Ben agreed, though he knew the higher-ups in the FFA, if they were smart enough to have remained undercover and undetected by the U.S. counterintelligence agents for this long, were not going to be fooled by any plan as simple as that.

He got up from his chair at the table and smiled at Jersey. "Come on, Jersey. It's time we got back to the base before our Scouts take off on their missions."

"Roger that, sir," Jersey answered.

Twenty-three

Achmed Sharif, the leader of Abdullah El Farrar's western contingent of terrorists, stood up in the passenger seat of his confiscated HumVee as it stood idling on the outskirts of Boise, Idaho. His second in command, Mohamed Omar, was in the driver's seat, and his FFA contact, Billy Wesson, sat in the backseat cradling his AK-47 in his arms.

It was just before dawn and the sky to the east was beginning to lighten with the coming of the sun, clouds on the horizon starting to color with brilliant oranges and yellows signaling the coming arrival of morning.

Scattered along the interstate highway behind the lead HumVee were over thirty trucks containing Sharif's original twenty Arabs and another 150 men and women of the FFA who'd joined up with the caravan as it made its way south and east from the coast.

All of the insurgents were armed with a variety of weapons that had been confiscated from Army depots, National Guard armories, police stations, and even gun shops that had been overrun and taken by the terrorists on their journey across the U.S.

"What do you suggest as our plan of attack, Mr. Wesson?" Sharif asked as he peered at the buildings of downtown Boise, barely visible in the early morning light.

"We have two objectives here, Achmed," Wesson said,

making Sharif's teeth clench at the overly familiar tone. "The most important is to take control of the airport without doing too much damage to the fields, so we can bring in more men and weapons when we're ready. The second objective is to take out the local authorities, consisting of the police station and the highway patrol headquarters."

"And how do you propose to do this?" Sharif asked, sitting back down on his seat and turning to look at Wesson over the back of that seat.

"Well," Wesson said, rubbing his chin. "The airport ain't gonna give us no real problem. Other than a few rent-a-cops, they ain't gonna have much security."

"Rent-a-cops?" Sharif asked, not being familiar with the term.

"Yeah, you know. Hired guards from a security company. They'll only be armed with pistols an' maybe a rifle or two. Nothin' we can't handle."

"What about the police and highway patrol?"

"There we're gonna have to be a mite more careful. Both the cops an' the highway patrol offices will have plenty of firepower, but it'll most likely be locked up. If we hit 'em fast an' hard, we should be able to get 'em 'fore they can open up the arms lockers an' get all their men armed with the heavy stuff they have on hand."

Sharif nodded slowly. "So, you would divide up our forces, with the strongest going to the police and highway patrol, and send a smaller unit to take the airport?"

"That's the way I'd handle it if I was in charge," Wesson said.

Sharif smiled slightly. At least the man was finally learning his place, which was in fact very low on the order of importance.

"Good, then that is how we will proceed," Sharif said, turning back around to face the front of the vehicle. He pulled a map of the Boise area out of the glove box of the HumVee and opened it on his lap.

Mohamed Omar leaned over and shined a small flashlight onto the map, watching Sharif's finger as he traced out the locations of the airport, the police headquarters, and the offices of the highway patrol.

"Mohamed," Sharif said, "I will command the attack on the highway patrol and you will lead the attack on the police station, since those are the two most dangerous assignments."

"What about the airport, Achmed?" the second in command asked. "Who will take command of that unit?"

Sharif glanced into the backseat. "Mr. Wesson, of course."

"Who, me?" Wesson asked.

"Yes. I want you to take a number of your FFA friends and go to take control of the airport while Mohamed and I attack the other two targets."

Wesson pursed his lips, and then he finally nodded. "Okay, no problem," he said.

The attacks on the police and highway patrol buildings were planned to take place between 6:30 and 7 o'clock in the morning. That way they could catch the men arriving for the morning shift in the building at the same time as the men leaving the night shift so as to maximize the number of policemen and highway patrol officers killed.

Achmed Sharif and his men surrounded the highway patrol building, which was set off by itself on the eastern side of town. They'd parked their trucks and cars two blocks away in an empty field so as not to draw attention to their presence.

Once the terrorists were in position, Sharif sent two FFA men carrying satchels loaded with fragmentation grenades to the front and rear entrances, while another made his way to the power box on the outside of the building.

At Sharif's signal, the lone man cut the power to the building, while at the same time the other two men stepped through the doorways.

As soon as all the lights in the building went dark, the men squatted just inside the doors and began to pull grenades from their satchels.

When the explosions began to ring throughout the building, the terrorists materialized out of the darkness and rushed into the doors, front and back, their AK-47's chattering a song of death and destruction as they spread out through the corridors.

Several of the invaders were wearing night-vision goggles to make it easier for them to pick out their targets.

The screams and yells of the highway patrolmen were punctuated with the explosions of the fragmentation grenades and the harsh guttural roar of the Kalashnikovs as they killed hundreds of patrol officers.

In less than thirty minutes, the highway patrol building was a mass of roaring flames, sending the acrid scent of burning flesh rising on the morning air.

Sharif lost only four men in the assault, while every patrol officer on the premises was either killed in the initial assault or burned to death as the building collapsed in a heap of smoldering ruin.

The police station downtown presented a more difficult problem for Mohamed Omar. It was part of a block of buildings and wasn't set off by itself, so the attack needed to be different from the one on the highway patrol headquarters.

Omar sent men into each of the neighboring buildings and out onto the roofs. From there, they crossed to the roof of police headquarters. It was an easy matter to cut the lock on the roof door and gain access to the stairs leading inside.

Once the roof men were ready, they signaled Omar, and he sent men into the front and back doors simultaneously.

Desk Sergeant Malcolm Watts looked up from his magazine to see a man of Arab extraction walk in the front door carrying what looked like a machine gun in his arms.

"What the . . . ?" Watts exclaimed, reaching for the pistol on his hip that he hadn't drawn in his entire fifteen years on the force.

The Arab grinned, leveled his AK-47, and fired from the hip, blowing Malcolm Watts backward off his chair, dead before his gun had left his holster.

As the cops milling around whirled at the sound, several more men began to swarm in through the doors, opening fire as they rushed into the building.

Policemen were mowed down where they stood, most not even managing to get a shot off before they were hit.

When he heard the shooting, Lieutenant John Smith, a twenty-year veteran of the force, ran to the arms locker and punched in the code to open the door.

Once inside, he grabbed an M-16 off a rack, jammed a clip into it, and pocketed two more. Thumbing the lever to full automatic, he eased to the doorway.

He was astounded to see dead cops lying everywhere, with black-clad figures running up and down the halls, shooting as they went.

"Son of a bitch!" Smith yelled, taking aim.

He pulled the trigger, and was satisfied to see three of the attackers dance a jig of death as the M-16 cut them down like grass under a lawnmower.

Hot lead splintered the wall next to Smith, and he ducked back into the arms locker room, slamming the door behind him.

He quickly took down a Kevlar vest and threw it on, picked up a couple of more magazines and a few stun grenades, and went back to the door.

Easing it open, he pulled the pin on one of the stunners, flipped it out in the corridor, and pulled his head back.

A tremendous flash followed by an ear-shattering blast rocked the corridor and filled it with smoke.

Smith took a deep breath, crossed himself quickly as he

said a silent prayer, and stepped out of the room, his M-16 held at waist level.

Three men in black were rolling on the ground, holding their hands to their ears and shouting in pain.

Smith bared his teeth and raked them with a quick burst from the M-16, ending their howling.

He ran up the corridor, jumping over bodies of his friends as well as the enemy, and looked for more targets.

Two men stepped around the corner, their eyes going wide when they saw him.

Smith let go with a burst, and knocked them onto their backs and kept running.

He got four more men before his magazine was empty. He stopped and flipped it out, and was ramming another one home when a volley of shots from ahead hit him square in the chest and blew him onto his back, the M-16 flying from his hands.

He lay there stunned and watched as another black-clad figure stepped out of the smoke to stand over him grinning. This was no Arab, but an American.

Smith jerked his .38 service revolver from his holster and shot the man three times in the face, blowing the look of surprise into bloody pulp.

Smith grinned and struggled to his feet, his pistol held out in front of him.

Behind him, Mohamed Omar took aim with his AK-47, and shot him in the back of the head, ending forever Smith's heroic actions.

Billy Wesson and ten FFA men and women pulled up in the parking lot to the airport.

He pointed to three of the men. "You three come with me. We'll take the control tower. You others, go in the front door and take out any guards or airport policemen you see, and anyone else who gives you any problems."

At this hour of the morning, the red-eye flights had already left and the incoming arrivals weren't due for another couple of hours, so the control room was relatively calm, monitoring only a few private planes in the area.

There was no guard on the door to the control tower, only a button combination lock to keep unwanted visitors out.

Wesson aimed his AK-47 at the lock and blew it out of the door, kicked the door open, and stepped aside as his men ran quickly up the stairs.

An elderly guard appeared at the top of the stairs, a pistol in his hand. He managed to get one shot off, wounding the first man up the stairs.

The second man in line emptied his entire clip of bullets into the guard, flipping him in a backward somersault out of sight and blowing out three of the windows of the control tower in the process.

"Be careful, goddamnit!" Wesson shouted. "Don't fuck up any of the equipment."

As they swarmed up the stairs, they found the rest of the air-traffic controllers sitting at their consoles, their eyes wide with fright and their hands in the air. The dead guard was leaking blood all over the floor.

Wesson stepped over his body and pointed to one of his men. "Get that body out of here," he ordered.

Once the guard was removed, Wesson walked over to stand in front of the controllers. "All right now, people," he said. "Just take it easy and no one else will get hurt."

"Uh . . . what do you want?" the oldest man in the room asked.

"We're gonna need for you to land a few planes for us later in the day," Wesson said. "Until then, I want all air traffic diverted to another field."

"But what will we tell them?" a younger man asked.

Wesson shrugged. "I don't care. Tell 'em you had a private plane crash and it fucked up your landing field or something."

The controllers looked at each other, knowing that wouldn't suffice, but none wanted to argue with the man holding the automatic weapon.

Once all the people in the tower were under control, Wesson walked to a far corner and took out the coded cell phone Sharif had given him.

He thought for a moment, trying to remember his personal code to make it work. Finally, he punched in six numbers, but the damned thing still wouldn't turn on.

"Fuck it," he said, and stepped over to one of the phones on the air-traffic-control console.

He picked it up and dialed a number. When the voice on the other end answered, he said, "This is Billy. We've got control of Boise Airport and you can get the transports ready."

They talked for another five minutes; then Wesson hung up the phone.

He turned back to the controllers. "We're gonna have some planes coming in later today," he said. "I'll give you their call letters so you can make sure they get here safely."

"What kind of planes?" the head controller asked.

"What difference does it make?" Wesson asked. "All you got to do is make sure they land okay."

"We need to know so we can assign them to the correct landing field," the man said. "Jumbo jets and large planes land on different fields from smaller prop planes."

Wesson nodded. "Okay. I'll let you know when the time comes."

Twenty-four

Ben Raines and General Maxwell Goddard were in a meeting, planning just where the Scout teams were going to be dropped and coordinating it with where the U.S. Rangers would be sent in, when Josh Currey, Goddard's Chief of Intel, burst into the room.

"Gentlemen," he said, a wide smile on his face, "we've finally caught a break."

"What is it, Josh?" Goddard asked, looking up from the maps he and Ben were examining.

"Someone aligned with the terrorists made a phone call on a regular landline this morning and we managed to intercept it," he answered, holding up a transcript of the call.

"Let me see that," Goddard requested, holding out his hand for the paper.

As he scanned it, his brow furrowed in puzzlement. "I don't understand this," he said, handing the paper to Ben.

Ben read it, his lips pursed in thought. "It looks like a group of the invaders have taken over the Boise airport and are going to use it to land some planes."

"But," Goddard said, "why would they need planes? From what our Intel has found, they're living off the land, taking whatever arms and supplies they need from the areas they've attacked."

Ben shrugged, staring at the paper. "I can think of a couple of possibilities, but you're not gonna like them," he said.

"Go on."

"One, they could be bringing in reinforcements from Vancouver Island. More troops or even heavy equipment and matériel such as tanks, half-tracks, or even attack airplanes and helicopters."

"Jesus," Goddard said, turning to Currey with a worried look on his face. "What other possibilities can you think of, Ben?" he asked. "As if that one isn't bad enough."

"It could be that this FFA faction has some people they want to transport down to help out with the invasion. They could've gathered from all over, and this would be the quickest way to get them in touch with El Farrar's men so they could work together."

Goddard slowly nodded. "That's right. Now, that wouldn't be quite as bad as thinking Farrar may be getting heavy equipment or air support."

Ben thought for a moment, then looked up, a sly grin on his face. "I've got an idea, Max."

"Spill it," Goddard said, looking hopeful.

"How about I send in one of my crack teams to Boise? See if maybe we can't throw a monkey wrench into those transport plans before the planes have a chance to land."

Goddard's forehead wrinkled and he bent over to look at a map of the U.S. "That's a pretty long run for a C-130 to make in the time we have left, Ben."

"We could use one of the Ospreys in your Air Force, Max. They've got both the speed and the range to make it before the other flights are scheduled to land."

Goddard looked up at Currey. "Josh, what's Intel say about the strength of the force that took Boise?"

"Close to two hundred men at least, and they were heavily armed to boot."

Goddard looked back at Ben. "Ben, the Osprey can only

take about thirty personnel if it's got a full load of fuel. Your people would be heavily outnumbered and outgunned."

"You don't know my people, Max. Five-to-one odds only makes it an even fight, and I'll still lay odds my men can take them out."

"Josh," Goddard said, "get on the horn and have an Osprey fueled up and ready to go in an hour. We don't have any time to waste."

He looked at Ben. "This is going to be a day drop, Ben. Your people will be awfully exposed."

"They won't be dropping, Max. The Osprey can land almost anywhere, like a chopper, so they can just let my people out a few miles away from the airport and then we'll see what happens next."

Ben went to the bachelor officers' quarters and met with his team.

After he'd explained what was going on at the Boise airport, he got down to specifics. "Since you'll be heavily outnumbered, we're gonna drop you several miles away and let you make your way to the hot zone on your own. Also, since you'll be working in among the enemy, instead of your normal BDU cammies, you'll be issued black outfits, similar to the ones both the enemy and the Scouts wear."

"How about our armament?" Harley asked. "Will we be able to use the same weapons we're used to carrying?"

"Yes, but since resupply will be a problem, you might at some point need to switch from your Uzis to the AK-47's used by the enemy so you can make use of confiscated ammunition and other weapons."

"What is our primary objective?" Coop asked.

"First to kill as many of the terrorists as you can. Secondly, to retake the airport before their planes can land and either warn the planes off or sabotage their landings in some way," Ben answered.

"Can we expect any help from local resources?" Jersey asked. "Such as cops or local citizens?"

Ben shook his head. "I doubt it. The U.S. citizens aren't like ours in the SUSA. They're pretty much used to the government doing everything for them. If the terrorists have operated as per their usual plans in the past, they will have taken out most if not all of the local law-enforcement personnel in their initial attack."

"So, it's us against about two hundred bad guys, huh?" Hammer Hammerlick observed.

"That's about it," Ben said. "All in all, I'm gonna put my money on you."

"That'd be a wise bet," Harley said with a savage grin.

The Boeing/Bell V-22 Osprey is a medium-lift, multi-mission, vertical/short-takeoff-and-landing (VSTOL), tilt-rotor aircraft. It can take off and land like a helicopter, but once it is airborne, its blades can be rotated to convert the airplane to a turboprop configuration capable of high-speed, high-altitude flight. It flies at 185 knots helicopter mode and 275 knots airplane mode, has a range of 2100 miles, and can carry a payload of twenty thousand tons of men and matériel.

As Ben's team was loaded into the cargo compartment, he stood there shaking the hands of each member of the team as they entered.

He pulled Harley Reno, the team's field commander, aside. "Harley, this is an important mission, but the most important part is to bring everyone back in one piece," Ben said. "Do what you can to disrupt the invaders, but if you have to abort due to overwhelming odds against you and the team, don't worry about it. We'll have plenty of chances to get them later if we have to."

"Ben, we've never failed you in a mission yet, and I don't

intend for this to be the first time," Harley said. "But I will make sure no one takes any unnecessary chances."

Ben slapped Harley on the shoulder. "Good. Keep in touch with your coded cell phones. I'll have Mike Post monitoring them constantly, day and night."

"Roger that," Harley said, and ducked his head as he stepped up into the cargo compartment of the Osprey.

As the big turbine engines of the Osprey roared and the craft began to lift off, the team sat on the metal benches arrayed around the interior of the cargo compartment making last-minute checks of equipment and armament.

"Damn," Coop groused as he shifted in his seat, trying to get comfortable, "I feel like I'm carrying a ton of shit in my pack."

He had been assigned the unenviable task of carrying the M-79 grenade launcher, known as Thumper or Big Thumper for the sound it made when it fired the grenades. The launcher and the fifty grenades Coop was carrying made quite a load in a pack on his back.

Jersey looked up from sharpening her K-Bar, a task she always did while on mission flights. "Aw, is it too heavy for you, Coop?" she asked sarcastically. "You want me to carry Thumper so you won't be overloaded?"

"Naw," he grumbled back at her, "I figure that tiny little Uzi is about all a delicate flower of womanhood like you can handle, darlin'. Wouldn't want you to do too much and get muscle-bound. It might ruin your feminine figure."

"I'll match muscles with you any time, little man," she fired back, staring at him where he sat next to her. "You look like that guy in the ads where some bully kicks sand in his face on the beach."

Coop glanced down at his arms, a slight grin on his face. He dearly loved the repartee between himself and Jersey. "Well, I've been kinda sick since I got wounded trying to save your butt on our last mission. That big Swedish physical therapist was working on developing my muscles when you made her stop."

Jersey let her glance fall to his lap. "Yeah, but the muscle she was working on is one you won't need on any of our missions, that's for sure."

Coop gave her a leer and waggled his eyebrows. "Don't be too sure, Jersey. Who knows? Someday, your hormones might kick in and you'll decide I'm just what the doctor ordered."

She gave a short, harsh laugh. "In that case, I'd sue the bastard for malpractice!"

After some hours in the plane, a green light lit on the forward wall, signaling the team the pilot was descending for a landing.

The Osprey didn't actually land, but hovered a couple of feet off the ground, and the cargo door was opened by the loadmaster, who gave the team a thumbs-up as they jumped to the ground one by one.

Twenty-five

Ben had ordered the pilot of the Osprey to let the team off near the Boise Fair Grounds, which were a couple of miles to the northeast of downtown and also several miles directly north of the Boise airport, which was to the south of the main business district.

After the Osprey took off into the night sky, Harley Reno gathered the team around him near the wooden seats of the main Fair Ground arena.

He turned on a small flashlight and played it over a map of the city and its environs that he'd spread out on the ground in front of them.

"Here we are at the Fair Grounds," he said, pointing to the area on the map. "As you can see, if we take Cole Road directly south and then take a left on Victory Road, it'll lead us onto the airport grounds."

He folded the map of the city and opened a more detailed one of the airport itself. "The airfield has only one main runway running north and south and three that intersect running east and west. The control tower is at the main intersection of all of the runways, giving it an excellent overlook of the entire area."

Coop leaned closer. "I don't suppose there's any cover to speak of around the control tower."

Harley grinned and shook his head. "Nope, 'cause that'd make our job entirely too easy."

Jersey leaned over. "From the scale of the map, it looks like we're gonna have to crawl on our bellies for several hundred yards if we want to get to the control tower unobserved."

Coop grunted. "Before I go crawling across several hundred yards of heavy grass fields, does anyone know if there are any poisonous snake species indigenous to the Boise area?" he asked, a shudder passing through his body. Coop's aversion to snakes of any kind was well known to the group.

"Probably none other than rattlesnakes, coral snakes, and pit vipers," Jersey said with an evil grin.

"Don't worry, Coop," Harley said. "We're not going to crawl anywhere."

"Then how are we going to take out the control tower?" Anna asked, placing her hand on Harley's shoulder.

Harley pointed to the map again. "See, the main terminal of the airport is less than a quarter mile from the tower. I figure, as small as the tower is, there won't be more than five or six guards among the air traffic controllers in the tower itself. Most of the terrorists and FFA types will be in the main terminal, guarding the roads into the airport."

"So, how does that help us?" Coop asked. "If we try to take out the main terminal first, the guards in the control tower will be alerted, and we don't have any idea of how many men might be holding the main terminal."

"Exactly," Harley said, "so here is my plan. . . ."

After Achmed Sharif's men finished looting the highway patrol offices and had taken everything they could use, Sharif had them disperse throughout the town in small groups of five or six men. They had orders to kill anyone in a uniform they came upon, especially cops or highway patrol officers. Sharif wanted to make sure all of the officers that hadn't been caught in the raids on the headquarters were taken out so they couldn't cause any trouble later.

As the groups took off, some actually riding in highway patrol vehicles so they could monitor any radio traffic from the escaped officers, Sharif stood on the front steps of the smoldering building and dialed in his code on his cell phone, followed by the number assigned to Mohamed Omar.

"Yes," the voice answered shortly after only two rings.

"Mohamed, this is Achmed," Sharif said. "Have you accomplished your mission?"

"Certainly, Achmed," Omar said a trifle smugly. "However, resistance was a bit stronger than we anticipated and I lost some men."

"They will be rewarded in the afterlife for their sacrifice," Sharif said without the slightest trace of compassion in his voice.

"How about you?" Omar asked.

"The highway patrol offices have been destroyed," Sharif said.

"What do you want me to do now?" Omar asked.

"I've sent my men out to search out and kill any remaining policemen or patrol officers," Sharif said. "I want you to take your men directly to the airport and make sure that fool Wesson has been able to carry out his orders."

"And shall my men take over command when we get there?" Omar asked, not liking the idea that he might have to take orders from the infidel FFA men, even though they were allies for the moment.

"Yes. Tell Mr. Wesson that you will be in charge. You may use his men for guard duty, but make sure to have one of our people assigned to each of his groups. I don't trust these traitors and I want to know what they talk about at all times, do you understand?"

"Yes, esteemed one," Omar answered. "When will you be joining us at the airport?"

"I will make sure all of our men are there by the time the

flights are due to arrive. These are very important arrivals and we need to make sure there are no problems."

"Certainly, I will go there immediately," Omar said, and clicked his phone off.

Achmed Sharif dialed another number, one that he hadn't used since the invasion.

Abdullah El Farrar answered and said, "Yes?"

"Abdullah, this is Achmed," Sharif said, his voice more deferential than it had been while talking with Omar.

"Ah, Achmed," Farrar said, evident pleasure in his tone. "How are things going on our western front?"

"Very well, your excellency," Sharif said, and he filled him in on the latest happenings.

"Then all is in readiness for the arrival of our airplanes?" Farrar asked.

"Yes, sir," Sharif answered.

"That is good. The reinforcements and heavy equipment will allow us to proceed to the next stage of the invasion, and we will be able to mount an attack on the very seat of President Osterman's government."

"How many men are you sending?" Sharif asked.

"That is not something to be discussed, even on these secure phones," Farrar said, "but it will be a substantial amount, along with some light tanks equipped with TOW missiles and other heavy armament."

"Excellent!" Sharif said enthusiastically.

"I am counting on you to make sure there are not going to be any problems, Achmed," Farrar said, his voice growing harder with the warning.

Sharif swallowed hard, for he knew what the price of failure would be. "Yes, I understand and all precautions have been taken, Abdullah."

"Good, then I will see you in a few days," Farrar said.

"I eagerly await your arrival," Sharif said, and he clicked off the phone.

Twenty-six

As the team moved silently through the darkness, they found the area between the Fair Grounds and the airport to be practically deserted.

As they moved through empty streets, Coop wondered out loud, "Where the hell are all the people? According to our information, Boise has a population of over half a million."

Jersey looked over at him. "What do you expect, Coop?" she asked. "You've got to remember, the economy of the States is in the tank. People don't have enough money for food, much less gasoline to go gallivanting around at night."

"Yeah," Hammer said, "they're all probably sitting around their television sets watching sitcoms about how perfect their world is and how good they've got it under the benevolent Administration of Babe Osterman."

Anna laughed. "And they're probably sponsored by cat and dog food companies, the only food most of them can afford to eat under her leadership."

Beth, by far the quietest and most compassionate of the group, objected. "I don't think it's fair to make fun of the citizens because of Osterman," she said heatedly. "It's not their fault she's dragged them into war after war."

"That's just it, Beth dear," Jersey said gently. "It *is* their fault. Last time I looked, the U.S. was still a democracy and its citizens have the right to vote anyone they choose into or out of office."

"But that's just it, Jerse," Beth said fervently. "Osterman controls all the media and information outlets. With her propaganda machine, the people are fooled into thinking the wars were all our fault."

"Then double shame on them for being so stupid and allowing the government to gain control of the press and media," Coop said, his voice totally unsympathetic to Beth's arguments for the citizens of the U.S.

"If you believe that way, you should be fighting for the FFA guys instead of against them," Jersey said. "After all, from what I can see, they're trying to get rid of Osterman by joining up with these Arab terrorists."

Beth shook her head. "No, the FFA is not the answer. That's like changing from a socialist form of government to a fascist one. Neither truly represents the will of the people or looks out for their welfare."

"Far as I'm concerned," Coop said, "any people that depend on the government to look out for them instead of doing it themselves deserve whatever kind of shitty leaders they get, until they grow the balls to take control of their own destinies and lives."

"All right, people," Harley said from the front of the group, "we're getting close to the airport road so hold it down. We could come upon sentries at most any time now."

As they came to the outskirts of the airport property, they found it surrounded by a ten-foot-high chain-link fence with triple-stranded barbed wire running along the top.

Coop stepped up to the fence. "You want me to make a door?" he asked Harley.

Harley shook his head. "No. Then we'd just have to cross all those fields out in the open. Let's move along the fence until we come to the road leading up to the main terminal. That's where we'll probably find the sentries."

* * *

Twenty minutes later, they came to a concrete road with a sign reading GOWEN ROAD. It seemed to lead straight toward the airport terminal visible a mile or so distant.

A hundred yards up the road, they could see large saw-horses stretched across the street, with a pair of HumVees parked nearby and five or six men milling around with AK-47's slung over their shoulders.

Coop sidled up next to where Harley squatted in the ditch next to the road, observing the guards through night-vision goggles.

"They don't seem to be too concerned about showing themselves," Coop observed. "You'd think they'd be worried about local cops or authorities."

Harley shook his head without looking around. "Naw. If they've acted as usual, the first thing they did was take out the local cops. That way, they can pretty much do whatever they want in the town until they're ready to move on."

"Too bad the government up here outlawed private ownership of guns," Coop whispered. "If they hadn't, the citizens could've taken care of these guys themselves."

Harley snorted through his nose. "Not the citizens of the U.S.," he said. "These bleeding-heart liberals would be too afraid of depriving the poor terrorists of their right to commit murder to do anything about them."

"Those guys look like Arabs?" Coop asked.

"Uh-uh, they're good ol' Americans," Harley replied.

He moved back to the group. "Now, here's what we're gonna do. . . ."

Twenty-five minutes later, Harley Reno stepped out onto the street and began to walk nonchalantly up to the group of guards stationed ahead.

"Hey," one of the men called, unslinging his AK-47 when he saw Harley approaching, and aiming it at him. "Who goes there?" the man called as the rest of the guards gathered around him, also aiming their guns at Harley.

"It's Harley Reno," Harley called, holding his hands out in plain sight so the men could see he was unarmed.

The guard who'd called out turned to the man next to him. "Who the hell is Harley Reno?" he asked.

The other man shrugged. "Damned if I know," he answered, "but it looks like he's dressed the same as us, all in black cammies."

When Harley got to within fifteen feet of the blockade, the head guard said, "All right, that's far enough, mister. What the hell do you want?"

Harley stood there, grinning at the men. "Hell, the boss sent me to check up on you guys and to make sure you're not sleeping on the job."

The men looked at each other, then back at Harley. "I don't recognize you, mister, and I'm damned sure I never heard the name Harley Reno before."

Harley shrugged. "I'm not accountable for your memory, or lack thereof," he said evenly.

"Okay, Reno," the guard said belligerently, "if the boss sent you, what's the password?"

Harley smiled slowly. "The password is, drop your weapons and put your hands up, or . . ."

The man laughed. "Or what?"

Coop and the other members of the team appeared from the darkness alongside both sides of the road, surrounding the men, their Uzis held at waist level and ready to fire.

"Or we'll blow the shit outta you," Coop said in a low hard voice.

"Holy shit!" one of the guards exclaimed as they all dropped their weapons. "Where did you come from?"

"Get down on the ground and put your hands behind you!" Harley commanded in a loud voice as Anna handed him his Uzi, which she'd carried for him.

The guards all scrambled to lie on their faces and put their hands behind them.

While the rest of the team kept them covered, Beth went along and fastened their hands together and feet together with plastic tie-wraps like cops used to secure prisoners.

Harley stood over the men. "I'm not going to gag you guys, 'cause it'd be a waste of time." He glanced around at the vast open spaces around them. "You can yell your heads off out here and no one will hear you."

"But what's gonna happen to us?" one of the guards whined.

"Depends on who finds you first," Coop said nastily. "If it's one of your men, you'll probably just get a tongue-lashing. However, if it's one of the Arabs, they'll probably cut your balls off for being captured."

"Oh, Jesus," one of the men cried softly.

"Uh-uh, wrong god," Jersey said. "Better pray to Allah, he's the boss of your new friends."

Minutes later, the team had divided up and were driving the two HumVees toward the main terminal of the airport.

Just before arriving at the terminal, the lead vehicle veered off toward the control tower a few hundred yards in the distance.

The second vehicle kept moving straight toward the terminal, with the team keeping their heads bent down so their faces wouldn't show through the windows.

Harley Reno, Anna, Beth, and Corrie were in the car heading to the control tower. As it pulled up next to the entrance, a man walked out of the door, his AK-47 still slung over his shoulder.

"Hey, guys," he called, a grin splitting his face, "what're you doin' here? It's not time for relief yet."

Harley opened the door and aimed his Uzi at the man's

midsection. In a quiet voice, he called, "Come on over here and act natural, or I'll cut you in half."

The man's face fell and he moved slowly toward the Hum-Vee, his eyes darting back and forth and sweat appearing on his forehead.

Harley noticed the signs of nervousness and stress. "I sure hope you're not thinking of trying to warn your friends, mister," he said. " 'Cause I'd surely hate to kill you."

The guard's eyes fixed on Harley's and he knew he meant what he said. "All right," he croaked through a dry throat.

When he got up next to the car, Harley asked, "Can your friends inside see us out here?"

"No, this is the blind side of the building. That's why I was stationed at the door."

"How many men in there with you?" Anna asked.

"Four guards, two air traffic controllers," the man answered shortly.

"What's your name?" Beth asked as she stepped out of the car and put plastic ties on the man's hands behind his back.

"Jim Short," he answered.

Beth bent and hooked his ankles together, and then stood and put a gag in his mouth. "Well, Jim," she said as she laid him in the back seat of the HumVee, "you be a good little boy, and you'll come out of this alive and well. Otherwise, I'll have to slit your throat from ear to ear."

They could all hear Jim swallow as he nodded his head vigorously up and down.

"Follow me," Harley said as he opened the back door to the tower and started up the steps, his Uzi cradled in his hands.

Just before they got to the top, a voice called, "Hey, what's goin' on down there?"

"It's me. Jim," Harley said. "They sent some grub over from the terminal."

"What's wrong with your voice?" the man above called, and stepped to the head of the stairs.

When he saw Harley and the women, he shouted and grabbed at the AK-47 slung over his shoulder.

Harley let go with a short burst from the Uzi and blew the man back out of sight.

Anna brushed past Harley, running full speed up the stairs and dove headfirst through the doorway.

A burst of AK-47 fire splintered the wall over her head as she rolled and let go with her Uzi.

She emptied her thirty-round clip in a matter of seconds, filling the small control tower room with the smell of gunpowder and cordite and blood and excrement.

By the time Harley and the others got up the stairs, Anna was on her feet, telling the air traffic controllers not to worry, they were in no danger.

Harley stepped into the room and looked around. Four men, dressed all in black, were scattered around the room, all as dead as they could be.

"Jesus," he whispered softly, looking at Anna. "Remind me never to piss you off."

She grinned at him. "Yeah, you wouldn't want to do that, Harley."

Hammer and Coop and Jersey, in the second HumVee, pulled up to the front door of the terminal.

Two men walked out of the door, holding their automatic rifles in their hands but not pointed at the car.

"Hey, what's goin' on?" the lead man asked. "Is there any trouble?"

"Yeah," Hammer growled as he stuck his Uzi out the window. "And it's all yours."

As the second man started to raise his weapon, Jersey stepped out of the HumVee and moved her right arm in a lightning-quick movement.

The man gasped, dropping his rifle and grabbing at the hilt of Jersey's K-Bar assault knife, which was sticking out of his throat.

He dropped to his knees, gurgled a couple of times, and then fell forward onto his face.

The other guard, his eyes wide with fright, quickly dropped his rifle and held up his hands.

"How many of you inside?" Hammer asked while Coop covered the door with his Uzi.

Suddenly, a man appeared behind the huge plate-glass window of the terminal. When he saw what was going on, he aimed his AK-47 and fired right through the window.

At the distinctive sound of the Kalashnikov firing, Coop whirled and let go with his Uzi on full automatic.

The plate-glass window shattered and Hammer was spun around, hit by one of the slugs from inside the terminal.

The man behind the window was flung backward with his arms outstretched by the blast from Coop's Uzi.

Jersey unlimbered her Uzi and ran and jumped through the shattered window, yelling and firing as she went.

Two men went down in front of her, their machine guns not even fired.

Coop was scant yards behind her, flicking out his empty magazine and replacing it with another as he ran.

Inside, three men were behind a concession stand counter, firing over it at Coop and Jersey, driving them to the floor as slugs pinged off the tile floors all around them.

As they squatted behind a row of chairs, Coop glanced at Jersey. "What now?" he asked. "They've got us pinned down here."

They ducked as they heard a loud thumping sound behind them. When they glanced back, they saw Hammer standing in the doorway. His left arm hung useless at his side and he was holding the M-79 grenade launcher in his right arm, firing one-handed.

"Hit the deck!" he yelled at Coop and Jersey, and they did so forthwith.

A tremendous explosion rocked the terminal's main room, and the concession stand disappeared in a brilliant flash of light and flame and smoke.

Candy bars, gum packages, and parts of bodies rained down on Jersey and Coop for several seconds.

A figure emerged, walking toward them from a cloud of black smoke. It was Hammer, still holding the M-79 Big Thumper in his right hand.

"That should be all of them," he said in a shaky voice, and then he collapsed onto the floor, a scarlet stain spreading out from his left shoulder.

"Jesus," Jersey said, running to his side. "He's bleeding like a stuck pig."

Coop knelt next to the big man and jerked a compression bandage from the pack on his back, slapping it into place over the hole in Hammer's deltoid muscle.

Twenty-seven

Mustafa Kareem entered the office the FFA man John Waters had provided for Abdullah El Farrar and Osama bin Araman to use to coordinate the eastern phase of the attack against the United States.

El Farrar and Araman were leaning over a table with a large-scale map of the U.S. spread out upon it. Farrar looked up and nodded his head in greeting to his second in command.

"Come join us, Mustafa," Farrar said. "We are busily puzzling over the response of the United States to our invasion, or more accurately, the lack of a response."

Araman frowned. "I've told you, Abdullah," he said, "the infidels are decadent and have no stomach for war when it is pressed on their home shores. That is why they have not counterattacked in force."

Farrar shook his head, his face puzzled. "No, Osama, I do not agree. I am a student of history and I well remember the Japanese general's strong warnings against the attack on Pearl Harbor in 1941. He said, do not attack the Americans, for you will awaken a sleeping giant."

"Bah," Araman scoffed. "That was many years ago, when the United States was a strong nation. Now they are divided into the U.S. and this SUSA on their southern borders."

He leaned over, picked up a tiny cup of Turkish coffee,

and took a sip, wincing a little at the bitterness. "It is my feeling that all of the citizens with balls moved south and left only sheep in the north, waiting to be sheared," Araman said, his voice dripping with scorn.

Farrar stared at him, his eyes doubtful. "You may be right about the leaders of the country, my friend," he said slowly and evenly, "but I still wonder at the total lack of response to our provocations."

Mustafa Kareem joined in. "I agree, Abdullah. This lack of response goes against all of our projections. Here we have moved across almost a third of the country without any real opposition to our destruction of their infrastructure." He shook his head. "It just doesn't make sense."

Araman laughed. "I think you two are borrowing trouble. At this rate, my troops will be in the capital by next week, and with the reinforcements and heavy equipment landing at Boise tomorrow, we'll own the country within two weeks."

Farrar dipped his head to study the map, which had small pins in all the locations where the various teams had been. The trail of pins lead steadily toward the center of the country, where President Osterman had her seat of government at Indianapolis.

"We'll see, Osama, but I fear this is just the quiet before the storm."

As Farrar was speaking, and Harley Reno and his team were taking control of the airport at Boise, hundreds of five- and six-man-and-woman teams of Scouts were being air-dropped across the country to intercept the Arab teams in their movements toward Indianapolis.

Each team had, in addition to the personal armament they carried, crates of weapons and ammunition to pass out to citizens who were willing to fight against the invaders. They would try to undo years of liberal thinking on gun control and put weapons back into the hands of ordinary citizens once again.

Major Jackson Bean hit the ground, rolled, and came up into a crouch, his Uzi at the ready in case they'd been spotted on their HALO drop just outside the city limits of Allentown, Pennsylvania. They'd been dropped there after reports had come in that the town was under siege by over fifty invaders—a mixed bag of Arabs and FFA traitors who were wiping out the police and other authorities in the town.

Bean, upon seeing no one was anywhere near the field they'd landed in, gathered up his black parachute and buried it in a shallow depression in the ground.

Once that was done, he whistled softly through his lips, and within moments his team was gathered around him: Willie Running Bear, descendent of the Sioux people; Mary Blackburn; Samuel Clemens; and Sue Waters.

As they gathered in the gloom of the early evening darkness, they could hear gunshots and explosions from the downtown area several miles away.

"Bear," Bean said, referring to Willie Running Bear, "you and Sam grab those crates of weapons and let's get moving toward town."

The crates were fitted with handles and wheels so they could be easily moved by one man, though they each weighed a couple of hundred pounds. The crates were filled with Uzi machine guns, M-16 rifles, Colt .45-caliber and Beretta 9mm pistols, ammunition, fragmentation grenades, and even some antipersonnel mines called Bouncing Bettys.

As they moved out of the field and into the suburban neighborhood nearby, Bean took the lead and knocked on a door.

A worried voice behind the door called out, "Who is it?"

"Major Jackson Bean," Bean answered.

"What do you want?" the person inside said, without opening the door.

Fed up with the whining he was hearing, Bean growled, *"If* there is a *man* in the house, I'd like to talk to him."

After a short hesitation, during which Bean could hear muted voices behind the door, a man opened the door and stood there, a large kitchen knife in his hand.

Bean grinned. At least the man wasn't afraid to protect his house and family. Now they'd see if he was up to protecting his country.

"I'm Major Jackson Bean, with a Scout unit sent in to help stop the invaders from sacking your town," Bean said shortly. "I need to know if there are any citizens around here with the balls to help us."

He raised his eyebrows at the man and waited for his response.

The man glanced around at the rest of Bean's team, then stepped back from the door. "Come on in," he said. "My name is Jim Watson, and this is my wife, Peg, and our two sons, Jeremy and Brit."

Bean entered the house and nodded at a small, sallow-faced woman and two boys who looked to be about sixteen or seventeen years old.

Once Bean and his team were seated in the Watsons' living room, he outlined the situation.

"I don't know just how much you people know, but an Army of Arab terrorists, mixed with some local traitors who call themselves Freedom Fighters of America, is sweeping across the country, looting, pillaging, and killing everyone in their path," Bean said.

Watson nodded. "There have been some reports on the television. The government is calling for all citizens to resist the invasion, but they don't say how since it's against the law to own a gun in the United States."

"We have weapons we can give you," Bean said, glancing around at the man's two sons, who were sitting on the edge of their chairs eagerly watching the exchange. "The important question is, are you ready to fight for your country?"

Watson glanced once at his wife, and then back at Bean. "Of course I am."

Jeremy and Brit chimed in simultaneously, "Me too!"

Bean nodded. "Good. How about your neighbors? Anyone around here with military or police experience who might be willing to join us?"

Watson thought for a moment, until Jeremy said, "How about Joey Pissaro's dad? He used to be a cop until he retired a couple of years ago."

Watson nodded. "He lives four houses down."

"Would he be willing to fight?" Bean asked.

Watson grinned. "Hell, yes. Retirement is driving him crazy with no heads to bust."

Bean pointed to the crate they'd brought into the house. "Jim, I'm gonna leave that box of weapons with you and depend on you to hand them out to people you think will be an asset to us. Meanwhile, we're gonna head on into town and see if we can't raise a little hell with the terrorists until you can get there with the reinforcements."

"Yes, sir!" Watson said, sitting a little straighter on the couch.

"Now, I want to warn you, there's some pretty sophisticated equipment in there . . . mines, grenades, things like that. If you don't know how to use them, and can't find anyone who does know, don't mess with them. They'll kill you if they're handled wrong."

"Okay," Watson said, "but there are plenty of older military types around here. We should be able to find someone to tell us what to do with them."

Bean got to his feet. "Good. Now remember, most of the terrorists are wearing all black, just like we are. I don't know about the FFA men, but you should be able to tell who they are, 'cause they'll be the only citizens around who have guns other than your group."

Watson nodded, and Bean and his team filed out of the door.

The Scouts followed their ears toward the sound of gunfire, and within an hour were crouched down the street from the police headquarters building, where a fierce battle was raging.

Parts of the building were on fire, and there were no lights on inside. There were men arrayed all around the building, peppering it with gunfire and moving slowly inward, closer and closer to the building.

Occasional shots would ring out from windows, but it was plain to see the cops who were still alive were badly outnumbered and wouldn't be able to hold off the invaders for long.

"Affix your silencers to your Uzis," Bean said in a low voice. He took his backpack off and opened it up on the ground in front of them. He handed each of the others a few fragmentation grenades to attach to their belts.

"Spread out around the building," he said, glancing at his watch. "In exactly five minutes, start picking men off. Remember to stick and move, stick and move. Don't get cornered or get in a firefight."

Willie Running Bear grinned, his teeth white in the scant moonlight. "Don't tell your grandmother how to knit a quilt, white eyes," he said with a chuckle.

Bean returned the smile. "Just be careful. Remember, we're outnumbered ten to one."

"That barely makes it a fair fight," Sue Waters said in a low, hard voice as she jerked back the loading lever on her Uzi with a metallic click.

Seconds later the team had melted away into the night.

Sue Waters made her way around the building until she was behind a group of seven men who were standing behind a large parked car and firing into the building across the street.

As Sue watched, she saw they seemed to be concentrating their fire on one particular window on the third story. A dark shape would pop his head up and return fire, but didn't seem to be coming too close to the men behind the car with his shots.

Sue grinned to herself and squatted behind a large trash can twenty yards to the rear of the men. "Let's see if I can't improve his aim," she said softly.

She took aim at one of the men behind the car and waited until she heard the man in the building fire.

She squeezed her trigger, and the Uzi made a soft coughing sound inaudible from more than a few feet away.

The man she'd aimed at grabbed his chest and flopped onto the hood of the car with a loud grunt.

The men standing next to him quickly ducked down. Two of them were Arabs and the other four appeared to be Anglos.

Sue figured to take out the Arabs first since they were probably the best-trained shooters and the most dangerous to her and her team.

After a few moments, the men stuck their heads back up and began to fire into the building again.

When the policeman again pointed his rifle out of the window and returned fire, Sue joined him, taking out one of the Arabs, who died a noisy death screaming something about Allah.

"Jesus!" one of the Anglos shouted to his friends. "That son of a bitch is getting better."

"Naw," another one said. "Just a couple of lucky shots."

"Hell, I'm not waiting around to see," a third said, and he began to inch away from the car.

"Time to quit fucking around," Sue mumbled, and she stood up.

She flicked the switch on the side of her Uzi to full automatic and held the gun on its side, so its natural tendency to rise would instead cause it to sweep from right to left.

She pointed the gun at the man standing most to her right and pulled the trigger. As the Uzi rattled quietly and moved sideways in her grasp, the line of bullets stitched across the men behind the car and they danced and jumped and screamed in a hail of silent bullets.

When the clip was empty, Sue calmly ejected it and jammed another in its place.

She looked around, saw some action off to her left, and moved slowly toward it, whistling softly to herself.

Running Bear operated a little differently. He liked to kill up close and personal, so he moved around until he found men who were firing at the building but were alone.

He'd then pull out his K-Bar and move silently up until he was standing behind the man. A quick motion with his left arm around the man's forehead, pulling his chin up and back, and then a lightning-fast slash with the razor-sharp edge of his blade, and Running Bear would be off to the next victim while the first was still gurgling and writhing and drowning in his own blood.

Mary Blackburn wasn't quite so elegant. She just walked around the building, pausing and shooting, and then moving on before anyone could see where the silent shots had come from. She killed or wounded over fifteen men before she was spotted.

A sharp-eyed Arab saw her as she aimed and took out one of the attackers, and he screamed something in Arabic and let go at her with his AK-47.

The first bullet took Mary in the right arm and spun her around so that the next three hit her square in the back, throwing her forward to land facedown in the gutter next to the street.

The Arab screamed in triumph and called to a couple of his comrades, and they ran over to her body.

"See," the Arab said, "even the infidel women die as easily as their men do."

His friend laughed and used the toe of his boot to roll Mary's body over onto her back.

She grinned up at them through bloodstained teeth and let go of the pin on the fragmentation grenade she was holding against her chest.

"Fuck you, rag-head!" she said.

"Aiyeeee," screamed one of the Arabs, and he had time to turn his back before the grenade went off, shredding all three of the men along with Mary.

Sam Clemens, who'd seen Mary go down and how she'd taken three Arabs with her, gritted his teeth until his jaw ached as he ran from tree to tree and car to car, firing and running and firing and running, taking out man after man. They rarely knew what hit them.

When his Uzi finally jammed because the barrel was too hot, he slung it back over his shoulder and took out his Beretta pistol. He had no silencer for it, and he had to get quite a bit closer to be sure of a lethal hit.

He moved around a corner of the building under siege and saw a group of nine men standing on a corner, discussing just how to finish off the cops inside.

Sam slid back the ejector lever on the Beretta, cocking it, and held it down at his side next to his thigh. Humming softly to himself, he walked nonchalantly toward the group, keeping his head down so they couldn't see his face as he approached.

When he was about twenty feet away, one of the men called out, "Hey, who are you?"

Sam looked up, grinned, and said, "Death!"

He raised his Beretta in the classic two-handed grip and

began to trigger off rounds, aiming for the biggest part of his targets, the chest.

Eight men went down before the ninth managed to get his AK-47 up and fire.

Sam fired just as he was hit, and took the last man out. His aim was thrown off by the impact of the slug from the AK-47 and hit the target in the mouth, blowing teeth, skull, brains, and hair out of the back of his head.

Sam had taken a slug in the left side of his chest, but he was lucky. The bullet had hit a rib and skidded just under the skin, and come out under his left shoulder blade without ever going into his chest.

Nevertheless, Sam was knocked off his feet and lay on his back, looking up at the stars in the night sky, barely visible because of the glare from the flames in the burning building across the street.

As Sam lay there with his left arm clamped tight against his chest to stop the bleeding, Jack Bean's face appeared over him.

"You just gonna lay there bleeding or are you gonna get up and fight?" Bean asked as he checked Sam's wound.

Sam took a deep breath. "Ah, if it's all the same to you, Major, I think I'll just lay here a while."

"Hell," Bean said after he'd checked the wound. "This is just a little ol' graze. Get on your feet, you pussy."

Sam's eyes rolled a little as Bean got him to his feet. "I'll get up, Jack," he said, "but I don't think I'm gonna be much good to you."

Bean laughed. "Listen to that," he said.

Sam cocked his head, and he could hear rapid fire coming from all around them, along with explosions of frag grenades among the attackers.

He glanced at Bean. "The citizens?"

Bean stepped out into the street. In the light of the moon, he saw Jim Watson, along with Jeremy and Brit and other men and women of the town, who were carrying Uzis and blasting away at scurrying terrorists and FFA men as if they were born to it, cleaning up the last of the invaders.

"Yeah," Bean said to Sam. "I guess they had the balls to fight after all."

The Arab invaders refused to give up, and were slaughtered where they stood, some of the citizens being cut down in the process.

For the most part, the FFA men didn't have the same conviction to their cause as the Arabs, and most of them, when they saw the citizens fighting and rising up against them, knew it was all over. They dropped their weapons and stood meekly with their hands raised over their heads.

As the people of the city threw them on the ground facedown and tied their hands behind their backs, Bean thought to himself he wouldn't want to be in the FFA traitors' shoes when it came time for their neighbors to judge their crimes.

In less than an hour, all of the attackers were either killed, wounded, or in custody of the citizens who'd come after them.

The police that were left alive took control and began to organize the citizens into groups, with each group assigned a different area of the city to defend.

Known FFA men or sympathizers were rounded up and put behind bars.

Jackson Bean, after seeing to what was left of Mary Blackburn's body and Sam Clemens's wounds, called the base and told them he was finished in Allentown and was ready for reassignment.

Twenty-eight

Similar happenings were taking place all across the United States, with varying degrees of success. In most cases, the citizens rose to the occasion as they did in Allentown, but some areas were peopled with citizens of less dependable patriotism.

California, long settled by people of a more liberal bent who expected the government to take care of them totally, had few citizens willing to risk life and limb to save themselves.

San Francisco, targeted hard by the invaders who hoped to use its port for importation of supplies and reinforcements, was one such place.

The Scout team sent in there, consisting of ten men and women because of the city's importance and the higher than usual number of invaders, found almost no one among the populace willing to help them in their quest to oust the invaders.

After being HALO-dropped on the outskirts of town, Major Jim Wilson, the leader of the Scout team, led his forces into the city by confiscating local vehicles.

Once in the city, Wilson approached numerous residents. After explaining the situation to them in detail, he asked for their help in arming others in the city to help in the attack on the invaders.

Other than a few older individuals, no one was willing to take up arms against the terrorists, citing their belief that it was the government's job to take care of national defense and that was what they paid their taxes for.

As the Scouts made their way down the coast road towards the famous Fisherman's Wharf, which even in these tough economic times was still a tourist mecca, Wilson was furious.

"These pacifistic sons of bitches," he groused to his second in command, Janey Goodall. "If it was up to me, I'd let the fuckin' Arabs kill every one of them."

Goodall, who was a bit more laid back than her commander, smiled and shook her head. "Yeah, me too, Boss, but that wouldn't help the rest of the country when they bring in those ships with reinforcements like they're probably planning to do."

Wilson grinned ruefully. "I know, I know. It's just that I can't stand people who won't stand up for the way of life they're enjoying."

"That's why you live in the SUSA and not the U.S.," Goodall reminded him.

"I guess so," Wilson said, pulling the truck containing his team over to the side of the road about three miles from the wharf area.

He stepped out of the vehicle and looked back up the hill toward the downtown area. Flames lit the night sky from the burning buildings that had been razed by the invaders in their destruction of the police and highway patrol offices. The nearby Army base, long deserted by a cost-cutting Administration, had been left alone since there were no soldiers there to protect the city.

Wilson climbed up on top of the vehicle and turned night-vision goggles toward the wharf area, trying to see just what kind of defenses the invaders had set up to guard the port.

He could see roadblocks on each road leading into the port, with teams of men standing guard to prevent access to the ship-docking areas.

"Looks like they got it pretty much blocked off," he said to Janey Goodall and the rest of the Scouts standing next to the car.

"Too many of them for a frontal assault?" Goodall asked.

"Yep," he answered shortly.

"Can you tell how many we're gonna be up against?" she asked.

He turned his goggles toward the dock area and saw it swarming with armed men. "Looks like a couple'a hundred at least," he said.

"You think we can get the job done with only ten people?" she asked, looking around at the team.

Wilson jumped down and put the goggles in a pouch on his belt. "Hell, yes. We're Scouts, aren't we?"

He fished a detailed map of the dock area from his pocket and spread it out on the hood of the car. "Now, here's what we're gonna do. Our job isn't necessarily to kill all of the invaders, but to make the docks unusable for off-loading of men and matériel in the event the invaders want to do that."

"So, all we have to do is walk in there and destroy the docks?" Goodall asked sarcastically.

Wilson smiled at her. "That's exactly what we're gonna do, my dear," he said. He reached into his backpack and pulled out a can of black shoe polish. "Put this on, people, 'cause we're gonna have to be invisible to get this done."

Once the team was ready, with backpacks full of packets of C-4 plastic explosive and timing devices, antipersonnel mines, and grenades, Wilson gave each member of the team an individual assignment, marking on the map fuel areas and docks that needed to be destroyed.

One of the basic strengths of the Scouts was their ability to work alone, without the need for backup and support on their jobs.

With their assignments committed to memory, the team split up and each of the ten men and women went their separate ways, moving alone so if one were discovered, the others wouldn't be put in jeopardy.

Janey Goodall, the straps of her heavy backpack chafing her shoulders, moved silently among and between groups of guards without being noticed. With her blackened face and hands and her all-black Scout's cammies, she was completely invisible from more than a few feet away.

Scurrying among ship's containers scattered along the dock area, she held her K-Bar assault knife in her right hand and her mini-Uzi in her left. The gun was to be used only as a last resort lest she tip off the terrorists to her team's presence on the docks.

Her nostrils picked up the scent of tobacco smoke just as she rounded a corner of a container just off the dock area. She found herself face-to-face with a fat man with a florid face who was leaning against the steel wall of the container smoking a cigarette. He had an AK-47 on a strap slung over his shoulder, and was just taking a sip from a flask as he saw her.

He stopped with the flask halfway to his lips, his eyes opened wide with surprise.

"Hey, what the hell? Who are . . . ?" he began.

Goodall smiled, her teeth flashing white against the blackness of her camouflaged face. "I'm nobody," she said, stepping quickly up to the man and burying her K-Bar in his throat up to the hilt.

She grabbed him as he sagged against her, the warm blood that spurted from his neck soaking her cammies and making her gag with its salty, coppery scent.

When he quit jerking, she lowered him to the ground, taking his flask so it wouldn't make any noise when it fell.

She held it up to her nose and sniffed. Smelled like whiskey to her. She took a quick sip to get the taste of the man's blood out of her mouth, and then placed the flask gently on his blood-soaked chest.

"Sorry, fellah," she whispered. "You were just in the wrong place at the wrong time."

She leaned out from behind the container and looked both ways. She could see no other guards, but she knew they were there, just waiting for her to make a mistake.

Crouching as low as she could, she ran across the bare area in front of the huge loading dock that was her target. Just on the edge of the wharf was a series of diesel fuel pumps. She squatted next to the pumps and checked her watch. It was midnight straight up and down.

Wilson had coordinated their attack to begin at one in the morning, so she set the timers on her C-4 packets for one hour. She placed one of the packets on the bottom of the nearest pump and stuck it there with a piece of duct tape.

Peeking around and seeing no one nearby, she crawled on hands and knees to the actual dock itself. Just as she was about to move onto it, she saw a tiny red flare fifty yards out on the very end of the dock.

"Damn, another guard," she muttered to herself. "Thank heavens for tobacco addiction," she added, knowing if the man hadn't stopped to take a smoke, she never would have seen him in the darkness.

She moved to the side of the dock and eased herself over, shimmying down one of the stanchions until her feet hit water.

A shock went through her body as she submerged up to her chest in fifty-degree water.

Goddamn, she thought, how do those surfers around here stand this shit? I'd be freezing my balls off . . . if I had any.

Treading water, she made her way out along the dock until she was about midway to the end.

She wrapped her legs around one of the support beams, gritting her teeth against the pain as dozens of razor-sharp barnacles shredded her skin.

Won't have to shave my legs for a while, she told herself with a tight grin.

She pulled another packet of C-4 from her pack and affixed it to the support, then dog-paddled under the dock to the other side support and did the same thing.

That oughta take the sucker down, she thought as she swam back to the shore end of the dock. She floated there in the water, wondering if she was going to be able to find a way to climb back up before she succumbed to hypothermia.

As she moved along the shore, she finally came to a rust-and-barnacle-covered metal ladder that ran from the water up to the top of the shore.

Thank goodness for small boats, she thought as she made her way quickly up and out of the freezing water. She pulled herself onshore and lay there shivering for a moment, waiting for her body temperature to get back up to survivable levels.

She checked her watch, its radium dial glowing in the darkness. It was twelve-forty. Damn, only twenty minutes to get shut of this place before it goes up like Hiroshima, she told herself.

On hands and knees again, she crawled back to the fuel pump where she'd placed her first packet of C-4.

She lifted the handle and laid it on the ground. After turning the lever at the top of the pump, she depressed the handle-lever and heard the soft sound of diesel fuel running out onto the ground all around her.

That oughta make a right nice fire, she thought as she moved silently away from the docks.

Ten minutes later she was back at the rendezvous point where they'd left their vehicle.

The rest of the team was already there waiting for her.

"Damn, Janey," Wilson said, "get a move on. We've gotta get outta here 'fore all hell breaks loose."

"Roger that, Chief," she said through chattering teeth.

She noticed most of the other members of the team were

soaking wet just as she was, and nodded thankfully when one of them handed her a woolen blanket to wrap around her shoulders.

"Where'd you get this?" she asked.

Her teammate grinned. "Took it off an Arab who probably ain't ever gonna be cold again."

"Get in the fuckin' car," Wilson hissed as he opened the door and started the engine.

They were five miles away when the dock area behind them went up in a tremendous explosion, sending flames hundreds of feet into the air and rattling windows for twenty miles around.

"I guess they won't be landing any boats in San Francisco for a while," Wilson said over his shoulder.

"From the size of that blast, it'll probably be raining fish all the way down to Los Angeles," Goodall said with a grin.

"Fish and Arabs," Wilson added, making the entire team laugh out loud.

Twenty-nine

Mustafa Kareem knocked, and entered the room where Abdullah El Farrar and Osama bin Araman were celebrating the steady advancement of their troops across what they assumed was an unresisting America.

Farrar and Araman, both devout Muslims, never indulged in alcoholic spirits, so they were drinking fruit juice and eating fish broiled in the Arab way, with heavy spices and curry.

Kareem looked down at the paper in his hand and gritted his teeth. It contained a message that he knew would end his friend and leader's celebration on an unhappy note.

"Sir," he said deferentially, as he always did when Farrar was with someone else.

Farrar looked up, a benevolent smile on his face. "Yes, Mustafa, come and join us. This fish is most elegant, even if it did grow under the feet of the infidels."

"I'm afraid I have some troubling news, my friend," Kareem said, his face a long frown.

"What is it, Mustafa?" Farrar said, his smile leaving as abruptly as his good mood did at the look on the face of his friend and second in command.

"I have received several reports that our troops have been stopped in their advancement. They are coming under heavy fire and have sustained terrible losses."

"Has the American government finally awakened to our threat and sent in troops?" Araman asked, a look of astonishment on his face.

"Not only that, Osama," Kareem answered, handing the paper to Farrar. "It seems in most areas the citizens of the United States are joining in the fight. They are proving to be more formidable adversaries than we first imagined."

"But how are they doing this?" Farrar asked, shaking the paper in Kareem's face. "I understood from our intelligence sources that the American government had disarmed its citizens some years back. Where are they getting the arms to stand against our troops?"

"From what little information I have been able to gather," Kareem explained, "the Americans are being aided by Ben Raines and his Scout troops from the SUSA. Evidently, they are not only bringing in arms for the American citizens to use, they are somehow convincing them to give up their pacifistic ways and join in the battle . . . with devastating results."

Farrar laid the paper gently on the table in front of him and stared at it for a moment. Finally, he looked up, a small smile of satisfaction on his face.

"Well, it is of no matter," he said. "Once our planes land with reinforcements and the ships we've sent to San Francisco disembark their cargo of more troops and equipment, we should be able to make short work of these infidel amateurs who think they can stand against our seasoned fighters."

Kareem dropped his gaze. He would rather bite off his tongue than give his friend this next bit of bad news, delivered by phone just minutes before.

"That is not all I have to tell you, Abdullah," he said, looking up with sorrowful eyes to meet the gaze of his best friend in all the world.

"What else is there?" Farrar asked.

"I'm afraid there will be no landing of troops at the San Francisco docks."

"What?" Araman almost screamed. "Why not?"

"The docks were destroyed in a late-night raid by some of Ben Raines's Scouts. The entire landing area is nothing more than twisted and charred metal. There is no place for the troops to be landed."

"Can't they be off-loaded in small boats and ferried ashore?" Farrar asked. "That was one of our contingency plans we had as a backup in case of trouble."

Kareem shook his head. "The commanders of the ships feel it would pose an unacceptable risk, my leader, with the shore under the control of the Scouts. The smaller boats would make easy targets for the snipers and Scouts on shore. They'd never make it intact, and the heavy equipment would need cranes to be off-loaded, a feat plainly impossible now."

"Allah forgive me for what I am thinking now," Farrar said with heavy feeling.

"There is more, Abdullah," Kareem said hesitantly.

"What else could there be, my friend?" Farrar asked suspiciously.

"I have been unable to make contact with our men in Boise since four hours ago."

"Boise?" Araman asked. "What is this place?"

"It is where our planes are scheduled to land in . . ." Farrar glanced at a watch on his wrist. "Three hours," he finished.

"Have you alerted the planes to divert to a safer landing spot?" Farrar asked, a worried frown on his face.

Sweat beaded Kareem's forehead and ran in rivulets down his face, though the temperature of the room was not all that hot. It was plain he didn't want to speak.

"No, sir," he almost croaked through dry lips.

"And why not?" Farrar asked, his face freezing in an unreadable mask.

"It seems the Americans are blocking our transmissions

with some scrambling devices we were not aware they had," Kareem answered slowly.

Farrar slammed his hand down on the table, spilling his carafe of fruit juice and making the remains of his dinner jump into the air.

"It is that damned Ben Raines again," he snarled. "Our intelligence was sure the Americans had no such technology. Raines must have brought his experts in to aid the Osterman government."

"Why wasn't this eventuality foreseen?" Araman asked in a nasty tone, glaring at Farrar.

Farrar returned his stare, his face flushing at the implied insult. "We had no idea the SUSA would join forces with a country they were just at war with months ago," he said firmly.

"This is an unforgivable oversight," Araman said, crossing his arms.

"Do you dare to dispute my leadership?" Farrar asked dangerously, his hand going to the hilt of the ceremonial dagger in his belt.

Araman's eyes saw the movement and his face blanched. He knew the Desert Fox was not a man to take an insult lightly, no matter the justice of it.

"No . . . no, of course not," he stammered, sweat now breaking out on his face. He knew he was moments away from a nasty death if he didn't speak just the right words.

"I meant no insult to your leadership, my friend," he said slowly. "It is the intelligence men who gave you bad advice and who should be punished."

Farrar nodded slowly, his lips turning up in an evil grin. "And so they shall be, Osama," he said in a hoarse voice.

He turned to Kareem. "Is there any way you can see to warn the airplanes off?" he asked.

Kareem shook his head. "No, I'm afraid not. We should have the scrambler code broken within hours, but by then it will be too late."

"Then let us pray to Allah that it is the scrambling that is keeping us out of touch with Boise, and that the Scouts of Ben Raines are not in control of the airport," Farrar said.

Thirty

President Claire Osterman called a staff meeting, to include Ben Raines, for eight o'clock in the morning.

When Ben walked in, the rest of Claire's staff was already present. He noticed she had her arm out of its sling for the first time and that her bodyguard, Herb Knoff, looked less pale and more fit than he had at their last meeting.

Ben nodded to those present: Wallace W. Cox of Finance; Gerald Boykin of Defense; Clifford Ainsworth of Propaganda; Josh Currey, the Chief of Intel; General Maxwell Goddard; and Herb Knoff.

Ben turned his attention to Claire. "I'm glad to see both you and Mr. Knoff are looking better this morning," he said.

Clair unconsciously flexed her arm and looked over at Herb, her eyes softening as she did so. "Me too," she said.

Herb just gave a small smile of thanks, and continued to drink his coffee from his corner position.

Ben noticed the look in Claire's eyes when she glanced at Herb and thought, There's more there than an employer/employee relationship. He considered the implications of Claire getting her ashes hauled on a regular basis, and came to the conclusion it was probably the best for everyone concerned—especially as it seemed to have mellowed her once-fiery disposition a great deal.

"Well, let's get started," Claire said, smiling. Evidently

she was in an exceptionally good mood this morning. "What do you have for us today, Josh," she asked the Intel chief.

Josh actually smiled for the first time since Ben had met him. "The news is pretty good this morning," he said, looking down at a sheaf of papers and radiograms on his lap. "It seems General Raines's Scouts have done an excellent job of stopping the invaders in their tracks. From what I can gather from our reports, many of the terrorist gangs have been completely obliterated, while a number of others have been stopped and are currently bottled up where they are, unable to move forward."

Claire grinned at the good news and looked over at Ben. "That is excellent news, Ben. How did so few of your Scouts manage to halt the progress of so many of the terrorists?" she asked.

General Goddard scowled in Ben's direction and cleared his throat. "I can tell you, Madam President, and I don't think you're gonna like it," he growled.

Claire frowned as she looked from one man to the other. "What's on your mind, Max?" she asked. "You seem particularly testy this morning."

"I am, Claire, and I'll tell you why. His Scouts took the unauthorized action of passing out military arms and munitions to our citizens over the past few days. Now we've got a bunch of untrained civilians running around armed to the teeth, shooting up neighborhoods and cities and doing no telling what with these very powerful weapons."

Claire chewed on her lip as she considered this latest information. Finally, she asked, "Is this true, Ben?"

Ben shrugged. "Yeah, it is."

"Weren't you aware that this country has a law against citizens owning or being in possession of firearms of any kind?" she asked.

"Claire, you asked for the help of me and my forces to rid your country of these invading terrorists," Ben said evenly, trying to keep his temper. "To do that job, I brought in our finest teams of Scouts and sent them up against an enemy who outnumbered them twenty to one."

"I'm aware of that, Ben," Claire said.

He shrugged. "Arming the citizens was the only possible way we were going to successfully halt the spread of the terrorists throughout your country."

"But Ben, the law plainly states . . ." she began.

"Would you rather have El Farrar and his terrorists sitting here in your office dictating new laws to you, Claire?" Ben asked testily. " 'Cause that's what you were staring dead in the face forty-eight hours ago."

He glanced at General Goddard. "And if you don't believe me, just ask the general over there."

Goddard's face flamed red as Claire turned to stare at him. "Is that true, Max?" she asked. "Could you have halted the advance of these invaders short of arming our citizens?"

Goddard hemmed and hawed for a few moments, and then he looked down at his hands clenched into fists in his lap. "No, ma'am, I don't believe so," he admitted.

"Well, then," Claire said, her face lightening up and her previous good mood reappearing. "No harm done. Once these terrorists are driven out of our lands, we'll just ask the civilians to turn in their weapons and all will be just as it was before."

Ben suppressed the smile that threatened to form on his lips at this naive idea, even as Clifford Ainsworth snorted loudly through his nose.

Claire stared at the Minister of Propaganda as if he were going crazy. "You had something to say, Cliff?" she asked with an edge to her voice.

Ainsworth took a deep breath. "With all due respect, Madam President, I'm afraid that will never happen."

Claire narrowed her eyes, noticed Ben's expression, and turned to him. "You agree with that, Ben?" she asked.

He nodded. "Yes, Claire, I do," he answered.

"Why, pray tell?"

"Freedom, and the ability to defend oneself and one's country, is a heady drug, Claire," Ben said, wondering how he could explain this to a woman who'd built her empire on the very fact of depriving her people of such a commodity. "Giving people a taste of freedom, a taste of self-respect and self-autonomy, and then asking them to give it up is kinda like giving a child a taste of candy and then saying 'no more.' "

"I don't believe it," Claire said stubbornly. "When I first took office and passed the laws about private ownership of weapons, the people were only too happy to give them up and let the government take care of defending them."

"Not to put too fine a point on it, Claire," Ben said gently, "but that was also when you lost almost half your population to the SUSA—the half that refused to give up their arms and live under the government's thumb."

She shook her head. "But that's just it, Ben. All of those barbaric malcontents left and moved to your country. The people who elected to stay here believe in a gun-free society."

Ben shrugged. "Maybe so, Claire, and maybe I'm wrong, but remember, that was before they found out that the government might not be able to defend them in all circumstances."

"If I may," Wallace Cox interrupted.

"Yes, Wally," Claire said.

"Why don't we table this argument until we get to the point we're discussing; then we'll know who's right and who's wrong."

"A good idea, I think," Claire said, though she still had a worried look on her face as if she thought Ben might be right after all.

She glanced at Josh Currey. "Anything else from Intel, Josh?"

"Yes," he answered, again referring to his notes. "We have information that several transport ships headed toward San

Francisco turned and headed back to Vancouver Island after the Scouts destroyed the docks there."

Goddard nodded slowly, a smile on his face. "Now there was a good piece of work. We may've dodged a large bullet by preventing those ships from landing."

"Count on it," Ben said. "My Intel was in contact with Canada, and they said those ships were loaded with heavy equipment and thousands of troops."

"Also," Currey added, "Ben informed me of a development near Boise, Idaho."

Claire looked at Ben. "Go on."

"My Scouts that took control of the airport there sent me word they had information several planes are due to land that are somehow connected to the terrorists."

"What kind of planes?" Goddard asked.

"C-130 transport planes," Ben answered. "It is their theory that these planes are also supposed to unload heavy equipment and troop reinforcements."

"Couldn't our Air Force shoot them down?" Claire asked the general.

He shrugged. "We could if we knew where they were coming from or when they were due to arrive. As it is, they could cross down from Canadian airspace and be on the ground before we could scramble a squadron to intercept them."

She turned back to Ben. "So what's going on?" she asked, frowning.

Ben smiled. "So far, my team is using a scrambling device to keep the terrorists from contacting the planes and warning them we have control of the airport. If we're lucky, the planes will come on in thinking the terrorists are still in control and we'll have them in our crosshairs."

"So," Claire said, stroking her chin thoughtfully, "you plan to let the planes land and then take the troops prisoner?"

Ben laughed. "Not hardly, Claire. Remember, I only have

a few people there. They couldn't possibly take a large number of troops prisoner and contain them safely."

"But what do you plan to do?" she asked.

"Have a surprise party for the planes when they try to land," he said quickly, a nasty grin on his face.

"You don't mean you'd deliberately crash them, do you?" Ainsworth asked incredulously. "Why, you'd kill all those poor men on the planes."

Ben looked at him as if he had a screw loose. "All those innocent men you're so worried about are on the way to your country to bury you, bub," he said sarcastically. "What do you want my people to do? Invite them in for tea?"

Claire held up her hands, trying to hide a smile. She too thought her Minister of Propaganda was a bit of a wimp, and was glad Ben had put him in his place.

"I'm sure Ben's Scouts will not do any unnecessary killing, will they, Ben?" she asked.

He shook his head, his face hard. "No, they won't kill a soul that doesn't deserve it," he said, leaving no mistake about what he meant.

Thirty-one

Harley Reno had the air traffic controllers help Jim Short, the captured FFA man, haul the mangled bodies of the dead guards down the stairs from the control tower and lay them on the ground.

Once that was done, he asked Anna and Beth and Corrie to assist the controllers in checking out the tower's equipment and making sure it was still in working order. Some of the machines had bullet holes in them, while others were dark, with none of their lights coming on.

"You think you can get it up and running?" Harley asked the lead controller, a man named Butch Gottlieb.

Butch scratched his balding head and gave a half grin. "Damned if I know, partner, but I'll see what we can do."

Harley smiled back. "That's all we can ask, Butch," he said as he prodded Jim Short in the back with his Beretta side arm.

"Come on, traitor, let's go on over to the main terminal and see how things are going," he said to the FFA man.

As they drove over to the terminal in Harley's HumVee, they could see flames inside the building and shattered glass where most of the windows used to be.

"Looks like they had a helluva party over here," Harley observed, more to himself than to Short.

When he and Short entered through the front doorway,

Harley felt a funny feeling in his stomach when he saw his best friend, Hammer Hammerlick, lying on the floor in a large pool of blood, with Jersey and Coop working over him.

Harley gestured with his pistol to a nearby chair. "Sit down over there and don't even think about moving," he said to his captive.

Short nodded and sat in the chair, glancing around at all the dead FFA men he'd planned and worked with over the years, now thinking what fools they'd been.

Harley rushed to squat next to Hammer, who gave him a lopsided grin. "Howdy, podna," Hammer said, his voice croaking through a dry throat.

Harley shook his head, trying to look severe. "Hammer, goddamnit, how many times have I told you, when they shoot at you, *duck!*"

Hammer squinted his eyes against the pain as Jersey increased the pressure on his combat field dressing. "I must've slept through that lecture," he said through clenched, gritted teeth.

Harley glanced at Coop. "He gonna be all right?" he asked, his face neutral.

Coop nodded. "Yeah. He lost some muscle and lots of blood, but Jersey got to him pretty fast and got the leaking stopped, so it should do okay."

"Any other casualties?"

Coop shook his head. "Nope. We were pretty lucky. Guess they weren't expecting any trouble or they would've been ready for us."

"You save any, or did you kill 'em all?" Harley asked, glancing over his shoulder at Short to make sure he hadn't moved anywhere.

"We got two still alive, but they're pretty badly shot up. Doubt if they'll make it unless they get to a hospital pretty soon."

"You doin' all right?" Harley said to Hammer, putting a hand on his uninjured shoulder.

Hammer nodded without opening his eyes. "Sure thing, Boss. You go on and take care of business."

Harley stood up, motioning Coop to follow him. They walked over to stand in front of Short.

"Come on, Short," Harley said. Then to Coop: "Show us the wounded men."

Coop led them down a corridor to an office where two men were lying on couches, covered with bloodstained blankets.

"You know these two?" Harley asked Short.

The captive nodded. "Yeah. That one's Sammy Sousa and he's Billy Wesson."

"Either one of them the man in charge here tonight?" Harley asked.

Short's lips firmed up in a tight line. "Under the rules of the Geneva Convention, I only have to tell you my name and rank . . ." he started to say.

"Hold on there, compadre," Harley said, stepping up until his face was inches from Short's.

"I'll bet you've never even read the Articles of the Geneva Convention, have you?"

"Uh . . . well, no, but . . ." Short said, an uncertain look on his face.

"First of all, when your country used germ and chemical warfare in the last war, they violated the articles and thus are no longer subject to their rules. Secondly, you're not a soldier in uniform. You're in civilian clothes, which technically makes you a spy."

"But . . ." Short stuttered.

"No buts, bub," Harley said, his voice hard as nails. "Under the Articles, I'm perfectly justified in shooting you on sight. Understand?"

Short dropped his eyes and stared at the floor, defeated. "Yes."

"Now, is either of these men your commanding officer?" Harley asked again.

Short inclined his head toward one of the men on the couch. "That one. Billy Wesson. He was in charge."

Harley nodded. "Good. Now we're getting somewhere. Now, all I see when I look around the airport here is white faces. I thought all you FFA guys were working in conjunction with Arab terrorist teams."

"We were," Short said. "The Arabs took the town while us FFAs were sent to take the airport."

Harley pursed his lips, thinking. "I see. So, are the Arabs supposed to come here later, or what?"

Short shrugged. "I don't know. You'll have to ask Billy what the plans were. The rest of us just followed orders. We weren't in on the details."

"Seems like I've heard that defense before," Harley said. "Do you know anything about some airplanes supposed to land here later?"

Short stared at him for a moment, as if thinking about refusing to answer or lying, then evidently thought better of it. "Yeah. Three or four big planes, C-130's I think, are supposed to land here early in the morning, at first light."

"You know what they're gonna be carrying?" Harley asked.

Short shook his head. "No, the Arabs didn't share that with us. But Billy told me he figured it was more troops and equipment of some kind."

"He tell you any passwords or codes to use when talking with the planes?" Harley asked.

Short shook his head again. "No."

Harley jacked the loading slide back on the Beretta and stuck the barrel under Short's chin.

"Say again?" Harley snarled.

Short began to sweat, and Harley could see white around his eyes. "No, I promise you . . . I don't know!" he cried in real fear for his life.

Harley eased the hammer down on the pistol. "I believe you, Short. You know why?"

"Uh-uh," Short mumbled, his eyes still on the pistol.

" 'Cause you have neither the balls nor the conviction to lie to me."

Harley whirled around and walked over to the couch where Billy Wesson lay.

He pulled the blanket back and saw three bloodstained bullet holes in Wesson's abdomen. He knew the man would never live to see a doctor.

He slapped him lightly on the cheeks to bring him to consciousness. "Billy, Billy Wesson," Harley said in a loud voice. "Wake up."

Wesson's eyes fluttered a few times, he smacked dry lips, coughed, and then his eyes came open. He stared up at Harley leaning over him.

"Who . . . who are you?" he croaked.

"My name is Harley Reno," Harley said in a neutral voice. "I have some questions for you, Mr. Wesson."

Wesson groaned and moved slightly on the couch. "I'm hurt . . . I need a doctor."

"We'll get you one, just as soon as you answer my questions," Harley said.

Wesson rolled his head back and forth, whining, "No, no answers until I get to see a doctor."

Harley stood up and shrugged. "Okay, pal, it's your choice. See ya later."

Wesson grabbed his arm. "Wait a minute. Aren't you going to get me a doctor?"

Harley shook his head. "No, and I really wouldn't want to be in your shoes, pal."

Wesson's eyes narrowed. "What?"

Harley grinned a nasty grin. "Yeah. You see, pal, you got three belly wounds. Now, since you're still alive, that means you probably aren't gonna bleed to death, which would be the easy way out."

Wesson frowned. "What . . . what do you mean?"

"Well, those bullets tore through your intestines, filling

your gut with lots of bacteria and other nasty stuff. Since you're not gonna bleed to death, that means you're gonna die from infection, and I got to tell you, pal, that is one really mean way to go."

Fear filled Wesson's eyes and he lay his head back on the pillow. "What do you want to know?"

Harley sat on the edge of the couch, glancing over his shoulder to make sure Coop was listening. "I need to know if there are any code words or passwords you're supposed to use to tell the airplane pilots it's safe to land."

Wesson nodded. "Yeah. When they radio in for final instructions, I'm supposed to end transmission with the words 'Thanks be to Allah.' "

Harley looked over his shoulder to make sure Coop had heard. Coop nodded, and Harley turned back to Wesson.

"Now, what about the Arabs who fought in Boise? Are they supposed to join you here later tonight?"

Again Wesson nodded. "The leader, Achmed Sharif, and some of his staff are going to be coming out here while the majority of his troops stay in town to keep the citizens under control," Wesson said, his voice getting weaker.

"Any passwords with this Sharif guy?" Harley asked.

"No . . ." Wesson said, his voice trailing off as he lapsed into unconsciousness again.

Harley stood up, motioning to Coop and Short to follow him out of the office.

As he walked rapidly down the corridor, he glanced at Coop. "We got to hurry. We've got a lot to do."

"Such as?" Coop asked.

"We've got to keep this Sharif away from the airport, and we've got to somehow get the airplanes to try and land so we can crash them, an' we ain't got a whole lot of people to do the job with."

"Why not just destroy the landing fields with our mines and get the hell outta here before the rest of the Arabs get here?" Coop asked.

Harley shook his head. " 'Cause then the pilots would see the ruined fields and abort the landings. They'd just go to their backup landing field and the troops and equipment would get delivered someplace else."

"Yeah," Coop said, "you're right. We've got to draw them into a trap so we can blow the shit outta them."

Harley looked at Coop and grinned. "Ah, a man after my own heart."

Thirty-two

Harley couldn't find any rope, so he used duct tape to secure Short's arms and legs to one of the metal chairs lining the walls of the airport terminal building.

Once the traitor was tied down, Harley met with the other members of his team. Hammer had been moved to a large easy chair in one of the airport offices, and that was where they had their meeting.

Harley filled them in on what the leader of the FFA traitors had said and what he planned to do.

Jersey shook her head. "I don't know, Harley. That's an awfully ambitious plan for only six people to carry out."

Hammer struggled to sit upright in his chair. "Hey, don't count me out. I can help too."

Jersey turned a hard face on the soldier. "You move around and get that wound to leaking again and I'll personally kick your ass, Hammer," she said in a voice that left no doubt she meant every word.

"Well, don't forget the air traffic controllers," Harley said. "They can pretty much take care of the control tower. I figure we can put four people on the road coming into the airport to take out the Arabs when they arrive, and that leaves two to cover the landing field."

"How are two men—or women," Coop added when Anna gave him a look, "gonna take out three or four C-130's when they land? We don't have any LAW rockets or SAMs or anything big enough to take down a BUF," he said, using the acronym BUF for Big Ugly Fucker, the name a C-130 was called by the grunts who had to ride in one.

"As much as I hate to admit it, he's right, Harley," said Jersey, glancing at Coop. "Those C-130's would just laugh at our Uzis, and even the Big Thumper could only get one before the others were warned off."

Harley nodded and walked to the window overlooking the airfield, trying to think of some way to do the job.

Anna walked over to stand next to him, her hand on his arm.

Suddenly she stiffened and pointed out of the window. "That's it!" she said.

"What's it?" Harley asked, trying to follow her pointing finger.

"The fuel trucks," she answered.

Hammer was carried up the stairs to the air traffic control area so he could help if the controllers ran into any questions from the airplane pilots they couldn't answer.

Once Hammer was situated, Harley and Anna rushed out onto the tarmac to start up the fuel trucks standing near the hangars, while Jersey and Coop and Beth and Corrie drove out to the guard station on the road leading into the airport, hoping they were in time to intercept the incoming Arabs before they found the tied and bound guards who had been left out there at the beginning of the attack.

The guards were still there, but had lost a tremendous amount of blood from the thousands of mosquito bites they'd had to endure.

As Jersey and her friends bent and dragged the men out of sight, putting gags on their mouths to keep them from yelling and alerting the Arabs, Coop looked at the swollen red bites all over the men and laughed. "War is hell, gentlemen. You should have thought of that before you decided to betray your country."

Achmed Sharif yelled at his driver, "Hurry up, you imbecile, or the planes will have landed before we get to the airport."

"The road to the airport is just ahead, your excellency," the driver called back over his shoulder.

They were riding in a large, black Lincoln Town Car, following a HumVee up ahead that contained ten of Sharif's handpicked men. He intended to take over from the infidel Billy Wesson and make sure the landings went off perfectly.

Finally, after what seemed like hours, they made the turn onto the airport road and approached a series of sawhorses placed across the road as a barricade.

The men dressed in black manning the barricades pulled them aside for the HumVee, and let it pull ahead a few yards so the Lincoln could pull up to the barrier.

As the Lincoln rolled forward, Sharif leaned up and stared out the window at the black-clad guards, who were wearing baseball caps pulled down low hiding their faces. They all appeared somewhat small, he thought. Perhaps that was why they'd turned traitor, because of their small stature.

The guard at the barricade stepped to the side of the Lincoln and gestured for Sharif to roll down his window.

"What is the meaning of this delay?" Sharif asked in his most demanding tone as he lowered the window. "I am Achmed Sharif and I am here to take over command from Mr. Wesson. Now let us through!"

Coop leaned down and peered in the window at the four men riding in the car with Sharif. He shook his head, an apologetic look on his face.

"I'm afraid I'm gonna have to see some ID," he said, reaching down to open the back door.

"You want to step out of the car, Mr. Sharif?" Coop asked humbly, swinging the door open.

"This is an outrage!" Sharif almost yelled as he climbed out of the car. "I will have you shot for this, you . . ." he began, until Coop backhanded him across the face with his Uzi.

As Sharif tumbled back into the ditch alongside the road, Coop dropped his Uzi and grabbed two fragmentation grenades from his belt, popped the pins in one continuous motion, and flipped them in the open window of the Lincoln.

He dove into the ditch, rolling up against the steep bank and using it as cover.

Seconds later the Lincoln exploded, blowing all four doors off their hinges and turning the four men in the car into hamburger meat.

Almost simultaneously, the HumVee up ahead lifted off its tires and came apart at the seams as four grenades from Beth and Corrie and Jersey went off inside the confines of the vehicle.

After bits of twisted, smoking metal quit raining down, Coop and the women climbed out of the ditches they'd been lying in and shook their heads. They were still almost deaf from the loudness of the explosions.

Coop glanced back down into the ditch. Sharif was still unconscious, a long gash on his right cheek still oozing blood from where the Uzi had hit him.

Coop motioned to the women. "Come on, maybe we can still get to the airport in time to help with the airplanes," he called, unable to hear the sound of his own voice over the ringing in his ears.

Mehmet Kececi, pilot of the lead C-130, radioed the Boise Airport on the frequency he'd been given on takeoff from Vancouver Island.

"Boise Airport, this is C76A2 Heavy calling."

"Come in, C76A2 Heavy, this is Boise. You are cleared to land on Runway A-2."

Kececi waited for the all-clear signal.

After a moment's hesitation, the radio squawked again. "And the weather is good. Visibility is seven miles, with winds out of the Northwest at five knots, thanks be to Allah," the voice said.

Kececi smiled and switched frequencies to inter-ship communication. "As you heard, we've been given the all-clear. We will land in tandem on my lead."

As he pushed the wheel forward, Kececi glanced through the windscreen at the field below. He noticed the landing strip looked wet, as if they'd had some recent showers.

"Glad we missed the weather," he said to his copilot, who nodded his agreement.

The three large planes began their descent, gliding in like a row of ducks coming in to land on a pond. . . .

The first plane, commanded by Mehmet Kececi, reached the end of the runway, and was making its turn toward the terminal as the second plane hit the midpoint of the runway and the third plane was just touching down at the far end.

Kececi wrinkled his nose and turned to his copilot. "You smell that, Farouk?" he asked.

Farouk Kaddoumi glanced at the pilot, nodding. "It smells like we're leaking fuel," he answered, cutting his eyes back to the instrument board to check the gauges.

As Kececi's eyes roamed over the instrument panel, he said, "I see nothing wrong, but I swear I can smell—"

At that moment, the wheels of the C-130 Kececi was piloting broke a line connecting two Bouncing Betty mines on either side of the runway.

Twin canisters containing explosives and shrapnel shot into the air, tumbling end over end until they reached a height of about six feet. They exploded almost under the cargo compartment of the big plane, sending thousands of razor-sharp shards through the metal skin of the plane, wounding and killing dozens of the men inside the aircraft.

The explosion of the mines also ignited the two inches of diesel fuel Harley and Anna had poured onto the runway, sending oily flames shooting three blocks into the night sky and surrounding the C-130 on all sides.

Kececi and Kaddoumi covered their faces and screamed as the tanks of the C-130, ruptured by the Bouncing Bettys' shrapnel, ignited and exploded, blowing the airplane into four tons of twisted, melting scrap metal and killing every soul on board instantly.

When the pilot of the second plane in line saw the conflagration up ahead, he slammed both feet down on the brake pedals of his C-130, locking the wheels until the rubber shredded off the tires and the rims screeched along the concrete, sending up showers of sparks.

The sparks ignited the fuel on the runway under the second plane and the fuel that had splashed up on the fuselage of the aircraft itself.

The plane roared down the runway, flames covering it and raising the temperature inside the cargo area to two hundred degrees within less than a minute.

The fuel tanks, still intact, took another minute to catch on fire and explode. The C-130 disintegrated in less than a second, flaming bodies and pieces of metal and seats flying through the air like so many Roman candles on a July Fourth holiday celebration.

When the pilot of the third plane saw the first two go up in flames and disappear, lighting up the early morning sky, he pushed his throttle levers all the way forward and tried to gain enough speed to take off again before he reached the flaming wreckage ahead on the runway.

The plane and the flaming fuel on the runway raced toward each other, the pilot screaming oaths at Allah to let him make it safely airborne again.

He took off just as the flames kissed the undercarriage of his craft, his wheels burning as they passed inches over the flames of the other planes.

He looked at his copilot and grinned in relief, until the flames on the underside of his plane ate through the cargo doors and billowed up the cargo compartment and into the cockpit.

The pilot had time to scream once before the rubber mask on his face melted in the intense heat and his eyeballs burst.

He flopped forward, pushing the wheel of the plane down and aiming the nose at the ground.

The plane hit nose-first five hundred yards past the end of Runway A-2, tumbling in a pinwheel of flames and smoke and debris.

The pilot and copilot were already dead when the tanks and light trucks and other equipment in the cargo hold landed on top of them, crushing them into the soft Idaho soil.

Thirty-three

Ben Raines's team was quietly jubilant as they watched through the plate-glass windows of the main terminal at the Boise Airport as the flames consuming the three C-130 aircraft slowly burned themselves out in the hot morning sun.

Jersey shook her head at the sight. "Those poor bastards," she said softly. "They never knew what hit them."

Coop, standing next to her, shrugged, phlegmatic as always. "Hell, sometimes I think it's better that way. One minute you're thinking about your next meal or your next liberty, and the next you're with whatever god or devil you subscribe to."

Jersey looked at him, an expression of surprise on her face. "Why, Coop. That almost sounds poetic."

He grinned. "Yeah, it does, don't it?"

She slugged him in the shoulder and turned to walk away. "I said *almost,* jerk-off," she told him in her usual taunting voice.

Coop followed her into the office where Hammer lay, snoring softly with a sheen of sweat on his pale face.

Harley looked up from the chair next to the couch. He hadn't left Hammer's side since the affair with the airplanes was over.

"I don't much like the way he looks," he said, a worried look on his face.

"Corrie was just on the cell phones to base," Jersey said. "She said Ben was sending the Osprey back for us, and Dr. Buck would be on board to start any treatment Hammer might need until the plane could get him back to Indianapolis and the base hospital there."

Harley nodded, somewhat relieved.

"Until then, what do you want us to do with our captives?" Coop asked. "You want to start questioning them or wait for the big boys back at base?"

Harley's face grew grim. "I don't believe I'd better have any contact with the men . . . I'm afraid they wouldn't survive it, and I know Ben will want to question them himself."

Jersey shook her head. "I don't think the Arab gentleman is going to be very cooperative," she said.

Harley grinned, but there was no mirth in it. In fact, it made the hair on the back of Jersey's neck stir. She'd never seen such an evil face on her friend.

"Oh, he'll talk. It's amazing what Intel can do with the chemicals they have available to them nowadays," Harley growled in his deep voice.

"Better living through chemistry is what I always say," Coop added irreverently.

"Meanwhile, you'd better keep a close eye on him until we get him safely back to base," Harley said. "These ragheads think if they martyr themselves it assures them a place in heaven, or wherever the hell they go when they die."

"He's tied up tighter'n a hog on slaughterin' day," Coop said. "I saw to that myself. He's even got a gag in his mouth so he can't swallow his tongue or something."

Jersey laughed derisively. "That's an old wives' tale, Coop. People can't really swallow their tongues."

"Bullshit!" he said, following her as she walked out of the office and down the corridor. "I once had an Uncle Festus who swallowed his tongue."

"Oh?" Jersey asked, her eyebrows raised.

"Yeah. It was on his wedding night. When his bride took

off her nightie, he noticed she had a . . . er . . . she was equipped like a man."

"What?" Jersey said.

Coop nodded. "Yeah, poor ol' Festus. He always thought it was funny her having a mustache an' all, but he put it down to a lack of female hormones."

Coop hesitated, then laughed. "Guess it was after all."

"You lying sack of . . ." Jersey began.

Coop held up his right hand. "Truth, I swear."

When they got to the room holding the prisoners, the FFA man, Jim Short, and the Arab, Achmed Sharif, Jersey walked over to Anna, who was standing there with her Uzi aimed at their midsections.

She leaned over and whispered in Anna's ear. "Harley says to watch the Arab real close. He figures he might try to off himself to keep from talking."

Anna snarled back, "If he does, I'll just start shooting off various parts of his anatomy until he gives it up as a bad idea or I run out of parts."

Jersey laughed and glanced at Sharif, who was straining to hear what they were saying. He tried to say something, but the gag made his words unintelligible.

Coop leaned over him. "Huh? What did you say? You've got a gag in your mouth and I can't understand a word."

This infuriated the Arab and he rocked back and forth, struggling against the duct tape Coop had wound around and around his body.

Coop soon tired of tormenting his captive and went to sit next to Jim Short, the FFA man they'd captured in the tower. The other FFA men who'd been guarding the road were similarly tied up out in the main terminal waiting room.

Coop stared at the man and said, "You look like you could use a cigarette. You smoke?"

"When I can get them," Short answered morosely. "Usually, they haven't been available in the U.S. since the last war." He grimaced. "In fact, most things that make life worth living aren't available either."

Coop fished in his pocket and brought out a pack of smokes. He put one in his mouth and lit it, then passed it over to Short, who took a deep inhale and let the smoke trickle out of his nostrils with a look close to ecstasy on his face.

"I've been wondering, Short," Coop said. "Why did you and the other guys throw in with these rag-heads anyway?"

Short cut his eyes up at Coop. "You wouldn't understand," he said.

"Try me."

Short shook his head. "No, you live in a place where you have some say in your government and your life. It's different here in the U.S."

"Oh?"

"Yeah. We're told when to work, what to do, what to eat, how to dress . . . that is, when food and clothes are even available, which is not too often."

Coop shrugged. "Last I heard, the U.S. is still a democracy. If the people are so unhappy with Osterman as president, why don't they just vote her out of office?"

Short gave a quick laugh. "Yeah, it's a democracy all right. Trouble is, the ruling class, the government, is in charge of counting the votes."

He leaned his head back and sighed. "After the last election, I asked around. I couldn't find one person who said they'd voted for Osterman and her Socialist/Democratic Party. Not one, mind you, and yet the official line was she won the election by seventy-five percent of the vote."

"I'm surprised more of the citizens didn't rise up and revolt like you did then," Coop said.

Short snorted. "Hah. Most of the people here are so demoralized by the way the government treats them, they're like little children. They are afraid to speak out against Osterman for fear of losing what few privileges we still have."

"Did you try protesting the results of the election to the United Nations?" Coop asked.

"Sure," Short said. "The leader of the FFA set up a meeting with representatives of the U.N. to discuss the voting irregularities, but for some unknown reason, he disappeared the night before the meeting."

"Disappeared?"

"Yeah, as in taken away by Osterman's Black Shirts to some dungeon never to be seen again . . . or worse."

"So, the U.N. did nothing?"

Short shrugged. "What could they do? After our leader was made to disappear, nobody else had the balls to make a formal complaint, and the whole matter just sort of died from lack of interest."

"So, how did you guys come to be working with these Arab terrorists?" Coop asked.

"Evidently, their leader, El Farrar, has some contacts in the U.N. Enough so he could find out the name of our organization and a few names of members. He sent some men over here last year to feel us out on the idea of working with him to get Osterman ousted from office."

"Didn't you realize that was just exchanging one despot for another?" Coop asked, amazed at the naïveté of the man and his organization.

"Of course, we knew that was a risk. But we figured in the confusion of the takeover, we might be able to get the upper hand." He shrugged. "At least it was worth a try. And if we didn't succeed, we figured having Arabs as our leaders would make it easier to recruit people to join us in opposition and eventually we'd be able to take our country back."

Coop shook his head. "Well, partner, I'm afraid you backed the wrong horse in this race. There's no way these assholes are gonna take over the U.S., not with Ben Raines joining in on the side of the present government."

Short stared at Coop. "Speaking of that, just why did Raines agree to help Osterman? We never for a minute figured on that happening."

Coop shrugged. "You got me, pal. That's way over my head. I'm just a grunt in this man's Army, and I goes where I'm told and I shoots who I'm told. That's the way the Army has always been and that's the way it'll always be."

Coop stopped as the sound of an airplane could be heard through the shattered windows of the terminal.

He stood up and motioned to Jersey. "Let the troops know, the train home has arrived."

Jersey got up out of her seat and went to tell Harley to wake Hammer up. His ride had arrived.

Thirty-four

When the Osprey landed at Fort Benjamin Harrison in Indianapolis, Hammer was taken off first. Dr. Larry Buck had an IV going, and quickly started intravenous antibiotics and painkillers.

Ben, who was standing on the landing field, asked Dr. Buck how he was doing.

"Okay, I think," Buck said. "The bullet passed through his deltoid muscle without hitting the bone, so it should heal all right. But I want to get him to surgery right away and clean away some of the damaged muscle to prevent any infection from setting in."

He hesitated as corpsmen working under him hustled the stretcher containing Hammer toward the base hospital. "The bullet left a pretty big hole in the muscle, so I might have to do a plastic repair and take some muscle from his gluteus maximus to fill in the defect."

"Gluteus maximus?" Ben asked.

"His butt, Ben, his butt," Buck said with a grin.

"Ouch!" Ben said, sympathizing with the pain Hammer was going to be feeling for some time.

Buck shrugged. "Other than not being able to sit down comfortably for a while, it shouldn't give him too much trouble if all goes as expected."

"Go on and get to work, Doc," Ben said. "When you're

done with Hammer, we'll discuss a chemical interrogation of our prisoners."

Buck gave him a thumbs-up and trotted after the stretcher as the other members of the team exited the plane.

Once Hammer was under anesthesia and his wound area and the possible donor site on his left buttock had been prepped, Dr. Buck stepped to the table and prepared to operate.

The wound on his left shoulder was a small entrance hole in the anterior portion of his left deltoid muscle, with a larger, more gaping hole where the bullet had exited on the back side of the muscle.

First Buck used a plastic brush to thoroughly scrub both areas, making sure to get out all pieces of cloth from Hammer's shirt that had been carried into the wound.

After that was accomplished, he used a pair of Metzenbaum scissors and some tissue forceps to grasp all of the grayish-appearing dead muscle and cut it away until there was a bed of fresh uninjured muscle slowly oozing blood across the entire diameter of the wound.

Using his fingers, Buck pulled the edges of the wound together to see if it could be repaired without having to take a chunk of donor muscle from the hip area.

He was pleased with what he saw. The damaged muscle had swollen to the point where he thought he might be able to bring the edges together by undermining the skin and subcutaneous tissue enough to free up the edges and make them more mobile.

He slipped the points of the Metzenbaum scissors under the skin, and using both blunt and sharp dissection, cut the skin away from its underlying soft tissue attachments. This loosened it enough that when he pulled the edges together, there was no tension on them, a necessary process for the wound to heal properly.

"Give me some three-O chromic suture on a large needle," Buck said to the scrub tech standing next to him.

The tech placed the needle with the attached suture on a needle-driver and slapped it into Buck's hand.

Using a deep vertical mattress-type technique, Buck made a deep pass through both sides of the muscle and gently pulled them together with several sutures.

Once this was done, he leaned over and had a nurse wipe the sweat from his brow. The temperature under the big operating lights over the table was twenty degrees warmer than the rest of the operating room, and the thick gown Buck was wearing made it even hotter.

Finally ready for the last part of the procedure, he stepped back up to the table.

"Four-O nylon on a cutting needle," he said.

The tech obliged, again slapping the needle driver into his palm with a smack.

Buck glanced at him out of the corner of his eyes. "Gently, son, gently," he said. "Put it in my hand and give a little push. You don't need to slap it like you see on television and in movies."

"Yes, sir," the embarrassed tech replied.

Buck again used the vertical-mattress technique for the skin sutures to keep tension off the edges of the skin so the wound would heal properly.

After an hour and a half, the surgery was completed. Buck stepped back from the table. "Would you dress that for me, please?" he asked the tech.

"Yes, sir," the tech replied, reaching for some Vaseline, gauze and sterile tape on the mayo table next to him.

Buck entered the command center still in his scrub clothes from surgery.

Ben Raines, the rest of his team, and President Osterman

and her cabinet were all in the large conference room when Buck walked through the door.

Ben stopped talking in mid-sentence to give him a worried glance. "How is Hammer doing?" he asked, speaking the question on each of the team members' minds.

Buck smiled widely. "Great! I was able to clean and debride the wound and close it without having to take any donor muscle from his hip."

"That's really good news," Ben said, a look of relief passing over his face.

Even President Osterman and her men smiled at the good news Buck had given them.

"Yeah," Buck said. "That means he'll heal much faster."

"When will he be operational again?" Harley asked, trying not to show his concern for his best friend.

"Oh, he'll be up and around with his arm in a sling ready for desk duty by tomorrow. No heavy lifting or exertion until the stitches come out in five to seven days," Buck said. "Otherwise, we'll be right back where we started if he busts those stitches loose."

"I'll make sure he doesn't use the arm too much," Jersey said, causing Coop to give her a look that had jealousy written all over it.

"Are you too tired to sit in on our discussion?" Claire asked the doctor.

Buck shook his head. "No, I grabbed a Coke on the way over here to get my blood sugar up, so I'm all right for another hour or so . . . then I need to get something to eat."

"This shouldn't take that long," Ben said. "We've been discussing the best way to proceed with the interrogation of Achmed Sharif, the leader of the Arab terrorists captured at the airport."

"You want my advice?" Buck asked, walking to the corner table, picking up a coffee cup, and filling it with the strong, black brew in the pot.

"Well, General Goddard thinks we should try to question

him first without chemicals to see if he'll give us any information that way," Claire said.

Goddard nodded. "That'd be much faster than chemical interrogation," he said.

Buck glanced at the general as he took a seat next to Ben Raines. "You want fast, or do you want effective?" Buck asked, sipping the coffee and making a face. He set the cup down without drinking any more.

"Effective, of course," Claire said.

"Then here are my recommendations. First, do not attempt to question him at all right now. It will just tip him off to what we're going to ask later, and will let him build up a mental resolve not to answer those questions, or worse, it may allow him to formulate accurate-sounding lies."

"Uh-huh," Claire said. "What then?"

"Strip him naked and put him in a completely dark cell for twenty-four hours with no sensory input to let him tell the passage of time."

"Why take his clothes?" Claire asked, interested in the reasons behind Buck's thinking.

"People, especially men, from a macho male-dominated culture like that of the Arabs, feel especially vulnerable when they are naked. Being dressed gives them a feeling of protection, of invulnerability. Keeping him time-disoriented and spatially disoriented, lowers his mental defenses and gives his mind all kinds of nasty things to think about—like what we're going to do to him when we come for him."

"That sounds barbaric," Claire said, a look of distaste on her face.

Buck shrugged. "It IS barbaric, but so is war, Madam President. The North Koreans established this protocol over seventy years ago during the Korean War, and the tenets of brainwashing and interrogation haven't changed a whole lot since then."

"Okay, so we strip him and keep him in the dark for

twenty-four hours. Then what?" Claire asked, leaning forward with her elbows on the conference table.

"The guards who come for him must be instructed not to talk to him at all, no matter what he asks or says. He is to be treated as if he is of no importance whatsoever. This will further lower his mental defenses. As a leader of the Arab terrorists, he will be used to being treated with some deference and respect. We must change that from the get-go."

"Go on, Doctor," Claire said.

"Tomorrow morning, after he's lain awake all night in the dark wondering what's to become of him, we'll take him from his cell and walk him naked through the corridors to my interrogation room, which will be filled with all manner of terrible-looking instruments and machines. I and my helpers will be gowned and gloved as if ready for surgery when he enters the room."

Buck thought for a moment, then smiled. "Also, it will be better if there are several females in the room."

"Females?" Claire asked, astonished at this request.

Buck nodded. "There's nothing to make a man feel insignificant and impotent like having women see him paraded around with his genitalia hanging out. It strips him of what remains of his pride in his manhood."

"Especially for an Arab who culturally has great disdain for women," Jersey added, a look of malicious glee on her face at the thought of the arrogant terrorist in this position.

"I see," Claire said, smiling herself at the mental picture this evoked.

"Then, when he is in the room, he will be blindfolded and strapped on an operating table. By this time, his mind will be conjuring up all kinds of horrible torture scenarios. In fact, it will most probably remind him of things he's done to enemies in the past, further helping to demoralize him," Buck said.

"You don't really intend to torture this man, do you?"

General Goddard asked, as if the very thought were foreign to his thinking.

Buck shook his head. "Not in the least, General. Once he's on the table, I'll start an IV and begin to infuse the chemicals I use for interrogation."

"You mean, like sodium Pentothal?" Claire asked.

"Naw, that's old hat, Madam President," Buck answered. "I'll start with sodium Amytal, a distant relative of Pentothal, but much quicker and more potent. Once the Amytal has him relaxed and calm, I'll add a pinch of scopolamine."

"Scopolamine?" Claire asked. "Wasn't that once used in childbirth?"

"You're correct, it was. It was used to cause a semiconscious condition called a twilight sleep. It completely relaxes the inhibitions part of the brain, and it has a further benefit of causing amnesia about the time the subject is under its spell. That way, Sharif won't remember what we did or what we asked or even what his answers were."

"So," Ben said, "we can repeat the process and double-check the answers to the same questions to see if he gives the same response?"

Buck nodded. "Sure. It's a way to make sure he wasn't able to lie to us the first time."

"You mean even with all this, some people are still able to lie under the chemicals?" General Goddard asked, as if he couldn't believe such a thing.

"Yes," Buck answered. "It depends on how strong-willed the subject is. Back in the days of Korea, the Koreans only had about a twenty-percent success rate with the Americans they tried to brainwash, because Americans were very strong-willed and had grown up in a country that prized individuality."

Buck paused. "However, since this man grew up under the Arab culture, where conformity and obedience at all costs is taught, he should be much easier to break."

Claire nodded. "So, you plan to start first thing in the morning?"

"Yes, ma'am. What I need from you is a list of questions you want answered and information you are seeking. It's best if only one person questions the subject."

"Can I be there?" Ben asked. "That way, if one of the answers leads to another question, I can let you know."

"Sure," Buck said, "but I have to be the only voice Sharif hears. During interrogation, there is a weird sort of transference that takes place between the subject and his interrogator. Too many voices spoils the effect."

Ben nodded, satisfied. "In the morning then . . ."

"Dr. Buck," Jersey said.

"Yes?"

"As one of the people involved in capturing this man, I'd like to be one of the women in the room when he's brought in naked."

"Me too," Anna said.

Both Corrie and Beth nodded that they wanted to be included in the audience.

Coop snorted. "You that hard up to see a naked man, Jerse?" he asked.

"No, idiot," she answered, "but I think it might make him feel even more insignificant if the women who aided in his capture were there to observe his humiliation."

Buck nodded. "You're exactly right, Jersey. I'd like all of you to be there in the morning. You too, Coop."

"Okay," Coop said, "but only if I don't have to look at his . . . equipment."

Jersey laughed. "Yeah, we wouldn't want you to feel inferior, would we, Tiny?"

Coop raised his eyebrows in disbelief at Jersey's statement. "Oh, yeah? And just how would you know anything about the size of my . . . er, uh . . . you know."

"Oh, it's not from personal observation, that's for sure," Jersey said, a look of distaste on her face.

"Then you're just guessing," Coop said triumphantly.

"No," Jersey replied, "but on the wall of the women's head back at our base, someone wrote, 'For an unremarkable time, call Tiny,' and under it was your phone number."

"That's a damned lie!" Coop protested as all the other members of the team burst out laughing.

Claire Osterman glanced from one member of the team to another, wondering how these fools could be so silly and yet be such devastating warriors. It was clear she just didn't get the camaraderie that existed among men and women who fought together and put their lives on the line together.

Thirty-five

After the meeting in the conference room broke up, Jersey stopped Buck in the outside corridor and whispered something in his ear.

He laughed and nodded. "A great idea, Jersey. I'm gonna make an interrogator out of you yet."

"What was that all about?" Coop asked.

"Dr. Buck says we can be the ones to escort Sharif to his new quarters," Jersey said, a glint of mischief in her eyes as she told the others what she had planned.

Achmed Sharif was sitting in his cell, wondering when the infidels were going to come to question him. He had prepared himself mentally to stand up to whatever torture they tried on him. After all, was he not the descendent of princes of the realm of Arabia? he thought with some pride.

The metal door to his cell banged open and several men and women filed in. Two of the women were holding Beretta pistols in their hands, the hammers back and ready to fire, he noted.

As he looked at them, he recognized them. They were part of the Scout team that had captured him and destroyed the airplanes as they tried to land at the airport.

In general, Sharif was opposed to the idea of women being

in the Army, thinking they were too weak to make good fighters. But, he had to admit to himself, these female Scouts of Ben Raines's Army made excellent warriors.

As two of the women covered him with their side-arms and the two men stood in a corner with their arms crossed and enigmatic smiles on their faces, the female with the dark skin and long black hair pulled out a K-Bar assault knife, its razor-sharp blade glistening in the pale light of the cell.

Sharif took a deep breath. He was determined not to show any fear, no matter what the crazy woman did to him.

She approached, a slight grin on her face and a weird glint in her eyes, causing his heart to beat fast and sweat to appear on his brow.

He stood up straight, his chest out and his lips in a tight line, determined not to let his fear show.

Jersey walked up to him, lightly running her finger along the blade of the assault knife. As she stepped in closer and raised the blade, Sharif could stand it no longer.

"What is the meaning of this?" he asked in his most imperial voice. "Don't you realize I am a prisoner of war and am to be accorded all the amenities of an officer?"

None of the troops spoke or even acknowledged his words.

"Wait a minute," he protested, taking a step back. "Just what do you intend to do?"

Jersey moved closer and raised the knife. In a lightning-quick motion, she sliced through his shirtfront, leaving it hanging open.

And then, she reached down and put her fingers in the front of his pants, pulling them out away from his stomach. Sharif's eyes widened and he opened his mouth to protest.

With another quick motion, Jersey sliced through his pants and underwear, opening his trousers and letting them fall to the floor, leaving him standing naked from the waist down.

"What . . . ?" he began, until she reached up and jerked his shirt off his shoulders, leaving him completely unclothed in front of the troops.

Sharif took another step back until his legs were against the corner of his bunk, and tried to cover his private parts with his hands.

His face blushed a fiery red as he noticed the women glancing down at his shrunken member, smiles of derision on their faces.

"This is unacceptable behavior toward a captive officer," Sharif began as Jersey took his shoulder and shoved him out of the cell and into the corridor.

Other troops were along the corridor, observing his nakedness and his futile efforts to keep his hands over his genitals as he stumbled down the long passageway.

"I am a prince of Arabia," he protested, trying to ignore the grins and laughs as he was paraded nude past dozens of men and women along the way.

Fear caused a terrible urge to urinate that he fought with all his strength, knowing that would be the final humiliation.

After a long walk and a descent down three flights of stairs, Sharif was shoved into a dank, dark cell with no window and no light in the ceiling.

"What are you doing?" he asked again as a solid steel door was slammed in his face.

He turned round and round, unable to see his hand before his face in the complete blackness of the room. With his hands outstretched, he moved slowly around the cell until he found a bare metal bunk against a far corner.

It was cold to the touch, the temperature in the cell being in the fifties. When he lay down upon it and placed his arm over his eyes, he shivered and could feel his genitals shrink with the cold.

These infidels were tougher than he'd been led to believe by the propaganda of his home country, which portrayed them as weak and vacillating creatures with no backbone in them.

As he lay there, his mind cast back to what he'd done to prisoners in the past to make them talk, and his genitals shriveled even more at the thought that now such things might be done to him.

"Allah, give me strength," he whispered, but could feel no answering solace in his words.

Sharif spent a horrible night. He slept fitfully, often awakened by terrible dreams of dismemberment and mutilation at the hands of the infidels, all with the terrible women warriors watching and laughing as his penis fell, shriveled and twitching, onto the concrete floor of his cell.

By the time the cell door opened—Sharif was unable to tell how many hours later—he was almost babbling and talking to himself. Even though he knew it was a sign of weakness, his terrorized mind was unable to stop playing pictures of his naked body being paraded sans penis among hoards of laughing, gesturing females.

When Harley and Coop and the women of the team walked into the cell to take Sharif to his interrogation, they found a much different man from the almost arrogant one they'd met at the airport.

He was sniveling, tears of rage and fear coursing down his cheeks, his body reeking of fear-sweat, puddles of urine on the floor next to his bunk.

Coop wrinkled his nose at the smell that permeated the tiny confines of the cell. "My," he mused, a smirk on his face as he stared at Sharif, "how the mighty have fallen."

Sharif put his hands together in front of his face. "Please, I beg of you. Do not do this. Contact my embassy. I am a prisoner of war!" he almost screamed.

The team didn't bother to answer his pleas. Coop and Harley grabbed him by the arms, bodily lifted him off his bunk, and force-marched him out of the cell and down the corridor.

Jersey and Anna and Corrie and Beth made sure to cast their eyes on his nakedness and smile snidely, as if they weren't much impressed by his manhood, or lack thereof.

By the time they made it to the interrogation room, Sharif was again talking and mumbling almost incoherently to himself. The team couldn't understand his words since they were in his native language, but they sounded full of self-pity and terror.

Just the state Buck had said Sharif would be in after a night alone in the dark imagining all sorts of terrible outcomes to his imprisonment.

When they entered the interrogation chamber, even the team, who knew it was all for show, was taken aback. There were rows and rows of saws and knives and terrible gleaming chrome instruments arrayed on a table next to a stainless-steel autopsy-type table, with gutters and drains for the blood to flow out of into a pot on the floor, which was already filled with a crimson liquid.

Sharif's eyes widened and he stifled a scream at the sight of the implements of what he supposed was to be his upcoming torture.

"No . . . no . . . please," he begged, dragging his feet and struggling not to enter the room.

"I'll tell you what you want to know . . . just don't . . ." he yelled.

Dr. Buck was standing next to the table, gowned and gloved and masked, looking ominous in the half-light of the room.

"Come in, Mr. Sharif. I've been waiting for you," Buck said in a deep, gravelly voice that sounded an awful lot like the actor who played Frankenstein in the old movies.

Coop had to turn his head to hide his grin at the overacting of Buck, but he could see it was having its desired effect on the terrorist, who turned his head rapidly from side to side, as if looking for someone to rescue him from this horror he was facing.

Coop and Harley hoisted him up on the table and secured his arms and legs with wide, leather straps.

Sharif's eyes looked like they were going to bulge out of

his sockets when Buck leaned over him, only his dark eyes visible over his mask.

"Are you ready to pay for your sins, Sharif?" Buck asked.

"No-o-o-o!" screamed Sharif, twisting his head back and forth and foaming at the mouth as Buck inserted a needle attached to an IV bottle into his arm.

As the clear liquid in the bottle dripped into his veins, Sharif subsided, his eyes half closing and his head lolling to the side as he became semiconscious.

Ben Raines stepped from behind a screen where he'd been hiding and whispered to Buck, "Jesus, he seems really spooked, Doc."

Buck nodded. "Yeah. He's probably been on the giving end of this sort of thing many times before, and so his memory is doing a job on his mind. He's expecting what he's doled out in the past to be done to him, and he doesn't much like the prospect of being on the receiving end."

Ben nodded to Corrie, who set up a video camera and pushed a button to record the session for later study.

Buck took a syringe off the table next to where Sharif lay and added five cc's of another liquid to his IV line.

Sharif smacked his lips and began to mumble to himself, his words slurred with the effects of the Amytal and scopolamine mixture flooding into his veins.

Buck consulted a list of questions prepared by Osterman's committee and Ben, and began to ask Sharif questions in a low, steady, nonthreatening voice. It was almost as if they were having a normal conversation, except that Sharif's eyes remained at half-mast, as if he were drunk.

Once Buck had gone through all of the questions about the leadership of the invasion and its ultimate plans and tactics, Ben thought of another series of questions to put to Sharif, and whispered in Buck's ear.

Buck nodded and leaned back over the table. "Mr. Sharif, what is your personal code for your cell phone?"

"The numbers 7615402 followed by the pound sign," he said tonelessly, as if discussing the weather.

"Are there any other codes necessary to get it to work?" Buck asked.

"No."

"What is the phone number you dial to get in touch with your leader, El Farrar?" Buck asked.

Again, Sharif spoke the numbers without any noticeable reaction.

"Do you know the names and phone numbers of any of your FFA contacts?" Buck asked.

Sharif nodded, but didn't answer.

Buck sighed, realizing he had to be very specific in his questioning. The subjects answered the questions very literally when asked, and didn't usually volunteer information unless they were asked.

"What are they?" Buck asked.

Sharif rattled off a series of names of Americans affiliated with the FFA and their cell phone numbers on the phones they'd been given by Farrar.

Buck glanced at Ben, who nodded that he had no further questions.

"When you awaken, you will remember nothing of what we discussed, Mr. Sharif. Is that clear?" Buck asked.

"Yes . . . remember nothing . . ." Sharif mumbled.

"Now for the coup de grâce," Buck whispered to Ben.

He turned back to Sharif. "When you awaken, you will have no feeling from the waist down. Your legs will be completely paralyzed and you will have no control over your bowel or bladder movements. Is that clear?"

Sharif nodded, but didn't answer.

Buck stepped back from the table. "Take him back to his cell," he said to Coop and Harley, who began to unfasten the leather straps.

After he was out of the room, Ben asked, "Why did you give that last command, Doc?"

"To further demoralize him, Ben," Buck answered. "He'll think he's paralyzed for life, and the loss of control of his bowel and bladder will humiliate him and make him much more manageable."

"But can you really paralyze him just by suggesting it to him?" Ben asked.

"Not really," Buck said. "The effect is more like the hysterical paralysis we see in neurotic patients, and it will wear off in a couple of days. But until then, our visitor will be as miserable a human being as it is possible to be."

Ben glanced out the door Sharif had been taken out of. "Good, Doc, it couldn't happen to a more deserving individual than our Mr. Sharif."

"I agree," Buck said. "From the way he acted when he saw my instruments, I have a feeling he's been here and done this a lot more times than I have."

"Yeah," Ben agreed. "And probably with a lot more long-lasting results than he's gonna have."

"I do have one regret, though," Buck said.

"What's that, Larry?"

"I feel really sorry for the soldiers who are assigned to clean up his cell for the next couple of days."

Thirty-six

Ben Raines and his team met again with Claire Osterman and her advisors after the initial interrogation of Achmed Sharif had been completed.

Osterman was a little miffed that Ben always insisted on having his team with him in these high-level meetings, and pulled him aside while he was getting his coffee before the meeting started.

"Ben, I'd like to talk to you a minute before we begin," she said, placing her hand on his shoulder as he was pouring his coffee.

He glanced at her. "Okay, Claire, shoot," he said in his typical no-nonsense manner.

She glanced at the conference table in the room behind them where Ben's team was taking their seats, Coop and Jersey as always gibing each other about one thing or another.

"Do you always have to have your . . . uh, soldiers present at these staff meetings?" she asked.

When he raised his eyebrows in question, she continued. "I find their irreverence somewhat off-putting to the seriousness of our discussions."

Ben pursed his lips and sampled the coffee, trying to decide how to explain his philosophy of leadership to this woman who obviously had no clue about the importance of input from men and women who toiled in the field.

"Claire," he explained, "I invite my field officers to my staff meetings for a reason. Staff officers, while often brilliant tacticians, are not field officers and usually are a bit removed from the real world of combat. Field officers, who have been out there taking fire and making decisions about how to proceed against an enemy, usually have some very good ideas about tactics and procedures the enemy is using that may have escaped the notice of the staff officers. In all my years of leading an Army, I have never been disappointed in the insights I've gained from listening to my men and women who do the actual fighting."

Claire nodded, evidently seeing the wisdom of such input from junior officers. "I agree, Ben, these people can be useful, but do they have to be so . . . boisterous?" she asked.

He grinned. "The exuberance of youth, Claire, should never be discouraged. They'll grow old and stuffy like us soon enough, so why rush it?"

She smiled and shook her head. "I should know better than to argue with you, Ben. You always have an answer for everything."

He shrugged. "Yeah, but my answers are not always right, Claire. That's why I like to have other opinions at my staff meetings—to help give me perspective when I miss the boat with my suggestions."

Claire turned away and went to take her place at the head of the conference table, with Ben following to sit across from her.

Ben put his coffee cup down and picked up the transcript of the interrogation, copies of which had been provided to each of the participants in the meeting.

After Claire finished reading her copy, she peered over the pages at Ben. "This is very interesting, and certainly gives us some insight into the workings of El Farrar's mind.

Do you have any immediate ideas on how to best make use of what he told us about their plans, Ben?"

"The first thing that comes to mind is the fact that El Farrar and his followers intend to double-cross their FFA allies as soon as they gain control of the country."

"Yes, I saw that," Claire said.

"And it's just what you'd expect from these assholes," General Goddard observed. "I can't believe the FFA traitors were dumb enough to think they could ever trust these terrorists to keep their word and share in the governing of the country if they won the war."

"From what our FFA prisoner Jim Short said," Ben said, "the FFA types were desperate and saw the invasion by El Farrar as their only chance to ever change the direction the country was taking. Of course it was naive of them to believe they could outsmart the Arabs, who are past masters at deceit and backstabbing and have been for centuries, but that's the way idealists often think."

"So, Ben, how do you think we can best use this information?" Claire asked.

"Show the videotape to Jim Short and let him see the treachery the Arabs had planned for their FFA allies once the battle was over. Then get him on television and let him make a statement to all his FFA comrades about what the Arabs have planned, and follow it up with calls to the leaders that Sharif identified, telling them they are fighting for the wrong team. Perhaps they will believe him and spread the word, and the terrorists' allies may just desert the sinking ship."

Claire shrugged. "It's certainly worth a try," she said, glancing at Goddard. "What do you think, General?"

He nodded. "I agree, though I don't know if it's going to do any good. Traitors are traitors and who knows if they'll listen to reason."

Clifford Ainsworth, Claire's Minister of Propaganda, cleared his throat.

"You have something to add, Cliff?" she asked, looking in his direction.

"Yes, Madam President. It is a basic tenet of propaganda that it never hurts to sow the seeds of distrust among one's enemies. Even if all of the FFA traitors do not believe what we tell them about the plans of the Arabs to double-cross them once the war is over, it will at least cause some discord and distrust among the two allies." He shrugged his shoulders. "In other words, it may cause them to work together less efficiently, and that in turn will be good for us."

"Okay," Claire said, "we're agreed then. Short will be shown the videotape and then asked to make a statement publicly calling for the FFA people to stop helping the terrorists."

"What if he refuses?" Ainsworth asked.

Claire shook her head slowly. "Then he'll rue the day he was born."

She glanced back at Ben. "Any other thoughts about the interrogation?" she asked.

"Yeah. Sharif gave us his codes for the cell phones the terrorists are using to keep in touch, and we have his cell phone in our hands. Is there any way your technicians can reverse-engineer the phone so we can eavesdrop on their conversations?" Ben asked.

Claire looked puzzled. "I don't know." She looked over at Josh Currey, her Chief of Intel. "What about it, Josh?" she asked.

He shook his head. "No, I'm afraid not," he answered, a disappointed look on his face. "I've already had our communications experts look the device over, and they say that even with the codes there is no way the conversations can be tapped. The satellite feed is just too secure."

"Damn," Ben said. "I was hoping . . ."

Corrie, Ben's own communications expert, interrupted. "Uh, Ben . . ."

He glanced at her. "Yes, Corrie?"

"As far as I know, El Farrar doesn't even know we have Sharif in custody. What do you suppose would happen if you gave the big man himself a call on Sharif's phone, letting him know we have it and have the codes to make it work?"

"Yeah," Coop added. "You could even drop a hint or two that we'd be listening in on his conversations with his group leaders and would be privy to his plans from now on."

"But," General Goddard said, a look of derision on his face, "you've already been told we don't have the technology to do that."

Coop's lips turned up in a sly smile. "So? How is Farrar going to know that?"

Ben agreed. "And even if he doesn't quite believe us, he won't know for sure."

He looked at Corrie and gave her a thumbs-up. "That's a hell of an idea, Corrie."

Coop glanced at the propaganda expert down the table. "And as us accomplished liars know, it never hurts to fuck with an enemy's mind."

Beth, who was Ben's team's most avid reader and researcher, looked up from the written transcript of the interrogation of Achmed Sharif.

"Ben," she said, "speaking of ideas, I have one that might be of interest to you."

Ben leaned back in his chair and smiled at Beth. She almost never spoke out in public meetings, and usually kept her thoughts to herself, being the most shy and retiring of his group of individuals.

"Go on, Beth. Let's hear it," Ben said.

"I notice that Sharif gave us quite a bit of information about El Farrar's background and family and stuff back in Iraq in his interrogation."

"Yeah, he did," Ben agreed, "but we haven't had time to go through it fully with our Intel people. Did you notice something that may be of immediate help to us?"

"A couple of things. First of all, Sharif said that most of

the money El Farrar is using to finance this invasion comes from his family's oil holdings in Iraq, most particularly a refinery near Al Basrah on the coast of the Persian Gulf. That's point number one," Beth said, glancing back down at the transcript on the table in front of her.

Ben nodded, wondering where she was going with this.

Coop interrupted. "Wait a minute," he said. "I thought the U.N. took all the oil fields away from the Arabs after the war."

"They did," Ben explained, "but the oil refineries were left in the hands of the previous owners. Even with less money being paid to them for the refining process, they still make a bundle off the oil fields, though not nearly so much as before."

"Oh," Coop said.

"Point number two, Sharif said that El Farrar was worth something in the neighborhood of a billion dollars or so, and that he'd recently taken his money out of his Swiss banks and put it in the Central Bank of Iraq so as to be able to use it more freely to buy arms and pay his troops."

"Uh-huh," Ben said, now really confused about what Beth had in mind.

"Dear," Claire said in a condescending tone, clearly impatient with the slow pace at which Beth was getting to the point, "this is all very interesting, but just how can this possibly help us deal with this fanatic?"

"There is an old adage in politics that can also be used in war," Beth said firmly.

"Now we're talking about adages," Claire said, smiling at her cabinet members.

"Yeah, it's 'Follow the money,' " Beth finished.

"As I said, that's very interesting, but please get to the point," Claire said a little testily.

"The point is, if you cut off Farrar's source of money, he can no longer finance his war. Once his funds dry up, so does his ability to hire troops and buy war matériel."

Claire started to speak, but Ben interrupted her. "For God's sake, Claire, let her talk. I have a feeling I know where she's going with this," Ben said.

Claire looked startled that someone would dare speak to her in such a manner, but she did shut up and let Beth finish her speech.

"What do you propose doing with this information, Beth?" Ben asked.

"First, either send in some Scouts from nearby Kuwait to sabotage the refinery, or bomb it into rubble with a couple of jets. That will cut off ninety percent of his family's and his income."

Ben nodded, smiling. "And second?"

"You remember that kid that Mike's got working in Intel back home? The one that's only about fifteen years old and is a computer geek?"

"Yes," Ben answered. "Mike uses him to monitor e-mail transmissions across the world. How can he help us in this matter?"

"Well, he kinda likes me and he's been trying to get me to go out on a date with him for several months."

"Oh, for God's sake!" Claire interjected, almost at the end of her patience.

Ben silenced her with a look, and told Beth to go on with her talk.

"Anyway, when he was trying to impress me with his computer knowledge, he told me he could hack into any banking system in the world, except the ones in Switzerland."

Ben grinned. "Ah-hah. Now I got you," he said.

"Would someone please explain to me what this is all about?" Claire asked, glancing at her cabinet, who all looked as perplexed as she did.

Beth leaned back and gestured at Ben to go ahead.

"Beth has come up with a great idea. We'll cut off Farrar's money in two ways. First, we bomb or sabotage his refinery so there will be no money coming in for the months it'll take to get it back up and running. Second, we get one of our guys to hack into the Central Bank of Iraq and transfer all of Farrar's savings to some other account, or if that's not possible, at least screw up the bank's computers enough so the money won't be available to him for some time."

Claire leaned forward, now clearly excited by what she was hearing. "Yes! And if this crazy terrorist has no access to money, he can't pay his troops and he can't buy more guns and ammunition. In short, he'll be out of business!"

Ben smiled. "You got it," he said, and then his expression sobered. "Of course, this will stop him from bringing in more men and equipment to replace those he lost in the airport incident, but his troops here will continue to fight until they are exterminated, money or no money. They won't have any choice."

Claire waved his objections away with her hand. "That's a relatively small matter," she said. "We can deal with a few thousand infiltrators and guerrillas. As long as he can't back them up with more troops and matériel, he's at a dead end as far as taking over the country."

"That's the way I see it too," Ben said.

"How soon do you think you can get your computer experts working on his bank account, and your men over to Kuwait to sabotage his refinery?" Claire asked.

"I'll have to check with Mike Post," Ben said, "but the computer stuff can be started immediately. I'll have to find out if we have any assets in Kuwait or if it'd be better to send a couple of our planes over there."

"I don't care how you do it, just please get it done as soon as possible," Claire pleaded.

"Yes, ma'am," Ben said, a touch of irony in his voice.

Thirty-seven

After the meeting broke up, Ben got to work on the assignments he'd been given.

He arranged for an airplane to take his son Buddy and Mike Post back to their headquarters in the SUSA so Buddy could arrange to take out the refinery in Al Basrah and Mike could get his computer guru to work on Farrar's bank account.

Once they were on their way, he hooked up Sharif's cell phone to a speaker device in the office Claire had provided for him and his team and gathered them around.

"I thought you guys might like to hear this," Ben said as he got ready to make a phone call to Farrar.

Abdullah El Farrar, Mustafa Kareem, and Farrar's eastern commander, Osama bin Araman, were in the middle of a strategy session with John Waters, the head of the eastern contingent of Farrar's FFA allies, when the cell phone on Mustafa Kareem's belt began to ring.

Kareem carried the phone so it wouldn't be a bother to Farrar, and he handled the more routine matters that didn't need Farrar's input.

They were all bent over a map on the table, studying troop positions and movements, when the phone rang.

Kareem stepped back from the table with a muttered "Excuse me," and pushed the button on the phone that would answer the call.

"This is Kareem," he said into the handset.

"Let me speak to Farrar," the voice on the phone said, without the customary deference the group leaders usually used when calling their supreme commander.

"Who is this?" Kareem asked harshly, intending to give the caller a rebuke for his insolent manner of speaking.

"It's somebody your boss will want to talk to," the voice said, evidently unfazed by Kareem's tone. "So, unless you want him to have your balls for breakfast, let me speak to him."

Kareem was stunned. No one had dared speak to him in such a manner for years. He held the phone out and glared at it for a moment, trying to decide what to do.

Farrar looked up from the map and saw the expression on Kareem's face. "What is it, Mustafa?" he asked, wondering which of his team leaders was on his private line.

"I don't know, excellency," Kareem said. "The caller refuses to give his name and is speaking in a very insolent manner."

Farrar held out his hand. "We will see about that," Farrar said, his expression darkening. He was not used to anyone treating him with anything less than the most abject respect and fear.

He took the phone and put it to his ear. "This is Abdullah El Farrar. Who is this?" he asked in a very harsh tone.

"Abdul, you old son of a bitch. How're you doin'?" the voice asked cheerfully.

Farrar's face flushed with anger. "How dare you address me so!" he exclaimed, his anger turning to rage at the insolence of the caller. He would have him executed for this.

"This is Ben Raines, Abdul. Just thought I'd call and have a chat with you."

Farrar's entire body jerked at the name. How in Allah's

name did the infidel Raines get a coded phone and the codes to use it, not to mention having Farrar's secret phone number?

He forced himself to calm down. He would get the answers soon enough. Now he must exercise extreme caution. Ben Raines had a reputation as a devil when it came to war strategy, and Farrar knew he would have to be careful how he handled him.

"Hello, Mr. Raines," Farrar said, struggling to keep his voice calm, even as the men in the room looked up at him with surprised expressions at the mention of Raines's name.

"How are you enjoying your visit to the United States?" Farrar asked. "I hear that you are assisting President Osterman in her efforts to retain control of her country."

"Oh, the visit has been fine so far," Ben replied, his voice still cheery, as if he were having a casual conversation with an old friend. "In fact, I might even say it has been very interesting."

"I am glad to hear it," Farrar said. "As for me, the country is entirely too cold for my liking, and the food is simply abominable."

"Yeah," Ben said, "I don't imagine you can find too many five-star restaurants in the States that serve goats' heads and dates, can you?"

Farrar's face flushed anew at the insult. Raines must know that only peasants and extremely poor people in Arab countries dined on goats' heads.

"Might I ask how you came into possession of one of our phones and my private number?" Farrar said, ignoring the insult for the moment.

"Oh," Ben said, "I almost forgot. Achmed Sharif says to tell you hello and to give you his regards."

The mention of Sharif's name and the fact that Raines evidently had him as a prisoner came as a shock to Farrar. His team leaders had been told that under no circumstances were they to be taken alive.

"Uh . . ." Farrar said, trying to stall for time while he formulated a response. "How is Achmed?" he asked. "Well, I hope."

"He's just fine," Ben replied. "I didn't realize your commanders were such talkative fellows, but I swear we're having a hard time shutting old Achmed up. Talk, talk, talk, that's all the man wants to do," Ben said, twisting the knife a little in Farrar's guts.

"I hope what he says is not boring you," Farrar said through gritted teeth.

"Oh, not at all, Abdul," Ben said, calling Farrar again by the diminutive of his name, a terrible insult. "In fact, what he's been telling us has been most illuminating."

"I do hope you are treating Achmed with the respect a prisoner of war deserves," Farrar said, while actually wishing the man to die a thousand deaths.

"Prisoner of war?" Ben asked. "Now that's a strange term to use for a terrorist caught in our country without uniform or insignia of rank. That sounds more like a spy to me, and spies certainly don't rate prisoner-of-war status."

"Nevertheless . . ." Farrar began, but Ben cut him off.

"Nevertheless, nothing!" Ben said sharply. "None of you qualify as soldiers, Farrar, so you'd better inform your men they will be treated as terrorists if captured and will be executed on the spot, as will the FFA men working with you."

Farrar bit his lip, trying to decide how to answer this, as Ben continued.

"But, I must say, what Sharif had to say was not nearly as interesting as this little gadget he gave us to play with," Ben said, a taunt in his voice.

"Gadget?" Farrar asked, not understanding the term.

"This cell phone," Ben answered. "My technicians say it's quite a nice little toy. After they took it apart and learned all its secrets, they tell me it'll be no problem to program its codes into our satellites so we will be able to talk to you any time we want to in the future. In fact," Ben continued after a slight pause to let what he was saying sink in, "they tell me all you have to do is talk on any of your phones and we'll be able to hear you."

"That's impossible!" Farrar blurted out before he could stop himself.

"Not really," Ben said mildly. "As a matter of fact, my technicians tell me it was easy as pie once Sharif told us all of the phone numbers and codes of your men."

Farrar cast his eyes heavenward, silently cursing the day Achmed Sharif had been born.

When Farrar didn't answer, Ben continued. "Old Achmed also told us quite a bit about your home territory, Abdul. In fact, he told us that the home your family lives in is quite exquisite and is just full of beautiful antiques and furniture, not to mention most of your blood relatives."

"My home?" Farrar asked, trying to understand what Raines was talking about.

"You know, Abdul," Ben said in a musing tone of voice, "if I had more money than I could ever spend, a nice family with lots of brothers and sisters and nieces and nephews, a beautiful home full of precious artifacts, and a steady income from an oil refinery, I don't think I'd risk all that just to try and take over a half-broke country that's long past its prime."

Farrar almost choked on the words that came from his mouth, his heart hammering in his chest. "What are you saying?"

"Just that what goes around comes around, as we say in America," Ben answered.

"Are you threatening my family?" Farrar asked, his voice full of rage.

"Not me, old stick," Ben said. "I personally don't believe in that sort of thing. But some people are kinda funny about having their country attacked for no reason at all and lots of fellow citizens murdered in the streets. In fact, I've heard talk that a man who does something like that deserves anything that happens to him . . . or to his family."

"How dare you threaten my family!" Farrar almost screamed into the phone.

"I wouldn't do that, Abdul," Ben said, his voice very calm and reasonable. "But we do have a saying over here that about covers it."

"What's that?" Farrar spat into the phone.

"A man who sticks his hand in a beehive to steal some honey shouldn't be surprised if he gets a few stings for his efforts, and he certainly shouldn't bother to complain about it to the bees."

"I will see you dead for this, Ben Raines!" Farrar hollered into the mouthpiece.

"Better men than you have said that, old son," Ben said, a chuckle in his voice, "and you know what? They're all food for the worms and I'm still here."

When Farrar had no answer for this, Ben continued. "Well, gotta go, Abdul. We'll be listening for you to make some calls, so if you need to talk to me again, just use that phone in your hand. Bye-bye."

Thirty-eight

Just as Farrar slammed the cover of the flip-phone shut, cutting off the connection to Ben Raines, the phone in John Waters's pocket buzzed.

He glanced at Farrar and shrugged as he pulled it out of his pocket and answered it.

"Hello, this is John," he said.

"John, this is Sam Jenkens," a voice said.

Sam Jenkens was a friend of Waters and one of his closest cohorts in the Freedom Fighters of America.

"Hi, Sam. What can I do for you?" Waters asked, wondering why Jenkens was bothering him when he knew he was in a strategy meeting with the Arabs.

"Are you watching TV?" Jenkens asked.

Waters sighed. "No, Sam. I'm really very busy right now. I don't have time for . . ."

"Make time for this," Jenkens insisted. "They've got one of Farrar's head men on the tube and he's spilling his guts."

"Oh, shit," Waters said, hanging up the phone without bothering to say good-bye.

He walked to a television set in the corner of the room and flipped it on.

"John, is something wrong?" Farrar asked.

"That was one of my men. He says they've got one of your men on the TV and he's talking."

Farrar, Osama bin Araman, and Mustafa Kareem joined Waters in front of the television set.

As the picture flickered and then cleared, a picture of Achmed Sharif appeared. It was a close-up, showing only his face and upper chest, but he looked strange. He was talking in a weird monotone and his eyes were half-shut, as if he were talking in his sleep.

"What's wrong with him?" Waters asked.

Farrar's heart sank. He'd seen this sort of reaction many times. In fact, he'd caused it himself when questioning dissidents in his home country.

"He is being drugged," Farrar said, as if to himself. "They are using chemical means to make him talk."

"Who is it?" Waters asked, looking at the three Arabs.

"That is Achmed Sharif, the commander of my western forces," Farrar answered, his eyes staying glued to the screen as an off-screen voice could be heard asking questions, which Sharif was answering.

"And, so you say your leader, Abdullah El Farrar, has enlisted the aid of American traitors in his takeover bid for the United States?" the voice asked.

"Yes," Sharif answered. "They call themselves Freedom Fighters of America."

"Shit!" Waters exclaimed. This was not good. He didn't want his organization's name plastered all over the television for everyone to hear.

"And why would Americans agree to help you foreigners take over their own country?" the voice asked.

"El Farrar has promised their leaders a voice in the new government. He told them they would be allowed to share the leadership of the country if they helped him overthrow President Osterman and her regime."

"So, these FFA traitors will be allowed to govern the country they betrayed?"

Sharif moved his head slowly from side to side. "No. El Farrar is lying to them to get their help. He has plans to dispose of them once he has control of the country. El Farrar will share command with no one."

"That means the FFA turncoats are not only traitors, they are stupid pawns of El Farrar in his invasion?"

"Yes," Sharif said.

"And they are to be disposed of, you say?"

"Killed," Sharif answered. "Just as soon as Osterman and her forces have been defeated."

The image cleared and a picture of Claire Osterman sitting behind her desk came on the screen.

She smiled and spread her hands. "There you have it, my fellow Americans, from the terrorist's own mouth. I have an offer to make to these so-called FFA men, traitors though they are. If you lay down your arms immediately and quit helping the terrorists, you will be forgiven for your treason by your government. Once the terrorist invaders are killed or driven from our shores, there will be nothing further said about your involvement with them."

Waters turned to glare at Farrar and his men even as Claire continued.

"However, if you persist in your misguided efforts, once the Arabs are defeated, and defeated they will surely be, you will all be hanged as traitors, along with any of your friends and family members who knew of your treachery and didn't inform on you."

She leaned closer into the camera until only her face was visible, her eyes as hard as flint.

"Our prisoner has given us the names of many of your leaders in the FFA, and as soon as they are arrested, I can assure you they will give us the names of all of the members. You will have no place to hide once this is over. So, be forewarned, your time is at hand unless you rededicate yourselves to serving your country."

The picture of Claire flickered off and an announcer came on to restate what had been seen.

Waters reached down and turned the television set off.

And then he turned back to face the three Arabs, his arms crossed across his chest.

"Well?" he asked, his face stern.

Farrar shook his head. His entire plan seemed to be coming down around his head. He glanced at Kareem and then at Waters. "Well, what, John?" Farrar asked.

"Is what Sharif said true?"

Farrar laughed, a low, nasty laugh without any mirth in it whatsoever.

"Of course it is, you fool," Farrar said, turning to walk back to the table with the maps on it. "Did you really expect me to share my government with fools like you who would betray their own country?"

"But . . ." Waters stammered. "We had a deal."

Farrar shrugged. "I don't consider deals made with traitors to be binding."

Waters's face froze in an expression of rage as his skin turned bright red. "I'm getting out of here," he said. "I'm gonna tell all my men to quit helping you as of now."

"No, you're not," Farrar said gently. He glanced at Kareem, who had his hand on the hilt of the dagger in his belt.

"Mustafa, take Mr. Waters into the next room and deal with him."

"What? No . . ." Waters said as Kareem grabbed him by the arm, the blade of his dagger at his throat.

"It will go easier on you if you don't struggle," Kareem said in an even voice, his eyes as flat and dead as river ice in winter.

A few minutes later, Kareem came back into the room, wiping the blood off his blade with a hand towel from the bathroom.

Farrar didn't look up from the map he was studying.

"What are we going to do now?" Araman asked, his face a mask of worry.

"Should I call our commanders and warn them of this

message to the FFA men?" Kareem asked as he sheathed his dagger.

Farrar shook his head. "No, I am afraid our phones are no longer secure."

"But how will we keep in touch with our group commanders to guide them in their attacks?" Araman asked.

Farrar sighed. "We won't. I will call them with one last message, and it won't matter if the infidels intercept it."

"What will you say?" asked Kareem.

"To press on toward the American capital and to take no prisoners and to spare no one. This is to be a war to the death and we will either win and survive, or lose and die," Farrar said, a glint of mania in his eyes.

"Then," he added, "I must make one other call."

"To whom?" asked Kareem.

"To my family . . . to warn them of possible retribution from Ben Raines," Farrar answered.

Kareem grimaced. "Do you think he really means to attack your home in Iraq?"

Farrar looked up at his longtime friend. "Of course," he said. "Ben Raines is a warrior, just as I am, and it is a thing I would not hesitate to do."

"But the United Nations would not allow such a thing," Araman said.

Farrar laughed. "Do you really think we are in any position to complain to the U.N., my friend?"

Thirty-nine

On the trip back to the SUSA, Buddy Raines and Mike Post reviewed their plans for the upcoming assault on Abdullah El Farrar's home turf.

"I've checked with my sources, and we don't have any assets in Kuwait that would be suitable for an assault on the refinery owned by El Farrar's family near Al Basrah on the Persian Gulf," Mike said.

"No problem, Mike," Buddy said, smiling. "I'll just take an insertion team over there and do the job myself."

"You're gonna have to be careful," Mike said. "If the Farrar family is as important as Ben says they are, they'll likely have spies and paid informers in the Kuwait government offices. You'll have to be very discreet to get your men into the area without Farrar's family knowing you're coming."

"I've already thought of that," Buddy said. "The oil minister of Kuwait has been trying for over a year to get President Cecil Jeffreys to sell him some helicopters to use to patrol their oil fields. I'm gonna go over there with some choppers in a C-130 and offer them to him at a very advantageous price. The technicians I take with me are gonna be SEALs, and after we've unloaded the choppers, naturally we'll have to take them on a field test to make sure they're working properly."

"You're not planning on flying all the way into Iraq on a

chopper, are you?" Mike asked. "They'd shoot you down before you got within fifty miles of the refinery."

Buddy grinned. "No, that's not it. I'll keep us out over the Gulf, and we'll drop into the water along with one of our jet-powered Zodiac assault boats. Once we're in the water and transfer into the boat, it shouldn't be too hard to find a place to land unobserved. Then we'll make our way overland to the refinery, blow the shit out of it, then back to the boat for our return to Kuwait by water."

"But that's a fifty-mile trip across an ocean that can be very tricky if the weather's bad," Mike said.

Buddy shrugged. "Then let's hope the weather holds, partner, or we'll be getting our feet wet."

Back at the SUSA headquarters, Buddy went immediately to contact the Kuwait oil minister and make arrangements for the transport of the helicopters, and to meet with and brief his SEAL team.

Mike went to his office and picked up the telephone. He dialed the number of his computer center control room.

When the phone was answered and a high-pitched voice said, "Mac the Hack," Mike could hear raucous rock-and-roll music playing loudly in the background.

"Mac," Mike said, speaking to Johnny MacDougal, the fifteen-year-old computer genius that practically ran his computer center.

"Hey, Mike, how're they hangin'?" Mac asked irreverently. He'd never quite gotten the idea of rank and the respect that was due it, but his skills made him irreplaceable and he knew it, so he continued in his informal ways.

"I've got a job for you," Mike said.

"Hey, I'm pretty booked up right now," Mac said, a whining tone in his voice. "I'm tryin' to debug your latest scrambler program and it's a bitch."

"This is more in the way of your . . . hobby," Mike said.

"Oh?" Mac asked, sounding more interested to know the job wasn't a routine one.

"Yeah. I need you to do some hacking for me," Mike said, knowing that would trip Mac's trigger.

"But Mike," Mac said, sounding a bit suspicious, "you know hacking is illegal and you made me promise last month not to do it anymore."

Mike laughed. "So you haven't been hacking lately?" he asked.

"Of course not."

"Then you won't mind if I send a couple of experts over to your room to check out the three machines you have there, will you?" Mike asked.

"Uh . . . wait a minute . . ." Mac stalled.

"Don't worry. This operation has been cleared all the way to the top. And," Mike added, "I think you'll have some fun with it."

"Well then, my man," Mac said, sounding more chipper, "take a jaunt down to the cave and let's talk."

The cave was the name Mac used for the basement computer center that housed the SUSA headquarters' banks of mainframe computers they used to monitor all of the intel that Mike relied so heavily upon.

When Mike entered the room, he found Mac leaning back in his chair, his feet up on a desk covered with candy-bar wrappers, empty potato-chip bags, and several empty bottles of a high-caffeine soda popular with teenagers.

"Jesus," Mike said, "what a mess."

"Hey," Mac replied, sitting up and putting his feet on the ground. "This is a high-stress job. I need my carbs and my caffeine to keep sharp."

Mike smiled and nodded. "Yeah, right." He handed Mac a sheet of paper on which he'd outlined the task he wanted him to do, complete with the names of El Farrar and all of his family members.

Mac read the sheet silently for a minute, then looked up and grinned. "This is all?" he asked sarcastically.

"What do you mean?" Mike asked.

"You want me to break into the Central Bank of Iraq, somehow get past all the firewalls and encryption codes, and steal these guys' money and transfer it somewhere else, all without knowing their bank account numbers or codes or anything?"

"Yes," Mike said quickly.

"Jeez, Mike, do you realize what's involved in doing all that?"

"Oh, well," Mike said, reaching for the paper. "If it's too tough for you . . ."

"Wait a minute, wait a minute," Mac said, pulling the paper back. "I didn't say it couldn't be done, just that it's gonna be hard."

"You want me to give the job to somebody else?" Mike asked, knowing Mac would rather cut out his tongue than admit anyone else was better on a computer than he was.

"Are you kidding?" Mac asked, a smirk on his face. "You know there's not another soul who could pull this off."

"How long will it take you?"

Mac shrugged as he turned his chair toward the large computer console in front of him. "Depends."

"Depends on what?"

"Depends on how good the security of the Iraq bank is, depends on how long it takes me to identify the Farrar family's account numbers, and most of all it depends on whether the bank will allow me to transfer funds out of the country, and one other thing."

"What's that?"

"What am I going to get out of this?"

Mike hesitated. The boy was right. This was not part of his job description and was highly illegal to boot.

"What do you want?"

Mac pursed his lips, thinking for a moment. "Let me decide who gets the money I steal."

Mike thought about that. It didn't make any difference to him where the money went, as long as the Farrar family couldn't get to it.

"Deal," Mike said, sticking out his hand.

Instead of shaking it, Mac slapped his palm. "Deal."

Mac turned back to his computer, the screen casting an eerie flickering glow throughout the room, like ghosts dancing on the walls.

"Now, get out of here and let me get to work."

Buddy Raines made the deal with the delighted oil minister, and he and his team of SEALs were on the way across the world by supper time in a C-130 loaded with three state-of-the-art Bell Kiowas and one Boeing CH-47 Chinook. It would take the C-130 almost twenty hours for the flight, and it would take multiple in-air refuelings before it would land at Kuwait Airport the next day.

Captain Matt Stryker, leader of the SEAL team, sat next to Buddy on the metal benches along the wall of the cargo compartment of the C-130.

"Now that we're airborne, you wanta tell me and my men what the mission is?" Stryker asked.

Buddy had not told anyone of their objective, lest the news somehow get to the Farrar family.

"We're gonna take out an oil refinery in Iraq," Buddy said, glancing at Stryker to see how he took the news.

"Any particular refinery or will any one do?" the captain asked.

"It's one at Al Basrah, near the coast of the Persian Gulf," Buddy answered.

"Airdrop or go in by water?"

"Water insertion, then a short trek across the desert until we get to the refinery."

"Can we expect any help from the locals?"

"Nope. We're on our own."

"That figures," Stryker said.

"Hey, if it was easy, I wouldn't need the SEALs to do the job, would I?" Buddy asked, a grin on his face.

"Ain't that the truth?" Stryker replied, a smile of pride on his face as he glanced down the cargo hold at his team of men, who were busy checking their equipment, over and over.

"Any chance of us getting out?" Stryker asked, as if it really didn't matter much.

"Oh, there's a chance," Buddy replied. "All we have to do is sneak into Iraq without being detected, cross God knows how many miles of desert on foot, blow up the refinery without getting killed, walk back across the desert to the Gulf shore, and then cross fifty miles of the Persian Gulf in a twenty-foot Zodiac with the entire Iraqi Air Force looking for us."

Stryker grinned. "Hey, sorry I asked."

Forty

Johnny MacDougal grinned to himself after Mike Post left his lair. He'd deliberately made the task seem harder than it was. In fact, he already had most of the bank codes needed for international transfers of money committed to memory, something Mike didn't need to know.

Mac booted up his computer and logged onto a personal program he'd encrypted with an unbreakable cipher-based code so no one else could ever read it. It contained all of the phone numbers of computer systems around the world that he'd gathered in almost three years of intense hacking.

He scrolled down the list and wrote several numbers down on a scratch pad he kept on his desk, and then he exited the program and logged onto his modem dialer.

Punching in the numbers for the Central Bank of Iraq's computer, he hit enter.

Several various high-pitched tones sounded as Mac's computer dialed the bank in Iraq. When the familiar squealing sound of a connection sounded, Mac glanced at his scratch pad and keyed in the proper number sequence to give him access to the computer program of the bank.

He'd found the number the previous year when he was hacked into the First National Bank of London. The London bank's computer had a list of various codes it used to connect to other banks across the world, and so, of course, Mac had copied all of the numbers against the day when he might need them.

Mac had been in the London bank's computer playing one of his favorite tricks. He'd hacked into the computers of several large corporations in England and changed their payroll programs. Usually, when the computers calculated payroll amounts, if the amount ended in a fraction of a cent, or shilling in England's case, the computer rounded it off either up or down to the next cent. Mac had changed the payroll programs so that all fractions of pennies or shillings were sent instead to another account in the London bank. As the money accumulated, Mac had it then routed to various charities he was fond of, like Save the Whales, Boy Scouts, and his personal favorite, Computers for Schools, which bought used computers and donated them to schools that otherwise couldn't afford them. The account was currently donating in excess of a hundred thousand dollars a year to the charities without any of the corporations realizing the good they were doing.

As the Iraq bank accepted his code, a menu appeared on Mac's computer screen.

The first thing he had to do was acquire the account numbers and codes to access the accounts of the Farrar family members.

He went into the customer database and scrolled down until he'd collected account numbers for everyone with the last name Farrar.

Mike had told him the most important was a man named Abdullah El Farrar, so Mac started with that account.

He exited the database and went back to the main menu. He punched in the number for Account Services, and then plugged in Abdullah El Farrar's account number and Personal Identification Number, or PIN.

When the account information appeared on the screen, Mac whistled through his lips. The man had over a billion and a half dollars in the account.

"Jesus, this is one heavy dude," Mac whispered to himself.

He looked at the menu of services at the top of the screen and found one saying, "Transfer of Funds."

When he keyed that in, he was presented with another menu listing various banks. Most of the banks listed were either in Iraq or one of the other Arab emirate states. The only bank not in the Middle East was Credit Suisse, a Swiss bank that Mac had never been able to hack into because of its strict security measures.

He leaned back in his chair and thought for a moment. It wouldn't do much good to transfer Farrar's money to another Arab bank because with his power he'd be able to get it back without too much trouble.

Mac had an idea. He exited the Iraq bank's program and dialed into the non-secure public portion of Credit Suisse's on-line banking service.

While there, he opened an account under the name Abdullah El Farrar, and was assigned an account number and then asked to pick a PIN for the account. Mac did so, and was rewarded with all the information needed to wire-transfer funds into the account.

Exiting the Swiss bank's program, he again dialed into the Iraq bank and accessed Farrar's account. He transferred all but a hundred thousand dollars into the Swiss bank account he'd just opened. He didn't want to completely bottom out the account because that would set off alarms and Farrar would be notified of the account activity.

After that, Mac entered the other Farrar accounts and transferred at least eighty percent of the monies in each of the accounts to the one in the Swiss bank under Abdullah El Farrar's name.

"Boy, they're gonna really be pissed when they think old Abdullah took all their money," Mac chuckled to himself.

When he was done, he sat back, popped the top on one of his caffeine-laden drinks, and sipped it thoughtfully. He had to figure out something to do with all that money in the new account before anyone got wise and started to trace it.

He leaned forward and re-accessed the Swiss bank and opened five more accounts under fictitious names. The Swiss bank would cooperate with Iraq and Farrar as far as information about the original transfer, but once the money left that account, the Swiss wouldn't divulge its whereabouts to anyone.

Using his original Farrar PIN, Mac transferred the money from the Farrar account into the other five accounts, dividing it up equally. Each of those accounts were then instructed to wire the money to an account Mac had set up in the Cayman Islands the previous year.

He'd set up the Cayman Islands account with no real purpose in mind, but just to have in case another scheme presented itself to him.

Now, the Farrars and the Iraq bank would have to penetrate two of the most secretive banking systems in the world to track the money, a feat he didn't think was possible.

Now, what was he going to do with over three billion dollars he had sitting in a Cayman Islands bank?

Finally, he laughed when the idea came to him. He turned his computer back on and accessed the payroll accounts of the Army. This was going to be a hoot!

Buddy Raines and the SEALs got the choppers unloaded and reassembled without any trouble. He'd thought to bring along several real aviation technicians who did the majority of the work while Stryker and his SEALs tried to look like they knew what they were doing.

Inside the Chinook, the jet-powered Zodiac and all of the equipment the SEAL team would need was neatly tied down under tarps so it couldn't be recognized.

After a gourmet lunch with the oil minister of Kuwait,

Buddy said he and the technicians were going to take the Chinook for a test ride.

When the oil minister asked why, Buddy told him the engine was having some hydraulic problems and they wanted to check it out under the conditions it would be operating in.

By the time Buddy and two technicians climbed up into the Chinook, the SEAL team was already hidden aboard down in the cargo space with the boat and their weapons and explosives.

"We'll just take it for a spin out over the Gulf," Buddy called down to the minister, who grinned and waved goodbye.

As the Chinook hovered fifteen feet above the choppy waves of the Persian Gulf ten miles offshore, the SEALs shoved the Zodiac out the door. It splashed down without any problems, followed in short order by several waterproof packets of weapons and explosives and then by the SEALs themselves.

Once they were all safely aboard, the Chinook's pilot waved through the Plexiglas and veered off back toward the base.

The jet engine, powered by two powerful marine batteries, made its customary whooshing sound and the Zodiac took off at thirty miles an hour toward shore, handling the waves like a racehorse.

Buddy had timed their arrival so as to reach shore just after sundown. He had with him satellite maps of the region, a compass, and a satellite-tracking device called a GPS that would tell them their position within fifty feet at all times. It was all he needed to make his way across several miles of desert to the refinery at Al Basrah.

Glancing at his watch, he said to Stryker, "We've got twelve hours to cross the desert, kill the refinery, and get back here before dawn."

"That's cutting it awfully close, especially if we meet with any significant resistance at the refinery," Stryker said.

"That's not the hard part," Buddy said.

"Oh?"

"Yeah. The tough part's gonna be crossing fifty miles of the Gulf in that dinghy without being spotted by the Iraqi Air Force if we don't get back before sunrise."

"In that case, let's get a move on!" Stryker said.

He looked over at his men to make sure they'd pulled the Zodiac up on the bank past the high-tide mark, covered it with a sand-colored canvas sheet, and were loaded up and ready to go.

His second in command, Sam Little, gave a thumbs-up and the men walked over to join Matt and Buddy.

Buddy keyed their present position into the GPS's memory so they'd have no trouble finding the hidden Zodiac if and when they made it back from their mission.

Then, holding the GPS pointed north and south by the compass, he keyed in the coordinates of the refinery that was their goal. On the tiny screen of the GPS, a map appeared with directions on how to get there from their present position.

Matt shook his head at the wonders of the new technology. "Kinda takes all the fun out of exploring, doesn't it?" he asked with a grin.

"Not if somebody's shooting at you and you have to make tracks in a hurry," Buddy said as he glanced at the map and started off across the desert sand.

Forty-one

The moon over the desert of Iraq was half full, which was both a blessing and a curse. On the one hand, Buddy Raines and the SEALs could see where they were walking, and there was enough light to read the dial of the GPS and not lose their way, but on the other hand, when it came time to infiltrate the security of the refinery, the light would be a distinct disadvantage.

Luckily, soon after starting on their way, Raines and his men came upon a road crossing the desert sands. It was little more than a pair of ruts in the dirt, but it was hard-packed and made for easier walking than the sand did. It even went in the right direction.

A little over an hour and a half after setting out, they began to see lights on the horizon. Soon, the refinery itself came into view. It was lit up like a Christmas tree, with thousands of lights covering every part of the structure, which spread out over half a mile in each direction.

"Jesus," Stryker said to Buddy as they stood there staring at the well-lighted refinery. "Here I was cussing the moonlight and it turns out it didn't matter a bit. That place is brighter than a whore's eyes when you pull out your wallet."

"I wonder if it's always that lit up or if they were warned we're coming," Raines mused, almost to himself.

Stryker shrugged. "Well, if they're expecting us, it's gonna be a hot time in the old town tonight."

"Come on," Buddy said, crouching a little though they were still a couple of miles from the refinery. "Let's get a little closer and see what the situation is."

Stryker spoke over his shoulder. "Spread out, men. We're going in. Keep a sharp lookout for guards and sentries."

Raines and the SEALs were wearing their black night-ops fatigues and had their faces blackened, which made them all but invisible from more than a few yards away, which was all that saved them when they came suddenly upon a sentry post five hundred yards from the perimeter of the refinery.

They would have walked right up on the men had one of the sentries not decided it was time for a cigarette.

Alerted by the flare of the match and the strong smell of Arabian tobacco, Stryker put out his hand to signal his men and went down to the ground.

The SEALs carried Uzis and Berettas, all fitted with silencers, as well as K-Bar assault knives in scabbards on their calves.

Stryker signaled his men to stay put, and he crawled forward until he was a dozen yards from the sentries. There were two men sitting on folding stools, smoking and talking in low voices.

They weren't speaking in English, so Stryker couldn't understand what they were saying. He slipped his knife from its scabbard and was about to take them out, when the harsh sound of static and a tinny voice erupted from a small transceiver on the ground next to the men.

One of them picked it up and spoke a few words into it, then keyed it off and laughed as he said something to his companion.

This was bad news. Evidently the sentries surrounding the

refinery all were equipped with two-way radios and were made to check in periodically. If Stryker took them out, it would alert their commanders the next time they failed to answer their call on the radio.

He backed up until he could turn around, and then he went back to his group and explained the situation to them.

"What do we do?" Raines asked. "If we leave the sentries out here, it's gonna be tough to get past them after we blow the refinery."

"Can't be helped," Stryker said with a shake of his head. "Better to be tough to get out than alerting them to our presence and making it harder to get in."

Moving slower now that they knew there were sentries on the outskirts of the perimeter, Stryker led his team in a circular approach to the vast lighted structure up ahead.

They passed two more guard outposts, but the men evidently weren't really expecting to see anyone because they were either sleeping or talking and smoking and not really paying too much attention to what they were supposed to be doing.

Finally they made their way to the southeast corner, and came up against a ten-foot-high chain-link fence that looked as if it had been erected in the last few days.

Stryker pointed at the fresh dirt around the posts. "This is new. Guess they are expecting company."

Raines spread out a drawing of the refinery on the ground and pointed at some structures at one end.

"This is the cracking plant," he said. "According to the experts, this is what we want to hit."

"What's a cracking plant?" Stryker asked as he peered at the drawing and then at the refinery, trying to pick out the structures in the plant.

"It's where the crude oil is heated up to various temperatures in a staged sequence," Raines explained. "The various compounds that make up crude oil all have different boiling and vaporization temperatures, so as the oil is heated, different chemical compounds are taken off and stored in these tanks," he said, pointing to circles on the drawing.

Stryker pointed off to one end of the refinery where a series of tall, vertical towers or tanks could be seen. "That look kinda like what we're after?" he asked.

Raines nodded, checking the drawing against what they were looking at.

Jerry Shaw, one of Stryker's men, spoke up. "Why not just blow the shit outta everything and be done with it?" he asked, looking at the other men to see if they agreed.

"Because Ben doesn't want to completely destroy the refinery," Raines said. "The world needs the oil too much to put it totally out of commission. He just wants us to shut it down for six or eight months, long enough to defeat the man whose family owns it."

"And taking out the cracking plant will do that?" Stryker asked.

Raines nodded. "Yeah. Ben figures it'll take the Iraqis at least that long to get someone to sell them the equipment to repair it, and by then this war with Farrar will be over, one way or another."

"Bolt cutters," Stryker said, holding out his hand.

Shaw pulled a three-foot-long pair of bolt cutters from his pack and handed them to Stryker, who used them to cut a large hole in the fence.

He turned back to his men. "Okay, guys, here's the deal. If we can get to the cracking plant and set our explosives without being seen, we'll set the timers for an hour. That'll give us a good chance to get away before the shit hits the fan. If we get in a firefight and the guards are alerted, then all bets are off and we blow the plant right away and worry about our escape later."

"Fat chance of that," Shaw said grinning. "I have a feeling when this thing goes off, it's gonna make the Fourth of July look like a picnic."

"All right, let's get started. We'll go single file with everyone keeping a sharp lookout for guards or workers. If you have to fire, make sure your silencers are attached and try to keep your bursts short."

As they rounded the last corner before coming to the cracking plant, the men came face-to-face with two Arabs in coveralls who were carrying large wrenches.

Stryker didn't hesitate, but let go with six rounds from his Uzi. The men crumpled without a sound as the machine gun spat bullets into them while making only a soft coughing sound.

"Pull them over there behind that pipe outta sight," Stryker whispered while looking around to see if anyone had heard anything.

Once the workers were hidden from sight, Raines and the SEALs ran weaving around and between tanks and pipes and small buildings until they were at the base of the cracking plant.

Raines checked his drawing again. "This must be the furnace room that heats the oil," he said.

Stryker gestured to one of his men. "Johnny, put a couple of packets of C-4 on each of these walls."

While he was doing that, Raines led the rest of the men around the building. "Each of those vertical tanks has gotta go," he said, pointing to a series of huge pipelike structures sticking straight up into the air.

Stryker nodded and his men fanned out, one to each of the pipes, and began to attach canvas sacks containing a couple of pounds of C-4 plastique and a timing device and fuse to the metal with duct tape.

The packets were expertly placed in corners and behind other pipes so as to be out of sight and not easily found in case an alarm was raised.

The timers were set for one hour, and then the men were done, mission so far accomplished.

"Now to see if we can get out of here without being seen," Stryker said, setting off back the way they'd come.

They were almost back to the hole in the fence when a shout rang out behind them, followed closely by the sound of a rifle shot.

Billy Bartlett, one of the SEALs, cried out and was thrown onto his face.

The SEALs circled around him and began to return fire, shooting first at the large spotlights arrayed around the refinery.

Stryker walked over to Billy and saw a spreading stain of crimson in the small of his back.

"Billy, Billy," Stryker said urgently.

Bartlett opened his eyes, his face a mask of pain. "Damn, I can't move my legs, Chief," he said.

Stryker glanced at Raines as his men poured round after round of automatic fire at guards who had come running to the sound of gunfire.

"He's been hit in the spine," Stryker told Raines.

He looked back down at the wounded man. "Billy, put your arms around my neck and I'll carry you outta here."

Billy pushed him away. "Bullshit, Chief," he groaned. "You can't carry me five miles across the desert and you know it."

Stryker, knowing the man was right, just looked at him without speaking.

"Here," Bartlett said through clenched teeth. "Prop me up against the fence and leave me a couple of extra magazines for my Uzi, then get the hell outta here."

"Shaw," Stryker said in a harsh voice, "gimme a couple'a magazines."

Shaw reached into his pack and tossed three magazines to Stryker, who handed them to Bartlett.

Bartlett laid them on his lap, gave a lopsided grin, and said, "Hoist one for me when you get back to base."

Stryker punched him lightly in the arm. "You know it, pal," he said through a tight throat.

"Now get outta here before the whole place goes up," Bartlett said, holding the Uzi up and beginning to fire.

Stryker waved his arm and his men followed him through the fence, running crouched over and immediately spreading out to make less of a target for their pursuers.

As they jogged across the desert, looking for the road they'd followed in, they kept a sharp lookout for sentries.

Shaw was suddenly knocked to the ground by a burst of automatic-weapons fire from the left, but the two sentries there were shot dead by the other SEALs before anyone else was wounded.

Stryker knelt next to Shaw, who was dead from a head wound.

Raines picked up his Uzi and waited while Stryker took the dog tags from Shaw's neck and put them in his breast pocket.

They ran another hundred yards before stumbling almost by accident onto the road leading back toward the sea.

Twenty minutes later, as they jogged down the road, a mighty blast went off in the distance behind them and sheets of orange and red flames shot hundreds of feet into the air.

The men all stopped and stared in awe as secondary explosions rocked the refinery, cutting off all the electric lights and spreading flames throughout much of the structure.

"Shit!" Stryker said. "Looks like we mighta used a bit too much C-4."

Raines shrugged. "That's all right. Better too much than not enough."

He glanced down at the dial on his GPS. "We've only got another couple of miles until we get to where we hid the Zodiac," he said.

"That's good," Stryker said, " 'cause we're gonna have company soon."

He pointed off in the distance where the searchlights of several helicopters could be seen circling near the refinery.

Forty-two

When the team was less than a mile from where they'd stashed the Zodiac, their luck ran out. A search helicopter came out of nowhere and swooped low over them, pinning them momentarily in its thousand-candle-power searchlight as it passed.

"Shit! Take cover!" Stryker hollered to his men as he dove to the ground.

"What cover?" Jacob Samson hollered back as he hit the sand and rolled over onto his back, his Uzi pointed at the sky above him.

He was right. There were no trees or boulders or anything else that would offer even marginal protection against the helicopter attack they all knew was coming.

As he watched the chopper make a broad sweep to the left in preparation for its strafing run, Stryker yelled, "Put your Uzis on full auto and go for the tail rotor. It's about the only thing these little nine-millimeters will hurt."

The men spread out in a wide circle so as not to give the helicopter gunner a single mass to target, selected full automatic on their weapons, and lay on their backs, waiting for all hell to break loose.

"Well," Raines said to Stryker as he assumed the same position, "we almost made it."

Stryker gave a harsh laugh. "Don't give up yet, Buddy. As long as we're breathin', we got a chance."

The helicopter tilted forward, its nose down and its tail in the air as it came screaming at them low over the ground, its 20mm canon under its nose chattering away, sending out streams of orange flames ahead of it.

As the ground all around the SEALs began to geyser under the onslaught of thousands of shells, the SEALs began to fire their Uzis, aiming at the nose so by the time the shells got there, they would hit the tail . . . hopefully.

The noise of the chopper's big turbine engines, its 20mm cannon, and the firing of the Uzis was deafening, and the smell of cordite and dirt and av-gas filled the desert air.

One of the SEALs screamed in pain and buckled under the impact of fifteen bullets, dead before his scream stopped echoing in the chaos of the attack.

Just as the chopper passed, it began to wobble and jerk and jive uncontrollably as its tail rotor was shattered by the combined bullets from below.

The pilot fought the stick and collector with all his might as the big bird jogged up and then down and then began to gyrate in a wide circle.

For a moment, it looked as if he might make it down safely. Then the chopper dropped straight down the last twenty feet, exploding in a giant fireball of flame and oily black smoke.

Stryker got to his feet and ran to check on his man. When he saw the dead SEAL with multiple gunshot wounds, he snapped his dog tags off, stuffed them in his pocket, and yelled, "Come on! We gotta get moving before the other birds arrive."

By the time they got the Zodiac uncovered and pulled into the water, there were four more helicopters nearby, crossing back and forth searching for them.

As Raines got into the Zodiac, he shook his head. "There's

no way they're not going to see us out on the water," he said to Stryker.

Stryker grinned and said, "You reckon not with the SEALs' ingenuity, my friend."

Once all of the men were loaded and the boat was easing away from shore through the small breakers, Stryker turned the sand-colored tarp over and on its other side it was coal black.

He gave a corner of the tarp to two men in the front and two men in the back of the boat.

A helicopter dipped out of the night sky and began to course toward them, its searchlight illuminating a broad swath of ground as it crossed the beach and headed out to sea.

"Now!" Stryker yelled, and ducked as the men pulled the tarp over the boat and held the corners down close to the water all around the boat.

The chopper passed fifty feet above them and never slowed down as its light passed over just another dark spot on the ocean.

Raines was sweating heavily in the mugginess under the tarp, but he laughed as he heard the chopper's engines retreat into the distance.

"Damn!" he exclaimed, slapping Stryker on the back. "We've got it made."

Stryker grinned slightly. "Yeah, if we can make it to Kuwait before dawn. This black tarp ain't worth a damn in the sunlight."

"What?" Abdullah El Farrar screamed into the cell phone he was holding, making both Mustafa Kareem and Osama bin Araman wince in fright.

Their leader had received so much bad news lately, they both thought it might drive him mad.

"When did this happen?" Farrar asked, his knuckles white where his hand gripped the phone.

He listened a few more minutes, pacing the room with eyes wide and wild with anger.

"What about the additional troops and equipment I ordered? Are they on their way here?" he asked, trying to force his voice to become calmer.

Kareem and Araman flinched again as they saw his face blanch and become even paler with what looked to be more bad news.

"But Father," he said, a note of whining coming into his voice. "There was over a billion dollars in that account."

He listened for a few more minutes, then nodded, as if the caller on the other end could see as well as hear him speaking.

"Yes, Father. I will do what I can with what I have. Let me know if your inquiries at the bank find anything out about the theft of the money."

He pressed the disconnect button on the phone, looked at it for a moment, then whirled and threw it against a far wall with all his strength.

The phone shattered into a hundred pieces, which showered Kareem and Araman like so much shrapnel.

Kareem hesitated, wondering whether he should ask about the news from home or wait for Farrar to decide to tell him in his own time.

Finally, Farrar walked over to sit at the table with Kareem and Araman. Kareem noticed his leader's eyes were red-rimmed and inflamed from his anger.

"What is it, my friend?" Kareem asked, his voice gentle and unassuming.

"My family's refinery at Al Basrah has been attacked by the infidels." His eyes looked up from the table to fix on Kareem's and Araman's. "It has been almost completely destroyed."

"Do they know who is responsible?" Kareem asked.

Farrar sighed. "They found several bodies, but they had no identification or national markings on them. They appear to be Anglos, probably Americans."

"How about your family's home?" Araman asked. "Didn't that devil Ben Raines threaten to destroy it also?"

Farrar glared at him. "So far it has been left alone. My father has doubled the security around it and has it under constant air cover, but he is not sure that is enough. He has decided to move the family members to secret living quarters until this is over."

"I heard you also mention something about our troops and equipment that were to be sent," Araman said. "Is there some problem with that too?"

Farrar slammed his hand down on the table, making Kareem and Araman jump.

"Yes. When my father attempted to wire payment for the equipment the Germans and the South Americans were going to sell us, the bank informed him all of the money from my account had been transferred to another account in a Swiss bank," Farrar said in a low tone, as if he were too depressed to be angry any longer.

"Has he checked with the Swiss bank?" Kareem asked, knowing that Farrar did indeed have some other accounts at various banks in Switzerland.

"Yes. The bank denies all knowledge of where the money is. It was transferred into a new account set up in my name, and then almost immediately transferred out to another account in the Cayman Islands."

"What does the bank in the Cayman Islands say about the account?" Araman asked.

Farrar shrugged, a defeated look on his face. "They will, of course, say nothing. No amount of pressure from my father has been able to sway them."

"How much did they steal?" Kareem asked, knowing Farrar had been financing their war against the Americans out of his own pocket.

"Almost a billion and a half dollars," Farrar answered, his voice hoarse.

"A billion and a half?" Araman asked incredulously, thinking that if he had that much money he would have been more than content to live his life in indescribable luxury and leave the fighting of wars to less fortunate men.

"What about your father?" Kareem asked. "Can he lend you the money to pay for the equipment against your future oil revenues?"

Farrar laughed, though the sound was more sad than mirthful. "That's just it," he said. "They also took all of the money out of my father's account in Iraq. The family has no money left for war equipment."

"What about his and your money in Switzerland?" Kareem asked.

Farrar shook his head. "Father says that money will be needed to pay for the repairs to the refinery and he will not authorize me to use any of it for our war efforts here."

"Your father was always against our plan to take over America," Araman said bitterly.

"Be careful how you speak of my father, Osama," Farrar said dangerously. "Your very life depends on showing my family the proper respect."

"But Abdullah," Araman protested, "what will we do now? We have no more money to pay the troops or to buy supplies or ammunition."

Farrar stroked his chin. "As for the troops, now that they are here with no way to return home, they will fight without pay. They will have to forage for food and ammunition to keep fighting, or else they will die at the hands of the infidels," he said. "They have no other choice."

"Then," Kareem said, standing up and trying to look hopeful, "we will just have to defeat the infidels with the troops we have and do without the hoped-for reinforcements."

Farrar stood up also. He placed his hand on Kareem's

shoulder and smiled, though it was clear to his friend that his heart was not in it.

"You are a good and true friend, Mustafa, and you are right. We will continue our battle against the infidels until it is clear we have no chance of winning."

Osama bin Araman got to his feet, a fierce grin on his face, his teeth showing white against the dark brown of his skin. "You are both mad," he said, stepping around the table to stand next to them. "But then, so am I. We will continue to fight and to die for Allah!"

Forty-three

When Buddy Raines and the SEAL team finally made it to the shores of Kuwait, they pulled the Zodiac up on a beach where hundreds of families were bathing and lying in the sun.

As a friendly crowd gathered around the disheveled, sweating, exhausted men, Buddy held up his hands. "I've got a really nice little boat here I'll trade for a ride to the city," he said.

A potbellied man with a full beard pushed his way to the front of the crowd. He examined the boat and stared at the men with narrowed eyes. He pointed at the stack of Uzis in the bottom of the boat, and then in the direction of Iraq from whence they'd come.

"Have you been on a . . . mission to our neighbor Iraq?" he asked.

Buddy looked at Stryker, not sure of how to answer. After a moment, he nodded his head slowly.

"And this mission, was it successful?" the man asked as the crowd hushed.

Again, Buddy nodded.

"Then, my friends, you may keep your fine boat. I will take you to the city—no charge!" he said laughing, causing the entire crowd to break out into cheers.

* * *

When Buddy and the SEALs arrived at the airport where they'd left the helicopters, they were met at the gate by the general in charge and the oil minister Buddy had dealt with before.

"Ah, Mr. Raines," the oil minister said, his face frowning. "So nice you could join us again. We've been worried about you since you didn't return after your helicopter ride."

"Uh . . ." Buddy said. "We, uh, decided to take a ride on the Gulf and kinda got lost."

"Yeah," Stryker said, his lips turned up in a half grin, "we were lucky to find our way back at all."

"Have my men left yet?" Buddy asked while some soldiers loaded the Zodiac onto a truck and he and the team were escorted to a large SUV for the ride back to the base headquarters.

"No," the oil minister said. "They've been killing time making unnecessary adjustments to the helicopters until you could return."

Buddy tried to suppress a smile. The wily old minister had seen through their plan from the beginning.

"In fact, I've just been informed," the minister continued, "that there was a terrible explosion at one of the refineries in neighboring Iraq while you were gone."

"Is that so?" Buddy asked, wondering just how much trouble he was in.

"Mr. Raines," the minister said severely, looking over the back of his seat at the team, "I am not a fool, and I resent being used in this way so you could mount a strike against the Farrar family."

Buddy opened his mouth to speak, but the minister held up his hand. "In fact, I plan to file a formal complaint with the United Nations about your conduct in this affair."

Buddy sank back in his seat. Now the fat was really in the fire.

"However," the minister continued as he turned back around to face the front of the car, "my desk is extremely full just now, and it may take a while before I get around to preparing the paperwork necessary for such a complaint."

"How long a while?" Buddy asked.

"Oh, a year . . . possibly two," the minister replied. He looked over his shoulder and grinned at Buddy. "Our friends the Iraqis are sticklers for protocol, the bastards. I must make sure the complaint is worded exactly right, and these things take time."

Buddy looked at Stryker and grinned. They were in the clear after all.

"I am sure your report will be most accurate, your excellency," Buddy said.

"Yeah," Stryker said, "you wouldn't want to make a mistake and spell any of our names wrong."

Back at base headquarters in the SUSA, Buddy shook hands all around with Stryker and his team. "Good job, men," Buddy said.

Stryker nodded. "All in a day's work, sir."

"And Matt," Buddy added.

"Yeah?"

"I'm putting all of you, including the men who died, in for Bronze Stars for heroism."

Stryker stood up straight. "That's not necessary, sir. We were just doing what we were trained to do."

"I know it's not necessary, Matt, but you and your men earned it."

Stryker saluted, and left to report back to Mike Post about the mission and its success.

In Mike's office, Buddy filled him in on the mission, including the oil minister's reaction to their little deception involving the helicopters.

Mike grinned. "That is a relief. I was more than a little

worried about how kindly Kuwait would take to being used in such a manner."

"Evidently they don't have any more love for Iraq than we do, Mike," Buddy said.

"Well, you did a good job and your dad's gonna be proud of you," Mike said. "Now, why don't you take a couple of days of R and R. I've got to fly back to Indianapolis and fill Ben and President Osterman in on the details. This is too sensitive to trust to transmission over open lines."

Mike was taken straight from the base's landing field to a meeting of Claire Osterman's cabinet and Ben and his team that was going on when he arrived.

"Ah, Mike, glad you got here in time to join us," Ben said, waving him to a seat.

While he was getting settled, Coop got up from his chair, poured Mike a cup of coffee, and carried it to him.

"We were just discussing the progress Claire's country is making against the terrorist invasion," Ben said.

General Maxwell Goddard stood up. "To continue," he said. "General Raines's Scouts along with our Rangers have stopped the invaders' advance. They've been contained along lines that they had forty-eight hours ago and haven't moved significantly since then."

"From reports I've received from my Scout commanders," Ben said, "the citizens have been more than a little help in containing the terrorists."

The general cleared his throat and glanced at Claire. "Yes, uh, that is my understanding also. While I still don't agree with your plan of arming the ordinary citizens, General Raines, it seems to have reaped big rewards in defeating the invaders."

Ben grinned. "Yeah. I seem to remember an old document that says there's nothing like a well-armed populace to make it tough for tyranny," Ben said.

"Well, as far as I can see, barring any reinforcements of men or matériel, we should have the last of the terrorists either killed or captured within a week at the outside," the general said.

Ben glanced at Mike. "You have any news for us concerning the possibility of reinforcements?" he asked.

Mike nodded. "There will be no reinforcements of either men or equipment," he said.

"How can you be so sure?" Claire asked, joining the conversation for the first time.

"The Farrar family has suffered a series of rather devastating setbacks recently," Mike said, a small smile curling the corners of his lips.

"What sort of setbacks?" Claire asked.

"The main source of the family's income, a refinery at Al Basrah, was destroyed two days ago by an explosion of undetermined origin."

"But surely they have other assets?" Claire asked, smiling at Mike's choice of words.

"Unfortunately, through an unexplained series of bank errors, all of their bank accounts have disappeared," Mike said, openly grinning now.

"Disappeared?" Claire asked.

"Yes. It seems through a computer glitch of some sort, over three and a half billion dollars of their money was transferred to offshore accounts in the Cayman Islands, and no one seems to know what happened to it after that."

"So, the men who started all this are broke?" Claire asked with a smile.

"Poor as the proverbial church mice," Mike said. "In fact, the Canadian government has rescinded their leases on the lands off your coasts due to nonpayment, and informed Iraq the men and equipment left there are to be removed immediately, if not sooner."

"That's a relief," Claire said, "not to have them sitting there waiting to cause more trouble."

"Claire," Ben said, "in light of this news, I'd like your permission to begin recalling my Scouts and replacing them with your regular troops. I'd like to get my boys home as soon as possible."

Claire glanced at General Goddard, who nodded. "Sure, Ben," she said. "I think the general can handle it from here on out."

Ben and his team stood up. "But before you leave," she added, "I'd like to give you and your men and women a little party tonight . . . as a token of our appreciation for what you've done. There'll be dinner, drinks, even a band. We'll have a real going-away party, so to speak."

Ben laughed. "Okay, as long as I don't have to dance."

Claire made a pout. "Oh, and I was *so* looking forward to that."

After Ben and Mike and the team left the conference room, they headed for the barracks where they were all staying to get ready for the night's celebration.

As they entered the main doors, Mike held up his hands. "Hold on, gang. I've brought something for all of you from home."

He sat his briefcase on a nearby table and opened it up. Taking out a large stack of envelopes, he began passing them out to each of the team members, and even handed one to Ben.

"Wow!" Jersey shouted after ripping her envelope open and pulling out a piece of paper. "What's this for?" she asked.

Ben opened his envelope and looked inside. There lay a check made out to him for thirty-five hundred dollars. The payer was a bank with an address in the Cayman Islands.

He held up the check and waved it in the air in front of Mike. "Mike?" he asked.

Mike grinned and shrugged. "I don't know. All I know is

everyone on active duty for the SUSA got one in the mail. I don't have a clue as to why."

Beth, standing at the back of the crowd, began to laugh out loud.

Ben looked over at her. "Beth, you know anything about this?" he asked.

She looked at him, tears of laughter in her eyes. "Ben, how many active-duty personnel do we have?"

Ben shrugged. "Oh, a million, give or take a few hundred thousand at any one time. Why?"

"And Mike, how much money did you say we stole from the Farrar family?"

"About three and a half billion dollars."

"There's your answer," Beth said. "Our friendly computer expert had the bank in the Caymans divide up all the Farrar family's money and send it out to all our troops."

"But we can't keep this," Ben said.

"Why not?" Coop asked. "Who better to get it than the very people who had to risk their lives because of its owners' actions?"

Ben thought about it for a moment. "Yeah, Coop, I guess you're right. Besides," Ben added, "I'd hate to have to go to a million soldiers and ask them to give it back."

"The chances of that happening are slim and none," Coop said.

"And slim left town," Jersey added, kissing her check.

After the team filed out to go to their rooms, Ben turned to Mike. "I hope you're keeping a close eye on this computer expert of yours."

Mike nodded. "I am, but why do you say so?" he asked.

"Because I'd sure as hell hate to get him mad at us," Ben said. "There's no telling what the little shit would do."

Mike grinned. "Amen."

Forty-four

The mood was one of desperation and gloom in the room where Abdullah el Farrar, Mustafa Kareem, and Osama bin Araman were having their final meeting.

Farrar had been unable to contact most of his field commanders by phone after having decided that, even if the Americans were monitoring the frequencies as Ben Raines had said they were, he needed to find out what the status of his units was.

The men he did manage to contact gave him terrible news. His field units were being systematically decimated by the Rangers of the U.S. and the Scouts of the SUSA, not to mention the unexpected ferocity of the American citizens who'd risen with a vengeance after being armed by the Scouts.

When their FFA partners began to desert the cause in droves after the televised account of Farrar's planned treachery, the Arab terrorists had no chance. They were in a strange land with even stranger customs, and they simply couldn't make any headway against the combined forces of Army troops and armed and aroused citizens.

Farrar put down the phone after his last call, a look of inevitability in his eyes.

"I am afraid we are doomed to failure, my friends," he said, his voice heavy with defeat.

"There may still be a chance, my leader," Kareem said. "Perhaps we can get more troops from home. . . ."

Farrar shook his head. "No, Mustafa. There comes a time when even the most optimistic leader must accept defeat at the hands of his enemy . . . for now at any rate."

Kareem slammed his hand down on the table. "It is all the fault of that infidel devil Ben Raines," he said bitterly. "If it had not been for his intervention, we should even now be sitting in President Osterman's chair."

Araman raised his eyes. "Mustafa is correct, Abdullah. We owe our defeat to one man and one man only, Ben Raines."

"Do not feel too bad, my friends," Farrar said. "Once my refinery is back up and running and the money flowing again from the coffers of the infidels who have an unquenchable thirst for our gasoline, I will rise from the ashes of this defeat with a new and better Army and will avenge what has been done to us. It is but a matter of time."

"And we will be by your side again, Abdullah," Kareem said.

Farrar stared at his friend. "No, Mustafa, I have another, more important assignment for you. One which will take all of your courage to carry out."

"You have but to ask, my leader," Kareem said, his eyes burning with the fervor of the true believer.

"Here is what I want you to do. . . ." Farrar said, leaning forward across the table.

Six weeks later, with the Arabs defeated and all of their troops either dead or in prison, Ben and his troops and team were back home enjoying a much-needed rest from the rigors of their war experiences.

It was just after dawn, and Ben was jogging along one of the roads of his base with his malamute dog, Jodie, running alongside him.

He was sweating, his T-shirt and shorts dark with sweat as he pushed his body to the max, trying to get back in shape after going without running for the months he'd spent in America fighting against the Arab invaders.

As he rounded a corner, he glanced to the side and saw a gaping hole cut in the chain link fence running along the road.

"Uh-oh," he muttered, slowing to a walk and catching his breath. "Looks like trouble, Jodie," he said, bending over to pat the dog on its back.

Suddenly the hackles rose on Jodie's back, and she curled her lips back in a savage snarl and began to growl deep in her throat as she looked to the side toward some heavy weeds near a ditch.

A dark figure, well over six feet tall, rose from the weeds, an AK-47 cradled in his arms as he walked toward Ben and Jodie.

Jodie tensed, and Ben knew she was about to attack.

"Jodie, easy, girl," Ben said, not wanting her to get shot. "Sit! Stay!" he commanded.

Jodie sat, though it was evident from the way she glanced up at Ben that she didn't want to obey, sensing the danger her master was in.

"General Ben Raines," the figure said as he stopped fifteen yards away on the edge of the road, the barrel of the machine gun pointed at Ben's midsection.

"Yeah," Ben answered, breathing slowly and deeply to replenish his oxygen level in case the man gave him any chance at all. "Who are you?"

"I am Mustafa Kareem, second in command to the Desert Fox, Abdullah El Farrar," Kareem said.

"I see," Ben said evenly, keeping his hands at his side. He had no weapons with him, not even a knife to defend himself with.

"I guess your boss sent you here to kill me for kicking

his ass 'cause he didn't have the balls to do it himself," Ben said, his voice filled with contempt.

"How dare you speak of El Farrar like that!" Kareem screamed, raising the rifle and pointing it at Ben's face. "He is a prince of Arabia!"

"Hah," Ben laughed. "A prince of cowards maybe." He pointed at Kareem. "And look at you, aiming a gun at an unarmed man. You don't even have the courage to face me man-to-man."

Ben leaned to the side and spat on the ground. "I spit on you and your cowardly leader!"

Kareem was so angry he trembled, the barrel of the AK-47 moving up and down as he shook. Finally, his face red and flushed, he lowered the rifle to the ground and pulled a wicked-looking dagger with a curved blade out of his belt.

He took a deep breath. "You are right, Ben Raines. It will be much better if I return to El Farrar with your infidel blood on my blade to show him."

As he walked slowly forward, Jodie growled and started to rise. "Sit!" Ben commanded, not wanting her to get hurt.

He moved away from the dog out into the center of the road, crouching and holding his hands low out in front of him as Kareem moved the knife from side to side, his lips bared in a grin.

"Tell me something, Kareem," Ben said, his eyes never leaving the knife Kareem was wielding. "Do you Arabs insist on your women being covered from head to toe because they are so ugly, or is it because it keeps the flies off them?"

Kareem's eyes widened and he growled as he lunged forward, furious at Ben's degradation of Arabian women.

Ben stepped lightly to the side, levered on his left leg, and swung his right in a powerful side-kick at Kareem's right hand.

Ben's shoe connected, snapping Kareem's wrist and sending the knife flying to the side of the road into the weeds.

As Kareem whirled around, holding his right wrist with

his left hand, and glared at Ben, Ben smiled. "I don't know why that made you so angry, Kareem," he said mockingly. "From what I hear, you Arabs all like young boys better than women anyway."

Kareem screamed and raised both his hands and ran at Ben, mindless in his anger.

Ben stood his ground, ducked under the hands, and forming his right fist into a rik-hand, with the fingers bent and stiff, he rammed it up under Kareem's rib cage with all his might.

Kareem stopped as if he'd been hit by a truck, his eyes bulging and his mouth open as he gasped for breath.

Ben whirled around and slashed with a flattened hand at Kareem's exposed throat.

A loud crunch could be heard as his thyroid cartilage was crushed and smashed back into his larynx.

Kareem raised both hands to his throat and gasped and gurgled as he strangled on his own blood.

After a few seconds, his eyes became vacant and he toppled forward onto his face.

Jodie whined and inched forward, waiting for Ben to release her from the sit command.

"Come on, girl," Ben said, patting his thigh.

Jodie ran over, stopped briefly to sniff at the already cooling body of Mustafa Kareem, then put her legs on Ben's chest until he bent over and let her lick his face.

He patted Jodie and glanced down at Kareem as he resumed his jogging.

When he got to the guard station at the end of the road, Ben told the guard there to pick up the body and take it back to the base hospital.

When the guard left, Ben patted Jodie and said, "Come on, girl, I'll race you the rest of the way back."

After a few moments, he looked down at the dog. "Just

like an Arab, Jodie, to bring a knife to a fistfight," he said
as she ran happily alongside him down the road toward the
base and home.

Look for
William W. Johnstone's
next novel

CODE NAME: GOLDFIRE

Coming in May 2002
from Pinnacle Books

Here's a sneak preview . . .

Iraq, January 15, 1991:

So barren was the area into which John Barrone, Lieutenant Colonel Arlington Lee Grant, and Sergeant David Clay had parachuted, that they may as well have been on the back side of the moon. Despite their seeming isolation, mission procedure dictated that they operate as if they were under observation; thus they made certain to use shadows and background to eliminate any silhouette. They called their progress across the desert floor a walk, but they were moving at a ground-eating lope of better than eight miles per hour.

"You are certain he is there?" Colonel Grant asked John.

"He is there," John replied.

John Barrone was the only nonmilitary member of the team. John, Colonel Grant, and Sergeant Clay were engaged in a covert operation, also known as a black ops, though not entirely because the three men were dressed in black and had their faces covered with camouflage paint in order to absorb any ambient light.

John had been operating inside Iraq for several days, looking for General Abdul Sin-Sargon. Once he found him, he'd slipped back across the border to U.S. Army "Task Force Ripper," to report on the general's location. When asked if he would return with the special operations team, John had agreed. One hour earlier, he, Colonel Grant, and Sergeant Clay had made a night parachute jump from a C-130, and were now moving swiftly through the Iraqi desert.

U.S. intelligence sources believed General Sin-Sargon to be Saddam Hussein's most capable battle tactician. He had been the architect behind the Iraq-Iran war, and was now charged with deploying a defense against the coalition forces. Taking out Sin-Sargon would deny the Iraqi Army his leadership and save hundreds of American lives, once the invasion started.

Exactly ninety minutes after the three men touched down, they reached their destination. Utilizing the darkness, they were but shadows within shadows as they eased out onto a rock precipice to look down at Sin-Sargon's encampment, three hundred yards away.

John and Colonel Grant were carrying M-16 rifles with four double-sized ammo clips. Sergeant Clay was carrying a Heckler & Koch PSG-1 sniper rifle, with a light-gathering telescopic site. As the three men lay there, observing the camp, Sergeant Clay began unloading his magazine, pushing the 7.62 ammunition out, one bullet at a time.

"What are you doing?" John asked quietly.

Clay opened a little cloth bag and dumped out a handful of bullets. "I prefer these over the military issue," he said. "I bought them myself, .308-caliber, 168-gram, hollow-point, boat-tail, match-quality ammunition."

He reloaded the magazine, then clicked it into place just forward of the trigger assembly.

With his rifle loaded and ready, Sergeant Clay deployed the small bipod, then took up a prone firing position, with his left hand just touching the fore stock and his right hand wrapped around the pistol grip. He put his cheek against the receiver, pressed the padded butt into his shoulder, then looked through the scope.

"I'm ready," Clay said quietly.

"Look for a man carrying a carved cane," John said.

"A cane?"

"Sin-Sargon is never without it."

Inside the tent of General Sin-Sargon:

Sin-Sargon took a sip of water, then put his cup down beside him. He was sitting cross-legged on a rug, an AK-47 rifle lying across his lap, his jewel-encrusted, gold-headed cane alongside. The tent was dimly lit by a small battery-powered lamp, and there was a double entrance to the tent so that whenever someone entered or exited, they would pass through two flaps. That way, there would be no chance for the light to escape.

"General, if the Americans attack, there will be many of them and they will be strong," Sin-Sargon's aide-de-camp said. "If President Hussein cannot come to some peace, I fear that many of our brave young soldiers will die."

"Those who do not die by the sword will eventually die by some other means," Sin-Sargon replied calmly. "There are many causes of death, but there is only one death. Therefore, if death is a predetermined must, is it not better to die bravely and for a cause? Our cause is righteous and blessed by Allah."

"I believe that as well," Sargon's aide said. "But we are professional soldiers. Many of our men are shopkeepers and goat herdsmen. They have not chosen the art of war, and it is they who fear what lies ahead."

Sin-Sargon stood up. "Perhaps you are right. I will visit them, and remind them that they are fighting for a righteous cause," he said. "Bring my cane." He pointed toward his walking stick. The aide picked the cane up and held it reverently.

"Is it true what they say about this cane, General?" the aide asked. "Is it the cane of the Prophet?"

"Yes, that is true. This was the cane of the Prophet Mohammed himself," Sin-Sargon said proudly. "Of course, such a thing is not written, but it has been passed down through many generations of my family, and each of us who have been blessed to own it know in our heart that it is a true relic of the Prophet. It was also carried by Mohammed II when he wrested Istanbul from the hands of the infidels. And now, it has fallen upon me to safeguard."

Sin-Sargon and his aide stepped into the small canvas alcove. The first flap was closed before the second flap opened, thus preventing any light from escaping. Then the two men moved out into the night air.

"Here is your cane, General," the aide said once they were outside. He handed the walking stick to Sin-Sargon. "I am honored that you have allowed me to hold it."

"I have a target," Sergeant Clay said quietly.

"Take him out," Colonel Grant ordered.

"Damn," Clay said.

"What is it?"

"Mr. Barrone said shoot the man with the cane. But one man has just handed the cane to another. I don't know which one is which."

"The first man was probably General Sin-Sargon's aide, Lieutenant Kahli," said John. "Don't bother about him."

"Kill them both," Grant ordered.

"Colonel, Sin-Sargon is the one we want," John said. "There's no need to kill just to be killing."

"You heard Sergeant Clay. Both men have handled the cane. The success of this mission is my call. We must be certain. Kill them both, Sergeant."

"Yes, sir," Clay replied.

The PSG-1 rifle boomed, then recoiled against his shoulder, but the flash-suppressor prevented a big muzzle display.

Lieutenant Kahli heard an angry buzz, then a thump. A puff of dust flew up from General Sin-Sargon's shirt, followed by a spewing fountain of blood.

"Uhnn!" Sin-Sargon gasped, his eyes opening wide in shock.

"General!" Lieutenant Kahli shouted, still not comprehending what had just happened. Puzzled, he looked off in the distance, where he saw a quick wink of light. It was the last thing he ever saw, for even as that strange sight was registering with him, the bullet entered between his eyes, then blew tissue, blood, and bone through a half-dollar-sized hole in the back of his head.